Motor

Girl

Motor Girl

And the Endless Race

A. A. Achibane

Published by R. L. Pub
Date of publication: May 8th, 2024
Copyright of book: April 2022
Copyright of cover: December 2023
ISBN: 979-8-9892581-2-3

Untouchables

Tier 10	Gilded	
Tier 9		
Tier 8		
Tier 7		
Tier 6		
MUTED	Tier 5	Tier 5
	Tier 4	Tier 4
	Tier 3	Tier 3
	Tier 2	Tier 2
	Tier 1	Tier 1

Don't forget your place

ALLO' ARLOVED

plunges.

Hyperdetailed holographics and 2k MB of data, send as many diginotes as you want!

Get the new Holophone 6.
Coming Soon

Nothing says love like a
Digipic or Digivideo

Digipics, the only means of
communication you need.

LIGHTCYC

New and improved mixer syste
For a smoother ride, get a Pryc

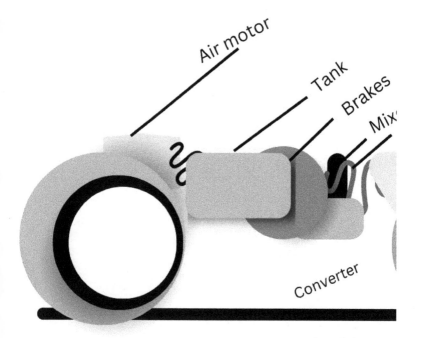

Air motor

Tank

Brakes

Mix

Converter

Nothing

Pryce A

n!

e.

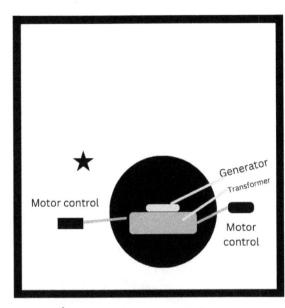

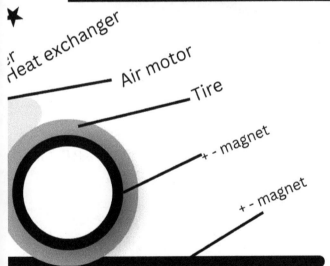

Heat exchanger

Air motor

Tire

+ - magnet

+ - magnet

ides like a Pryce!

utomotive ®

Electotrain

Magtram

SAVE YOURSELF THE
HASSLE AND TAKE A
TRAIN

To my daughter.

My biggest fan and the original Mōtāgāru.

Amendments to the Bills of Absolutes: Effective Immediately

AA10: All local and regional law enforcement is hereby defunded. Independent Contractors may be used in the case of any unlawful actions by contacting the local Regulations Office. Payment for any procedures or processes shall be upon the complainant.

AA11: Historical National laws regarding relations between tiers take precedence and shall always be *enforced to the fullest extent of the LAW* and henceforth be *__Regulated__*.

Chapter One

"Great heroes need great sorrows and burdens, or half their greatness goes unnoticed. It is all part of the fairy tale."

— **Peter S. Beagle, <u>The Last Unicorn</u>**

"Josaline… is Rene with you?"

There was terror in my aunt's voice and it spread over me like ice. "No, I haven't seen her in person in years."

Aunt Caroline knew this, so for her to ask, she had to be desperate. The line was filled with sobbing and my body filled with emotions. Guilt, fear, hopelessness, anger. All because I knew that if Rene was missing then….she was already dead.

Jolting awake I found myself in an awkward position. I was sitting—all alone as the only person in first class. My

Pods, the small speakers everyone had implanted behind their ears, blocked out the world as far as sound while my eyes were trained on my Holophone. I had it opened to my diary, an entry from a few years ago. Before the reality of my world was presented to me. It must have triggered my dream from that night.

The images glowed and floated above the screen. A hologram video, just like when you had a call with someone, showed me the story in a three dimensional image. The dancing images of me and my cousin Rene showed nothing but joy, and if I were foolish or naïve like I had once been, it would be impossible to see why my family had separated us.

And if I had foresight, I would have cherished the moment more as the last one we would have together.

The diary entry ended and the hologram faded away. I stopped myself from hitting the play button again. I had cried enough today, so I decided on another move. Getting up, I left the 'comfort' of first-class and broke my parent's first rule. First class wasn't much different from business in looks. It was the same pale gray upholstery and dark wood veneer on the whole train. The windows in first were larger and the seats in business were closer together. But it was the exclusivity that you paid extra for; distance from who was in the cheap seats.

The electric train barely made a sound as it glided along its wire track, passing the uninhabited wasteland outside the city. There was nothing around to watch, hence my deep dive into my archived memories. The sea of mud and dust had become monotonous after the first hour. The occasional rock or swing of the cart had me tumbling from time to time but the ride was smooth otherwise. They pumped a calming lavender scent into the first-class cart. It was one of the distinctions between the different sections.

Along with the noise levels because as soon as the electric doors slid open, the sound of varying levels of voices hit my ears.

Business class smelled like its passengers (a strange mix of perfumes and food smells), which was a a blend of people you wouldn't find in the 'safety' of first. Some talked loudly with animated hand gestures while others whispered. Most were silent and on their holos. Those on their holos were Gildes and the ones talking were Mutes. It was easy to tell with how they sat and the clothes they wore. They were all different tier levels but I couldn't tell them apart. Maybe after some time spent in this world but for now, I was too sheltered. But I had to be careful or my parents would force me back into their protective shell—no bad grades and a lot of secrets if I wanted to stay free.

The pressure was high but worth it. I have been looking forward to this for years, planning and studying to move here, to go to school with Rene in *Ocresta*.

Too many eyes locked onto me. It made me feel see-through so I spun back and returned to my seat. We were nearing the city now, the endless brown landscape was slowly replaced with the cityscape that now stemmed from the ground before me. It was only a few minutes until we arrived, and it was still like standing just outside another world. Around us were brown dirt and thin trees, but tall, shiny buildings covered in lights of varying colors sat in the distance. The sun shone dimly on the thick electrical line the Ectotrain hung from above, but the city before us had a blanket of clouds as if in a dome with a completely different ecosystem.

It had been years since I was allowed to come here. Forbidden to see this side of our family. But, if you asked me, they were the best side of us. Uncle Haru, Aunt Caroline, Reglin, and… Rene…

Stop it. Don't think about Rene now. Not with Uncle minutes away from meeting me at the station. That was why I had spent the better half of my trip looking at old diary Holos of the two of us. To get all that out before I arrived. It wouldn't be good to have Uncle pick up a sobbing mess.

It would only serve as a painful reminder of what he lost.

The remaining minutes stretched forever as I waited for the station to come into view, using them to compose myself back into my cheery facade. A dotting of gray, short buildings welcomed us, rusted and worn. The signs of a Mute area—decay. There would be significant cracks in the walkway and I needed to pay attention to those. Falling flat on my face in the crowded station would hurt in more ways than one. It wouldn't be the first time the broken and unkempt world of Mutes tripped me up—my knee still had a scar.

Mom wasn't happy about that at all.

I struggled to balance my luggage and myself with the large crowd and the uneven platform. Getting off the Ectotrain was more complicated than getting on it. I was trying to watch for cracks but got distracted by the differences in the crowd. Tall, short, pale, dark, fat, and thin they all had different postures and hair colors. The smell was overwhelmingly worse than business-class with all the other smells of the crowd mixing with putrid scents of trash. And the noise was so loud, it made my brain buzz with all the voices and mixed conversations with suitcases rolling, dropping, and popping along. I really wanted to turn my pods on just to block out all the confusion.

"Josaline!"

The familiar voice of my Uncle cut through the noise and as I turned, someone knocked right into my shoulder, sending my purse and backpack flying. At least my things remained intact instead of spilling the belongings inside. I caught sight of Uncle Haru while on my knees, growling at the man who bumped me. The two could have been related. They looked far more alike than I did to him; black, coarse locks and brown, almond eyes, but mostly the noticeable slump to his shoulders as he walked or stood. They were probably in the same tier at one point.

Although I couldn't hear them, I knew a majority of Uncle's reprimand was warnings to the young Mute that knocked into a Gilded. At least I wouldn't call Regulations like other Gildes half my rank would have.

I had just gotten my things back in my hands when Uncle took them out again. "I'll carry those."

"I got it."

His eyes turned to slits, "Josaline, it's not up for discussion." I relented, knowing he didn't want to cause a scene. Or be seen walking with me as my equal. "You really went for it, huh?"

Uncle pointed to my hair, and I fingered a bright pink lock. "What can I say? I like to stand out."

"That you do. Finding you in this crowd was easy." He said with a chuckle, leading us away from the train platform.

The drive was quiet. The hum of the magnets that managed the speed of the Auto filled in time. The political AUD Uncle played in the background went on in length

23

about the struggles of Mutes—and how to accommodate.

I took in as much of the city as possible, but we were soon on the outskirts. The residential area looked like endless rows of boxes fitted into homes. But, as far as Mute neighborhoods went, this one was well kept and clean. The sidewalks were whole instead of a broken mess. And the electolamps hanging over the streets worked (last I checked, but I could have old info). I had never seen the lowest Mute communities but I had heard stories. They could be barely livable. I was glad Uncle had found this neighborhood and that it accepted his family. Things should have been a lot worse for them.

Uncle Haru was at the trunk, pulling most of my bags out before I could get a word out otherwise. It was a struggle to get my seatbelt off. The older auto or beater's antiquated system was not one I was used to. The car still worked and few had their own transportation like this. It would be public transportation for me with my parents insisting I get a rental everywhere. I rolled my eyes at the thought, but my Gilded parents hardly thought about costs, only image.

Glancing up, I took in the sight of the old, familiar

home of my childhood summers. It had been a while, but the pale yellow and white shutters still stood out amongst the other houses on the street. The rest were steel gray or bland white, as most places are these days. I had always loved that. This house was so different from the others. But now (instead of happy nostalgic memories), I only felt regret. Missed opportunities weighed on me like rocks in my heart as I made my way to the back of the beater. Uncle's dark and caring eyes flashed to me, standing near and looking over my things. He passed me a small but sad smile.

That was what I expected, and I was thankful for that much (at least), knowing he was feeling many of the same things I was, being back here with them for the first time in years. I watched as he bent over, his black hair gleaming in the sunlight. There was no point in fighting him on it—again. A few beaters passed loudly on the street next to us. It filled the hush between us. I glanced around the trunk and realized we were the only ones out on the street. The last time I was here, there were kids everywhere. But I guess, like me, they grew up.

Another auto passed as we carried my luggage up the

short set of stairs to the front door. If we were in any other neighborhood, I would worry about Regulations being called. However, no one would do that here.

I followed silently behind Uncle into what would be my new home. Like I had as a child, I did my best to copy his movements. If I wanted to fit in here in my new home, I would need to do all I could to look the part. That included how I walked and talked.

The small townhouse was impressive for its size—given its location. It stood tall and skinny in the middle of the Maan district, sandwiched between similar homes. With four bedrooms, it was a rare find in such an area.

The carpet was freshly vacuumed and the whole house smelled of cinnamon. No doubt, Auntie worked all hours to get this place in perfect shape for my arrival. She always did, but I didn't notice until I was older. She pulled out all the stops for me whenever I came.

The bedrooms were on the top floor, with three flights of narrow and creaky stairs to get there. I was given the last room in the hall. Auntie and Uncle's room was the first and cousin Reglin's second. While one door on the floor, the one I used to share when I came here, stayed shut tight and silent. Untouched from the outside and -what I suspected- the inside as well.

Auntie was waiting for us in my new room. The white walls stood out against the dark purple sheets she was currently dressing the small single bed with. The sheets and curtains didn't match but the light yellow brightened the room. The carpet was exactly as I remembered; gray and scratchy. It was easy to get rug burn from it but no one would be rolling around on it anymore.

I took in the sight of my Aunt. It had been so long that her honey-brown hair had some gray streaks in it now. If Auntie Caroline had been the one to collect me from the station, no one would question us. Her features were close to matching mine. We were the ones with similar backgrounds since she grew up a Gilded.

Her round, dark blue eyes found me a second later, "AH! Josaline, you're finally here!!" She shouted as she grabbed me up in a fierce hug as she spoke.

"Hello, Auntie. Long time no see." Which was a bit of an understatement.

Auntie's hold only got tighter, and I didn't fight her on it, letting her get her fill. I slowly pulled back a small distance, and my shoulders were held so Aunt Caroline could look me over. Even though Caroline smiled, she couldn't hide the sadness in her eyes. Agony twinkled back at me as if to wave and say, 'I'm here to stay'.

Aunt Caroline's attention shot to my locks. Her smile grew, but it was still not as encompassing as it once was. "Oh my. And I thought the Holo exaggerated the color?"

As I had at Uncle's comments, I gently touched my pink strands, long curls springing back in place after my fingers released them. "Nope. Thank you for allowing me to stay with you."

"Of course, Josaline. That was always the plan, wasn't it?" Caroline said, her smile slipping a bit.

"When you called and told us you were attending Utrius Omega, we were both quite surprised—to say the least," Uncle admitted.

"Come on now, Dad," we all turned to the new voice, "Jo has always been sneaky smart...and tricky!"

Creeping in from behind, my cousin Reglin joined us.

His wavy, brown hair was longer than when I last saw him, and he had a slight shadow on his chin of dark hairs. The beard attempt threw me the most, though, since he barely shaved the last time I was here. Also, his posture was more pronounced now, looking even more like a Gilded than before—taking after his mother.

Wrapping an arm around my neck, Reglin ruffled my hair in an immature show of affection. But knowing him and the situation, it all felt forced.

"Some of us hide that sort of thing while others flaunt it!" I squealed, acting along.

Ducking out of Glin's grasp, I gave him a slight shove while he smirked. "If I didn't, people would try to take advantage of this cute face!"

It was so good to talk with them like this. Like everything was normal. I hoped Uncle, Auntie, and Glin felt the same way about it as I did. Otherwise, all my acting was for nothing. Uncle sobered suddenly, pointing a finger at his son. "Speaking of, you need to keep an eye on your cousin, Glin. The city is *nothing* like the life you've lived. A Country Bumpkin like her will easily get taken advantage of."

He said 'Country Bumpkin,' but I knew what he meant. It was more than the crime rate that was different here in the city than in the countryside where I grew up.

It was the expectations set upon you based on who your family was.

But it wasn't as if I had never been here before, that I had never spent time in the city with this side of my family. Or that I lacked any street skills at all—not that I could tell them about any of that. As Glin said, I was sly.

So, I was only able to give a vague response. "I do have some street smarts, Uncle."

He gave both Reglin and me a glare. "A seventeen-year-old doesn't have street smarts. You may be old enough for career placement, and the government might see you as an adult, Josaline, but you're both still naïve to the real world. You two will be fine together but be careful who you associate with. I know you've lived as an *Untouchable*, Jo, but that's the big difference between here and your life in Renize." I cringed at my town's title on instinct. If anyone knew where I hailed from it would be bad. "Take care of each other because no one else will."

Reglin nor I could fight Uncle on that subject. Even if we did have the words for it, we knew better than ever to say them to Uncle or Auntie. I refused to let fear guide who I spent time with ever again. After what happened with Rene, all I had was regret. Regret that I wouldn't have if I hadn't been afraid to mix with a tier other than my own.

The gentle twinkling of a Holo interrupted what was a solemn moment. Reglin pulled out a Holophone. His whole demeanor changed as soon as he glanced at it. "I . . . have to go…."

"Go?! But…your Cousin just got here!" Aunt Caroline whispered with her worry clear.

Reglin went from the carefree guy I remembered to serious and determined in a flash. Or rather a diginote. "I know, and I'm sorry, but this can't wait."

Uncle Haru sighed agitatedly. "Your Mother prepared a feast in Jo's honor…."

"I'll be home late. Welcome home, Josaline."

He rushed out, avoiding any more conversation on the subject. I watched Glin's fleeting form -noting how he now walked with a pronounced slump- and tried to ignore the worry creeping up my spine, especially when I saw the looks on Auntie and Uncle's faces. How could Glin act so casually about walking out on his family? After what they'd been through?

"He is always going somewhere these days. And he never tells me where!"

Uncle wrapped an arm around his wife's shoulders and gently pulled her from the room. "I'm sure he would tell us if it was something to worry about. Reglin is a good boy."

There was little doubt in my mind that Glin was, in fact, a good boy, which made it all more strange. With loss, people change, so it wouldn't be odd for Reglin to have become a completely different person. But what kind of person had he become, and what kind of trouble had it gotten him into? When Glin read his Holo, the look on his face spoke volumes on how he felt about the message he received. Whatever it was that had him coming and going so much… Glin was facing it with so much determination. It scared me.

Chapter Two

*Sometimes the best heroes are the ones in your head—
but that doesn't make them any less real.*
**-Ashley Poston, <u>The Princess and the Fangirl (Once
Upon a Con, #2)</u>**

I needed a distraction. And there was plenty,

relatively new to the city and my new school to check out. It

took swearing not to go far and be back before dark to get

permission to leave the house for a while.

Honestly, I was surprised I got that much.

Part of me had worried I would never be allowed to

go alone. It had been almost a year, and even though there

was no real getting over it, Auntie and Uncle seemed to be

getting used to it. I didn't pretend to know how much my

arrival threw them off the new norm. But, I did know keeping

with the plan and coming here had a jarring effect on me that

I hadn't expected.

As promised, my journey was straight to the Utrius

Omega campus. It was a trip that passed the brightly lit and overcrowded streets of Ocresa as it flew by on the tram. Everything was tall and highlighted by lights that danced with a display. In the middle of the day, the holographics were burning away, trying to sell everything from Smokers to underwear. The thick layer of clouds hanging near the buildings' tops gave a little shade to the light show. It hid the tips of the buildings, making it look like they stretched on into space. I watched the lights reflect on the bottom of the fog, causing the clouds to look multicolored until the Magtram dipped into the covered track. When it entered the light again, I was in an oasis, surrounded by the lush green grounds of Utrius.

Utrius Omega (affectionately known as UO as in 'You Owe Us your life') was like its own world. It was sheltered from the harsh streets and shadowy buildings that towered over most of the city—sheltered so much that I had to press my forearm into the tram's ID reader again to be allowed off on their grounds.

A few gut-twisting heartbeats and it pinged my admittance, showing those on the tube with me -who didn't

34

already know from my clothes and posture- where I stood in this world (since it was *impossible* to fake an ID chip). I half expected it to be rejected. I barely got into this Career Placement and would have to work hard to stay in it. It was all additional proof of UO's elitism.

As well as how in the world of grit and grime, it stood untouched and clean. And although far shorter, the buildings on campus still loomed over me without touching the smog blanket above. Every building was gleaming with glass that was frosted to opaque.

"So much for getting a peek into the classrooms," I muttered to myself.

But the buildings weren't what was impressive. It was all the life. The whole campus gave off the vibe of being in the country. Even the air was fresher but that was likely my imagination. It was strangely relaxing but that was probably the point. A mixture of Mute and Gilde working hard to secure their futures, they would need a break from the stress.

The large dome-shaped buildings dotted along a perfectly paved pathway. There were many and they seemed to go on forever. One for every career path, at least. One side had a hover walk for anyone short on time, tired, or disabled to make it to class easier. Planned gardens added color instead of holo ads like the other buildings in the city. Trees covered the walk with shade that helped with the heat. If it weren't for the blanket of smog high above, giving the sun a soft glow, I would think I'd left the city completely. It felt like . . . home. I had mixed feelings about this sanctuary in the electric fortress.

With my class list glowing on my Holo, I roamed around, looking for each of my future classrooms so I wouldn't be lost on the first day. I was already at the bottom of the heap. The last thing I needed was to be the fool among fools. And I wouldn't have that dumbfounded look on my face –overwhelmed by the campus– for all to see.

I just roamed and ingested the many buildings and parks within the Elită Campus, which held the few arts offered and the 'top' science majors. It took me two directories to find UO's Art Museum, tucked away and tiny compared to everything else on the campus. Of course, why would art be high on the list for funding and support?

The massive Medical Research part of campus took

the longest to get through, and their Library was three times the size of the Museum I now stood in. That was predictable. The real stars of this place were in the medical and science fields. UO was famous for inventing Medi-mechs, so their credits went to medical and engineering colleges.

With my low scores, I only made it as a Humanities Career. I was far from the elite sharing the grounds with me. It would be nothing like Primaries and Fundamentals. At least here, no one would know who I was and wouldn't be fake or befriend me for my parents.

Being a Gilded while among Mutes would be new, and I would never be the lowest on the pole, no matter how dumb I was. But, that made my belly twist more with guilt and fear, not reassurance. The whole point of going to UO was to be with Rene. Now, it was just to escape the life my parents had planned for me. The last thing I wanted was to be another blind Gilded that married within her tier and did nothing but throw parties for her husband.

I didn't want to become my mother.

The sun was starting to set when I made for home, and it was still sticky with the heat outside. There was a slight reprieve on the Magtram from the sun but no climate control. The mixture of perfumes returned, just like on the Elecotrain, but this time the smell of sweat was strong. My thin cotton dress is doing as much as possible to keep me cool. However, I still have sweat forming on my forehead and back.

It didn't help that the tram was packed with no empty seats in sight. I took up a small corner near the door. I was running the risk of getting pushed out at the wrong stop, but if I didn't stand there, a pervert might touch me, and I would be defenseless in such a large crowd. One of the many things my visits here in the past had taught me.

One thing had changed since I was a kid visiting. There were no segregated tubes anymore. I didn't see any Mutes from where I stood. A quick stop and more piled onto the overcrowded box. I pressed hard into my corner. It was primarily professionals in suits making their way home. With all of them Gilded, I had the comfort of knowing that most would be gone before my stop on the edge of Gilded and Mute territory.

It was quiet with everyone on their Holos. The screen

flashing on their faces made them look hollow. It made the hum of the tram deafening, a comforting reminder that the Magnets were firmly attached to the track. On a few of the crowd, I could see the tiny light of their Pods under their skin just below their ears, telling me they were listening to something besides the hum with me. There were so many bodies around me. I couldn't even move and struggled to distinguish one person from another in the sea of dark, pristine fabrics.

So, I focused on other thoughts, ones I wasn't sure I should ever think about. But when I was alone, I couldn't stop myself.

Rene.

It had been five years since my last visit, yet our plans had always been the same: we would be together in career placement no matter what. It was my idea to go to UO, even though Rene had the grades for it—money or not. It was the only way I would ever get my parent's permission to go to career placement. The establishment would have to be someplace so elite that they couldn't say no.

I bristled at the thought. The only reason I hadn't

visited in so long was because of my parents! They didn't think it was good for me to be so close. Or near so many Mutes. I shook my head at their voices in my head. How calloused and simple-minded my parents were was disgusting sometimes; my stomach twisted with nausea. Even more, now that Rene had been missing for eight months.

The weight in my heart only grew, allowing them to keep us apart for so long. And if I was honest, I blamed my parents for Rene's disappearance a little bit.

"Josaline… is Rene with you?"

Aunt Caroline's voice still echoed in my mind. The desperation. The fear. Any thoughts on my missing cousin made my chest ache—it was filled with anger, regret, and sorrow, making my eyes sting with unshed tears. We had been best friends, practically twins, as the only females in the family our age. I looked up to Rene and her wild personality. Rene was brave in the world she was born into and always had her hair dyed bright and beautiful colors, standing out as much as possible with her differences. When I came home with pink hair, my parents forced me to cut ties.

How much of my disappearance from Rene's life

caused her to go missing from everyone else's? I couldn't think about things like that, not now. Even though they plagued me at night as I waited for sleep to claim me. Still four stops from mine, I prayed that at least some of the crowd would get off soon. As it was, I was struggling to breathe.

Breathing, I battled with even more when I felt a hand on my thigh.

At first, it seemed like an accident. A touch that brushed against my skin. But then it returned and lingered, searching my exposed flesh. Given my position, the most I could do was try and shake it off. But it persisted. I couldn't move with so many people around me, and I couldn't tell who the culprit was! I was close to screaming when the hand started to move upwards, planning on going up my skirt.

Struggling, I pushed against those around me who only glared in response. My heart was about to explode from my chest, and tears burned my throat. Meager squeaks of fear-filled upset escaped my lips while the rest of the world around me watched their screens and listened to their Pods.

I was getting assaulted in a room full of people, and no one was doing anything. Myself included.

"Hey!" A deep voice cut across the hum of the crowd. My eyes went to the man automatically. But he wasn't looking at or speaking to me. "I don't think she likes that. How about you stop so I don't have to come over there?"

I followed his stare and found a man -who paled at the man's words- a short distance from me. The hand on me evaporated like magic, and I tried to breathe easier. But after such a close call, it was a struggle. My heart refused to slow the more I thought about it.

Instead, I focused on my hero. His head poked out over all the others. His shaggy black hair looked unkempt and carefree, making me believe that he wasn't one of the businessmen around. Mutes didn't get office jobs often, but Uncle Haru worked in an office, so it wasn't impossible.

All I could see was his head. No way to know if he was in a suit or not. I had seen his face and eyes for a flash when he spoke up for me. But I barely focused, and now he was buried in a book. A small paperbound novel. It was a strange sight outside the stash I had (and was teased for most of my life) because no one read from a *book* anymore.

There was no way to get his attention unless I called

out, but that would be far too embarrassing, especially without knowing his name. It felt worth it to see the intriguing flash of gold from his eyes again, but he had just saved me, so it would be impolite to harass him. Right? A Gilded would take it as a service and never say thanks.

Three stops later, the train finally cleared to a bearable level. My hero stood unmoving, somehow keeping his balance while focusing elsewhere without support. I was sure now he was a Mute. Or at least mostly, his posture didn't look like that of a Mute but his clothes did. He had to be tier five Mute or tier six Gilde.

That explained the fear and complete compliance from the guy that touched me. It was hard to tell if this guy was a Mute or Gilded. As an Untouchable Gilde, I had no reason to fear him, regardless. Unless my hero was a purist who attacked anyone not of their tier? I had never feared anyone based on stupid stereotypes or rumors anyway.

There was little chance the guy would even talk to me. He didn't seem like he wanted to speak to anyone with his face in a book (ignoring everything and everyone around him). He had helped me, so maybe he would? I was careful

43

as I made my way to his side. With the next stop my last, I had a limited time to thank him for his kindness. It was now or never.

Now that there was room, and a small circle around him.

The other Gildes kept their distance, and I knew only a portion of it was because he called out threats a few minutes ago. He didn't flinch as I stood beside him, completely lost in his book. If he was a Mute, he had no apprehension of me. But I was trying to look and move like a Mute. Some things are impossible to hide (like the high-quality clothes I was wearing), and anyone paying attention would probably see right through me. However, it was nice to think I was pulling it off, coming to stand right in front of my savior.

I had to grab the support pole nearby as I took in his slim-fit jeans and loose button-up he wore open with a clear view. His shirt's dark red and black plaid stood out boldly against the white of his t-shirt underneath. And his jeans touched the tops of his pure white sneakers. Clearly, not a businessman like so many on the train today. He was too casually dressed. His clothes looked every bit the Mute that he was. Standing up for a Gilded made him different from most Mutes. He reminded me of my Uncle.

Now close and able to see him, I regret not just calling out to him. The guy is gorgeous, and it was even harder to speak. "Um . . . excuse me?" He either ignored me or didn't hear. The glow of his Pods was missing, so they weren't on. "Excuse me!" His eyes shifted slightly, looking at me for only a minuscule second, but I saw it. The flash of his beautiful golden eyes made my heart tremble this time. "I just want to thank you. For earlier? If you hadn't said anything…."

"I almost didn't. Dressed like that on a crowded tram? And then you said nothing to the guy."

I suddenly needed to smooth down my dress as if it would somehow make it longer. The material was soft on my skin and palms, except for the small buttons (top to bottom) in the middle. Did he know I was a Gilded? Is that why he questioned my silence–he thought I was a Mute? "No one else did or said anything either."

"They probably thought you wanted it. I wasn't sure

myself at first."

My anger swelled. It made my throat hurt again with angry tears I refused to shed. "Of course, I didn't!"

"How would anyone know? A tiny, Gilded girl with mediocre looks wears such skimpy clothes on the F? Maybe she's just lonely . . ."

Well, that answered that question. "I came over here to thank you, but now I feel like taking it back!!"

He shrugged, the lack of care clear on his pretty face and lackluster tone. "I don't need it anyway."

If he didn't want to associate with a Gilded, he could have said as much or given me a short 'you're welcome' and moved on. But no, he was a jerk and not out of any fear of being seen with me. He was one just to be one. I didn't know him, and he didn't know me, but it only took a split second to decide how we felt about one another. And I didn't like him— saving my skin be damned.

The tram slowed, the hum of the magnets fading the slower it got, and I couldn't get off it fast enough. I took one stomp away from my fallen hero, and he grabbed my wrist. It felt like a burn with his hot palm and fingers wrapped tightly around my skin.

"You're welcome, Gilde. Never say a Mute did nothing for you, alright?"

I didn't know how to feel, but I did feel a loss when he let me go. Somehow, I got off the tram, but his golden irises were melted to me, burning the entire time the car shifted away.

Chapter Three

"Being a hero means ignoring how silly you feel."
— **Diana Wynne Jones, *Fire and Hemlock***

Although UO was modern and sleek, I had to admit the Humanities buildings were clearly the least well maintained. The hall I sat in now with around a hundred other students barely had climate control. All the people around me looked miffed, either from the lack of cooler air or the hard built-in desks on risers we had to sit in. They squeaked every time anyone moved, so most of us were frozen. My desk had a few names etched in on the top. You had to be pretty bored to scratch in the name Alexander Zion Knowelby an inch deep. The school must be pretty cheap not to fix it too. It gave me something to do as I waited for class to start, running my fingertips along the letters.

Now day two of classes and the professors were

plunging into the curriculum. My New World History class followed suit as the room fell into darkness, the wall at the front lighting up with the projected lecture. It was like the holographics in front of City Center buildings, but smaller and more precise. The microscopic projector was in the floor, a piece of glass over it to protect it while it shined on a glass diamond above it. Two more projectors hit the box at different angles to complete the image.

Then a man stepped between me and my line of sight to the holographic. "Welcome to day two of New World History 101. For those of you who already forgot, I'm Professor Smith. Let's begin." There was a slight shift of anxiety within the classroom. "For those who think you can skate through this class, having grown up in said New World, think again."

Great, now I am looking forward to this required course. The image changed, a picture of what appeared to be the busy streets of Ocresta. Sidewalks were filled with a mix of people from different tiers as the professor began pointing at heads.

"Now, most of you are well-aware of basic History,

how the War of Class caused the entire World's economy to crash and sent the civilization into chaos. The Great Crash was over a century ago, and we all live in a rebuilt world. Right now, I want everyone in this room to take a good look around."

Like everyone else, I was doing as told. Eyes met mine before shifting off to someone else. A few lingered, but they were bored within seconds of making eye contact–quickly moving on to the next. They all varied, either blonde, brown, or black hair, but I was the only wild colored. Their features switched around, some with thick lips, others with big eyes, and a few with broad noses. The skin pigment was all shades. But one thing was clear, and I had noticed as soon as I entered the Humanities campus on the first day. There was a lack of a single Mute in the room—on the entire campus.

"Anyone notice something strange?" Professor Smith asked.

No one raised their hand, the silence slowly becoming humorous. But I couldn't take much more of the awkwardness and hated looking dumb.

I raised my hand (unsure of the rules) and waited before speaking. Professor Smith took his time, noticing me and then looking me over carefully before permitting me to talk. "There are no Mutes in this class."

Professor Smith nodded, and several eyes turned my way–glaring. It wasn't my fault, and it was true. There were no Mutes on the Humanities campus. Did they seriously not notice? Or not care? Maybe they were pissed because they thought I was one until they took a closer look? The 'natural' look costs more than the 'wild'. Add in the Mutes' need to stand out somehow, and any neon or unnatural color was a hit within the Mute community. Wild colors weren't something many Gildes did, and the classroom was filled with Gildes.

"And you won't find any on this side of the Elită campus. It is challenging to go from a Mute to a Gilded. Damn near impossible. As many of you know, going down in tiers is easy, but going up? Gilded are at the top in pay and control the law and money of the world. That is why you won't find a Mute wasting their time and money on a degree in Humanities. If they have the funds for Career Placement or are clever enough to get a scholarship, Mutes will put it towards a degree that will get them closer to the upper tiers."

The faces around me turned humble. Prof Smith's plan worked. He wanted us to feel a need to impress. We might be Humanities majors, but now we wouldn't be slacking off for the teacher that put us in our place. I already knew I was at the bottom, but I was still too happy to be where I was to care.

"Wish you could see this, Rene." I thought to myself.

Professor Cranky Smith continued his rant on differences while my eyes still swept the classroom. Until landing on one girl.

She didn't stand out physically. Her looks blended into the rest of the room, but she was still gorgeous. Platinum blond hair that was stick-straight and fell past her shoulders in a messy and sexy way I could only wish to pull off. Her skin was a porcelain color, making the bright red lipstick she wore stick out more on her thick lips. The girl may not have had wild hair like me, but the upturn of her chin in determination as she glared down at Professor Uppety Smith was a look I'd seen many times on Rene's face whenever someone expected her to be silent.

The lecture wrapped after a few more hits to our place in this society. Everyone's shoulders had a small sag to them as we empty the room. Not enough to be confused for a Mute, but still noticeable.

With all of us knocked down a tier (metaphorically), it seemed like as good a time as any to boost my new life here in Ocresta by making new connectors. A clump of girls from the class were paused before me and talking casually. I approached slowly, taking in their stance and clothing. My thread count was lower but that was on purpose.

I gave them a small wave and a smile; their frowns instantly made me shy. The friendly air that was there a second ago evaporated.

"What's with your hair? Are you ashamed of yourself?" One blonde with high cheekbones asked.

It wasn't anything new for me. People always questioned a Gilded with bright hair like mine. If I told them who I was, they would back off instantly. And I still refused to give up my name even if they beat it out of me.

Making friends was never a struggle for me back home but now, I was wondering how much of that was my title. If these girls were so quick to dismiss me then it was going to be a long and lonely semester.

I didn't want that, Rene wouldn't want that either. I had changed minds before, so maybe I could now. "I'm not ashamed. I love pink!" I said honestly. "What about you?"

I could hear their eye rolls. Being asked your favorite color was so Primaries but I couldn't think of anything else to say. What I said wouldn't have made a difference to these girls. We had a massive gap in our mentalities that would never be breached. It didn't matter how much money fed your family tree. We all bleed red. And these girls believed the Gilde lie that we had gold in our veins.

Their dislike for me was for not looking like them. It made me wonder how they would have treated me if I was a Mute?

I should be embarrassed or ashamed but I was only disappointed. And I wondered how much more I could take as the blonde girl I admired during class stepped in between them all. My heart jumped into my throat, worried my new 'hero' would soon disappoint just like the Mute on the tram. "You're in Humanities on your own scores, so don't take it out on her. It shows just how stupid you really are." I was shocked, but the girl just wrapped an arm around my shoulders like we were best friends. "Shift off before I have my Daddy fire all of yours."

There was no way to know if the blonde girl was serious or if her threat held any weight to these girls until they scattered like ice on a hot pan—fast and without real direction. We may have all been Gilded, but tiers mattered to most. And this girl showed how high up the chain she was compared to the rest in a single moment.

My apprehension settled out of my belly, and I pulled out of the stranger's grip to hold out my hand as a replacement. "Josaline."

"Camillia Trevor. And yes, I'm from those Trevors."

Well, that explained it. "Oh…"

Camillia's status didn't intimidate me in the slightest. I was surprised that someone from that family would be in the Humanities section… and talking to me without knowing who I was or my tier. For a split second, I had to wonder if my parents somehow set up Camillia coming into my life? It was something they would do, and I didn't put it past them to try.

Camillia and her family were in the ninth tier of the Gilded, but my family and I were still higher. The Trevors were one of the richest families inside the city. Those who lived in the countryside like mine were the richest in the world. If anyone knew who I was . . . it would be a different type of trouble that I didn't need or want.

The smile Camillia wore was genuine, and she'd just saved me from unnecessary stress. Even if my parents set it up, our friendship was inevitable.

She gently fingered a curl of mine in admiration. "So, how does one end up with pink hair these days?"

Camillia began to walk in the same direction I needed, so I followed along. "A cheap dye kit at home, that's how."

She smiled and nodded, turning into the classroom I had next. I dared to sit next to her and Camillia continued to hold my attention. "What did you think of Professor Smith's introduction today?"

I shrugged, "Honest…but not entirely fair."

"I know, right? I may not be bright but I still got into

Career Placement at UO. And my parents didn't lift a finger to do it either."

She glanced at the door and I followed her gaze. The clump of mean girls was just passing by. I giggled at the insult they would never hear and turned back to Camillia. She had her textbook up on her Hpad and groaned. "I'm going to have to work my butt off to stay here."

"Me too."

We left it at that, focusing on the lecture. When it finished, we walked out and to our next class. We had three out of four classes together and sat together for all of them. It was the beginning of a routine. One that continued (to my delight) a week later. And now, Camellia and I met up after classes too. I had made my first real friend.

The afternoon sun was nearing its peak, and the only place of refuge I could find from the sun was under a fan tree off the avenue. Although cold, the water bottle I held did little for the heat as I watched all those that filtered by, looking just as hot as I was.

I sat right on the grass in my lovely dress, too hot and tired to care. I'd been at it since seven a.m. and (at the moment) covered in sweat. It was hard to care about formalities on a regular day. Most of my classes were in outdated buildings. The Humanities department was far from highly funded, so all the facilities had climate control but not good air conditioning. And it never got this bad at home. So, I was exhausted after baking in most of my courses all day, only to walk home in the hot sun.

My new routine had become: rising at dawn, catching the tramway (while eating my breakfast most times), going to class, parking under a tree for a few moments, then heading home to study and eat. I had thought Reglin would show me around the city and spend time with me, but he was always in and out of the house. Auntie and Uncle were a bit gray each time he left without a word.

Another body joined me, plopping on the grass right next to me in a pair of tight denim shorts and a flowy halter top. "Anything worth mentioning?"

Camillia lifted her bright blonde locks off her neck and back for a few short moments, fanning her freed skin with her empty hand while I watched on in awe of her beauty. "Not sure. Why don't you tell me, Cami? See anything worthy of your affections?"

Camilla dropped her bundle with a loud huff and rested her elbow on her bended knees, placing her face on her palms. "There is nothing but dull and boring people here!"

"Isn't that a bit repetitive?"

I giggled while Camillia just stuck her tongue out at me. "You're the only interesting person I have met at this college, and even you're pretty dull, Josaline."

"Gee . . . thanks . . . "

"Let's do something this weekend at least?!"

Now I huffed loudly, "What are we supposed to do? Neither of us knows the area at all."

Standing abruptly, Camillia took a stance like a superhero cartoon, her fists on her hips and her chin up in the air. "Then we should get to know it! Together! We will meet at your place and go from there!!" She said in a haughty and loud voice.

I hesitated, worrying for a moment about Camillia seeing where I lived. I wasn't ashamed, but I also didn't want to lose my new friend. But if Camillia was that type of person to shun Mutes and my family, then we shouldn't be friends in the first place.

Standing next to her, I took the same stance. "That's right! Let's have an adventure!! Two are better than one when exploring, right??"

A mischievous giggle came from my friend that had me shrinking back towards the tree. "I'm so glad you said so, Jo. Because you and I are going to do some exploring this afternoon!!"

"Uhhh…. what?"

Camillia had a hold on my bag, taking it hostage before my brain could follow the action. "You and I will check out more of this campus now!"

"I don't know, Camillia. Shouldn't we do that on a day without classes? Won't we just get in the way of the other students?" I asked with genuine worry.

Camillia rolled her eyes, turning away to start our journey ignoring my protests. "Not if we are just strolling around outside. Besides, the point is to do with others on campus. To meet people. Come on! We can't spend all our days hanging around the Humanities' buildings! We will never meet anyone more intelligent than us!!!"

I hung my head in defeat, following along behind until Camillia looped her arm through mine and pulled me instead. Camillia was the only new friend I had made since school started weeks ago. The other girls didn't seem to like that too much, but they had already cast me out of their club, so what harm did it really do?

Cutting through a couple of the Humanities' buildings, we were soon deep in the Engineering department. A few people stood outside, chatting or reading, all deeply entrenched in their tasks. With a rainbow of colors, I fit in more here than in the Humanities section, with natural and wild tones on top of heads everywhere. Professor 'Sore Butt' Smith was right. Mutes were all over other parts of campus. But the Gildes still overshadowed them in this crowd.

All of it was magical. Having gone to a segregated Primary and Fundamental, I had only heard stories most of my life about mixed tiers. I found it beautiful face to face with it. It was a struggle for me to take my eyes off it. I was not paying attention to where I was going. Good thing that Camillia was leading.

Or so I thought.

A rigid body crashed into me, knocking me free of Camillia's grip and falling to the ground. But large hands grabbed me before I hit the hard pavement, pulling me back up to my feet before I could make heads or tails of anything.

"Sorry about that. I wasn't looking where I was going." He smiled sheepishly at us.

Bright greens eyes clashed with mine. "It's alright. I wasn't either." I gave him a short bow of apology, and it was awkward.

The guy wasn't Gilded (at least not at mine or Cami's level). His clothes told me so. He was a low-tiered Gilde or a Mute—how I wanted to come off. And clearly, bowing in apology was not done by Mutes anymore.

He broke the moment by running a hand through his messy chocolate locks. The action caused the sun to bounce off of them. The color matched the thick and healthy beard on his lightly tanned face. "And here I thought I knew all the pretty girls in the Engineering department."

His warm and kind smile (hidden slightly by the thick and bushy beard) caused me to relax immediately. And his thick accent told me he wasn't from Ocresta. "That's because we aren't in the Engineering department. My friend and I are doing a little sightseeing."

Camillia appeared at my side, looking up at the stranger with hungry eyes. "Hi there."

He chuckled, letting Camillia look him over. "Where are you two from?"

I hesitated, but this guy knew we weren't Mutes anyway. "Humanities . . ."

"Oh, I see." He continued to smile, not showing any signs of care from my admittance. I liked him instantly.

A short silence fell over us, and Camillia gave me a small elbow into my ribs. "I'm sorry. My name is Josaline, and this is my friend Camillia Trevor."

"Nice to meet you. I'm Jebediah Green, but everyone calls me Jeb."

I smiled politely this time instead of bowing, but Camillia stuck out her hand to him. "Green, huh? I've never heard of your family before. Are you from here, or did you migrate?"

My mouth dropped open in shock, and then I started to chastise Camillia for being so brash, but Jeb's laughter stopped me. "Alora. Let me guess . . . Trebridge?"

"Oh, so you've heard of my family then? It's been a couple of generations since we moved to Ocresta." Camillia said with a cheeky smile.

I knew all about Cami's family and I still never noticed an accent. Jeb slowly nodded, his whiskers dancing from his smirking lips on his face. "Grew up just outside of Basea. And you, Josaline? Where are you from?"

"I'm from around, but . . . I'm nothing notable." Everyone knew the top tier Gildes, the ones who made the laws and were 'untouchable', lived in Renize. So I wouldn't be sharing that information.

My cheeks burned as the confused look on his face grew. "But . . . your clearly a Gilded. Your hair doesn't fool me."

Running my fingers across the top of my head, my hands dragged across the loose strands, and my curls bounced from it. I found myself doing the unconscious action more and more since I went pink. "My family has been here since before the Reconstruction."

I didn't dare say more than that, fear leeching into my

chest that I had already said too much. If they found out I was from Renize, they would know I was high up on the Gilded food chain. Not exactly how high, but enough to make people uncomfortable.

Jeb opened his mouth, not getting a sound out before another man draped himself over our new friend. His arm went around Jeb's neck, bending as he did, forcing them to lower their heads a bit at the action. It was all fast, and all I caught was the hair color of the newcomer, light blond, catching the sun more than Jeb's.

When they popped back up, Jeb immediately removed the man from him, pulling his arm up and off. "Jeb, who are these lovely ladies you are talking so adamantly with?"

Jeb gave his friend an agitated shove and glared back at him. "Buri, this is Josaline and Camillia Trevor."

Much to Jeb's obvious displeasure, the one called Buri leaned an elbow on his shoulder. "Hello pretties, I'm Ziyad Green, but everyone calls me Buri."

How long would my lack of a last name bother them? I hadn't even told Camillia yet, and I hoped to keep it to myself for as long as possible. But Camillia appeared to be as agitated with me not sharing during this conversation as when we first met. Frankly, if I could change it, I would and never be associated with my family again. The few I could stand with the same surname as me would understand.

At some point, it would come up. After all, you didn't honestly know someone until you knew their full name. And their family. I could only hope that I wasn't judged too harshly when that time came.

"Buri?"

Camillia managed to make her confusion look cute. And Buri was eating it up. "Yeah, it's short for another name people call me."

"What name is that?"

The duo just smiled at me, ignoring my question altogether. So Camillia filled the void. "Buri, you are from Alora as well?"

"Aye, Miss, the two of us cousins been together since birth. Used to share pacifiers...."

"You never shared anything you just took." Jeb shoved Buri off him at that.

Buri righted himself, standing on his own now. "Don't be like that!" He turned his attention back to the two of us. "We're like brothers. Followed each other all the way here, we did."

The two reminded me so much of Rene and me that it hurt. But I still wanted to learn more, see how much they were like my cousin and me. "Something tells me you followed him?" Buri's accent was far thicker than Jeb's, and he didn't hold himself as straight as Jeb either. Which only made me like him more. I loved that Ocresta was a mix of people and backgrounds. It made it far less tedious, like back in my hometown.

Buri started to pout, and Jeb punched his shoulder hard. "Did you want something, you idiot?"

It was as if a switch was flipped, Buri becoming sober instantly. "It's about this weekend. I need your help with a bit of work…."

"Ah. I see. Ladies, it was nice to meet you. I hope we run into one another again soon."

We all waved, Buri a little after the rest of us as if he forgot and split ways. Camillia wrapped an arm through mine again, pulling me along. "See? That wasn't too bad, now was it?"

Chapter Four

"When you're truly awesome, you know that it's actually a burden and wish day after day to be relieved of such a curse. Think of about 95% of the superheroes."
— **Criss Jami, *Diotima, Battery, <u>Electric Personality</u>***

I was still working on my homework when I heard Reglin come home. Going straight to his room, I waited for a few beats, took a deep breath before leaving my desk, and stepped out into the hall. But as I stepped out, he did the same, looking genuinely surprised at the sight of me.

"Did I wake you?"

"No, I was waiting for you."

His hand was still on the knob of his door, but he was in his PJs, the same as me. "Me?"

"I was hoping we could . . . talk."

He pressed a finger to his lips and pulled his hand from his door to grab one of mine. Tiptoeing down, we silently made for the front door. I was confused when he pulled us outside, but then he took us to the garage, opening the gate after placing his forearm on the reader. The creek and whine of the old lifter had me worried we would wake the whole street, but Reglin seemed unphased.

Entering first, he called out to the lights to turn on, flooding us with bright fluorescents. On one side was Uncle's beater, a modest car that was black, aged, and nothing special. But on the other side, next to it, were two lightcycs. And by the look of them, the cycs were *railbroken*.

Reglin already had his toolbox out, crouching down to work on one of them, while I was trying to reign in my excitement at the sight of the two cycs. It was clear which one had gotten more love between the two, the one Glin currently squatted before a complete machine with black–colored metal for the covers.

"What did you want to talk about?"

I watched him for a few moments as he worked (curious beyond words), then pulled my attention to the lonely cyc sitting untouched. "Are both of these yours?"

Glin nodded, "Yep. Got them at a Regulations'

auction. Both crashed while trying to run from Regulators."

That explained why the cycs were rigged to break the speed barriers. My hand took on a life of its own, walking down with the seat's soft leather against my palm. Glin had stripped the one I touched of its coverings, exposing the machine's organs and bones. "They're beautiful. I didn't think you liked lightcycs? I remember you saying something about 'why have two wheels when you could have four'?"

"You could lend a hand, you know?"

Glancing up, I caught the raise of his brow. "Alright."

Taking a closer look, I crouched next to the other cyc before picking up my weapon and starting to work. "So . . . Glin . . . we haven't really . . . talked since I got here."

He chuckled, but there was a sadness to it. "Yeah, sorry about that. I got a . . . job, and it is very demanding. I never really have a free moment. "

"Do you think . . . you might have some time this weekend? A friend from school and I want to explore the city, and I thought you could show us a few cool spots?"

It had been years since I had spent even this much time with my cousin, and I found I was nervous. It was clear he wasn't the same person I once knew with his ins and outs. And I was afraid the new him wouldn't like me anymore. With what he'd been through with Rene…

He froze, leaning back and looking at me before a smile grew on his face. "I think I can give you some time. As long as it's early in the day. How about Saturday?"

My heart returned to normal, and my face hurt from the smile I gave him in return. "Sounds good."

Falling silent, we returned to our work. With grease on my palms and numbness in the pads of my fingers, I felt at peace. It had been too long since I had been allowed to do work like this. When I was younger, my father let me hang around him and my brother when they played with their lightcycs. Then, later, I snuck away to play with my cyc. It wasn't until they found out what I was doing that I had to stop.

My joy must have been showing on my face as Reglin came over to inspect my work. "Not bad. Keep this up, and you will have her running in no time." I grinned up at him and returned to my work. "Tell you what. You fix it, and it's yours."

"What?? Really?!"

"I know how much you love and miss riding." I ducked my head at the memory, yet another thing my parents took away from me for appearances. "Consider it a 'welcome' present, *Mōtāgāru*."

I bristled at the name, "I didn't think anyone remembered that name. Least of all you."

"Oh please, I was your biggest fan! After Rene, that is."

It was the nickname Uncle Haru gave me back when I was allowed to visit and ride a lightcyc. A lifetime ago, so much had changed, and I had stopped being the girl who raced for a cheap thrill. *Mōtāgāru*, or Motor Girl, no longer existed. Just like the language Uncle Haru spoke to give me the name. However, along with Glin and Rene, we forced Uncle to teach us bits and pieces, using it as code to speak to one another.

After the cold welcome Glin had given me upon arrival, ducking out moments after I had my stuff inside, it was hard to refuse the gesture, especially with his guilt so evident on his face and my overwhelming desire to ride the machine before me. Careful not to smear lubricant all over him, I leaped up and grabbed him, giving him a tight hug. Under it all, he was the same old Glin from my childhood. Just as sweet and giving, even if it was a bit strained. When I loosened my hold on him, I was bouncing with glee, pulling completely free to clap my hands together before getting back to work. It was all involuntary, too happy to care how foolish I looked as I acted the way I felt; like a little girl coming down the stairs on the first day of Primaries. Even more diligent, I had even more reason to work hard.

Classes were picking up their pace. At least with New World History I had Cami right beside me so we could roll our eyes together.

Professor Smith was yet to let up about the fact that we were all Humanities majors and how lame that was. A few in the class looked like they started to believe it. Some stopped coming and I assumed it was them giving up and going back home. I couldn't do that, so I had to push through.

The day seemed normal as the Prof turned on his holo projector and let it warm up. The expression on his face never changed causing the small grin on his lips to worry me. "Alright class, today we're diving into the only thing that matters in this world. Addendum AA001, the Tier system."

The classroom didn't have air conditioning, however, the topic made me shiver.

The projector queued up and soon a video began to play. It was shaky and the focus went in and out. It was an old video taken with an old phone. But, you could still make out the details like the location. It was an Electrotrain, just like the one I took to get to Ocresta. And they were filming inside the business class.

You could also make out who was in the video. At least the main characters. I saw two men standing with squared shoulders and a fight on their faces. There was no question what the disruption was over. I could tell because one man was a Mute while the other was a Gilded.

The Mute's nice but cheap clothing was a dead giveaway. The way he stood was also a clue. Mutes didn't get the same…education as the Gilded. There were a few mannerisms none could hide. And higher thread counts where something only Gildes could afford no matter what tier Mute you were.

"I don't want filth like you next to me. Go to the back!" The Gilde shouted.

The video suddenly paused. "The Mute in this fight was in tier one." Professor Smith explained. "You can tell by how dirty his shoes and hands are. He was probably returning from working a long shift in one of the food fields and just wanted to get home to rest."

My heart ached for the stranger in the video, but even if I was there, I or anyone else, couldn't protest or stand up, it was the law. If a Gilded didn't want to be near a Mute, the Mute had to listen.

No one said anything as the Mute took a new seat far away. "This is why they have the lovely name, Mute, as they are too poor and lowly to get a voice. Only those at the very top, Untouchables, have any say in the laws we follow today. The Gilded have the money and the power, so what they say goes. And those like the Mutes have to go along without a word and respectfully." Professor Smith smirked, and pointed to the tier poster on his wall. "Some people liked the Mutes where they were–lower economically and barely tolerated.

The laws reflected that, making it nearly impossible for a Mute to advance to the tier of the Gilded. It happened, but it was super rare. The Gilded hated the Mutes and believed they were lesser than them or feared them. The Gilded worried they would lose their spot in the golden sun."

I wasn't sure which group my parents played into—fear or hatred. They were the only reason I sat in first class. Their money and clout insisted on it.

"And that's why, Mutes will always be better than Gildes." Professor Smith finally said what he really felt about Mutes and Gildes. He was either a former Mute turned Gilde or he was a Mute supporter.

I was starting to like Professor Pain.

The group of girls I tried to befriend the first day were giggling the entire film. It was clear how they felt about Mutes. The rest of the room was silently scribbling down notes. Who didn't know what it was like for Mutes or the laws that made it that way for them? Everyone in the class acted as if they had never heard the word Mute before.

Everyone except me and Cami.

She was silent but she wasn't writing. Her arms were

crossed over her chest and she watched the screen intently. It was impossible to gage her feelings on the subject. I had hoped to get a clue before taking her to meet Glin and my family. The last thing I wanted was to be blindsided. But she gave nothing away and the rest of the class and week continued on.

I didn't let Glin forget his promise. We spent the rest of the week working side by side. I made sure to help him when I could. I was far more knowledgeable about cycs than he was. So he had no excuses when Saturday rolled around, and it was time for him to take Cami and me out.

It was nice seeing Reglin outside the house. Whatever had him so stressed since my return was no longer an issue. Or we were a good distraction which was a high possibility.

The sun shone bright and hot above us, but City Center's streets were continuously illuminated. The lights of animated billboards, holographic dancing, and neon signs added in. I watched as it reflected off the tops of my companion's light-colored strands. I was amazed by the switch Glin flipped inside himself. He was a completely different person as we walked around the city streets. If I didn't know him better (or didn't know his clothing's thread count), I never would have believed he was a Mute.

Glin soon took us to a more subdued area filled with bodies as they went in and out of storefronts. Some were overloaded with bags, while others held none. All were Gildes in this area, but Glin moved around easily, blending into the crowd. Even as a mixed blood, or *Alloyed* (*Plunge* as many mean-spirited people liked to call them), he could always blend into the Gilded crowd. Mine and Cami's apparent Gilded blood didn't matter even considering the area. No one would think we were mixing tiers and call Regulations.

Glin had gotten all his mother's traits and habits while Rene was more like their father. How unique their lives were, both Alloys and yet forced into two distinct societies due to mannerisms? I remembered how different the friends they kept were. Glin hung out with Gilded while Rene Mutes. Glin introduced me as his cousin outright whenever I met their friends, while Rene introduced me as a family friend. The one time Rene introduced me as her cousin… it had been bad.

"This is the Phey shopping district. It's one of the largest. " Reglin talked loudly to us, then veered into my ear while Camillia took in the sights. "I know this isn't your scene, but we can hit up some museums later when it's just the two of us. "

A shrug and a smile, and we set out to discover. I didn't mind going shopping, although I didn't love it as much as Camillia did. Soon the blonde was one of the many with her hands filled with bags. Somehow, she got Glin to carry most of them. Being the fashionable girl she was, Cami's shopping habit wasn't a surprise. What was, though, was her budget. The girl didn't even flinch as totals were read out to her. Camillia was a wealthy girl.

Far from destitute, I blinked several times when I read a few of the price tags and silently decided to keep my hands free for Camilla's purchases. I only wanted to use family money for school and nothing else. Even that much rubbed me the wrong way, but I had no choice if I wanted to go to school.

I was thankful for the small and cheap noodle shop

since my feet felt like they would fall off. One relaxed lunch later, and we slowly made our way back, the walk and tram ride taking the rest of the afternoon to arrive back at Glin's home.

This would be it, the moment Cami found out about my family. She had said nothing as we made our way into an Alloyed friendly neighborhood. But now, my palms were sweating as Glin walked before us up the small stoop to the front door. He was calm, either because he didn't know or care that Camillia was about to discover his mixed lineage. And my Alloyed family. It would be sad for me if she was disappointed. Suppose Cami turned out like so many who were disgusted to the point of being offended. I didn't think she would be like that, but I had been wrong before.

Cami was cool hanging out with those lesser than her or in a lower class. But how would she feel about hanging out in a home with a once Gilded mother and a Muted father?

Glin got his key in the door before it swung open, Auntie pulling us all in excitedly. "Come in, come in! Oh, I'm so excited to meet Jo's new friend!" Auntie was already gushing, laying it on thick in hopes of keeping my "new friend" from bolting. "Josaline has told us so much about you, Camillia!"

The blonde blushed, tucking a platinum strand behind her studded ear. "Thank you for having me inside your home. "

I knew this would be okay. Camillia was rich, and she hadn't so much as balked at our home, which was comfortable at best.

"Welcome," here was the final test, Uncle coming into plain view and giving a slight bow (where I got the antiquated notion), "it's a pleasure to meet you finally."

Cami was silent for a moment, but only a moment (and it was fleeting), stepping up without fear and a hand out to Uncle Haru. "Thank you for having me inside your home, Sir."

There was no need to worry. At most, I would lose a friend, and it wouldn't be the first time someone turned out not to be who I thought they were. But Cami was different. She was a good person and a true friend. The nervousness I had at this meeting melted away.

We were finishing dinner with Auntie and Uncle when

Glin's Holo went off, his face going paler than usual before shoving it back in his pocket.

"Everything alright, Sweetheart?"

I swore he flinched from Auntie's simple question. "Eh . . . yeah, everything is fine. I just have to go out tonight."

"Again? We have a guest."

Haru's tone was a warning, both Auntie and Uncle at the end of their rope with my cousin. "I'm sorry. I uh . . . just got called into work. It's an emergency."

They dropped the issue with no other choice, but I was far from satisfied. I watched Glin fidget in his seat for the rest of the meal. Dessert was before us when Camillia twisted over to my ear. "What's going on with Glin?"

"I don't know," I whispered, "this has been going on since before I got here."

"Where does he work? The morgue? Cause he looks like he might join the dead at any moment."

"I seriously doubt he is off to work. The hours are too weird."

Camillia got quiet, biting her lip in thought. "Why

don't we follow him?"

The more I thought about it, the more severe Camillia's face became. Even though I had a bad feeling about what my Cousin was getting into almost every night, I had no reservations about following him into that danger. If I didn't know what Glin had gotten himself into, I'd never be able to help get him out.

And the last thing I wanted was to lose another person that I loved.

Chapter Five

"I am of certain convinced that the greatest heroes are those who do their duty in the daily grind of domestic affairs whilst the world whirls as a maddening dreidel."

— Florence Nightingale

Although well at the age of adults, Aunt Caroline and Uncle Haru were the types that wouldn't let two Gilded women out at night alone. I was relieved when they went to bed an hour after dinner finished. My (as Camillia put it) cute cousin, who was far prettier before he got his so-called 'work' call, was still messing around the house.

Cami and I milled around my room, keeping the door cracked and listening for any sounds of movement. "So . . . your family?" I turned my head to look back at Cami, who sat on my bed looking at me. "Glin is Alloyed? I would never have known. That's some lucky posture he's got." She was right, but I shrugged, keeping my attention where needed. "How's it possible?"

I knew what she was talking about even when she said nothing more. The laws on romantic relationships set decades ago made it hard for anyone to be together. Especially, Mutes and Gildes, which were illegal. "They forced my grandfather's and grandmother's hands. Allowing them to get registered and married."

"Forced? How did they do that?"

At some point, I had started to pace without realizing, "how else?"

Cami gasped but was grinning. "So Glin was illegal?!"

"For his first two months, he was. Instead of getting my Aunt Caroline arrested and having her baby in holding, grandfather signed off on their registry, and they got married right away."

"Are you Alloyed?"

Cami did not shy away from what she really wanted to know. I just shook my head slowly, not giving her anything more than that. I wasn't mixed, but I still didn't want to go into my heritage. Not now.

It seemed like my disappearing family, even with our adventure plan, would stay home. Reglin hadn't moved much since dinner wrapped. Out of nowhere, he made for the door, and we almost missed it. Following close behind, I bolted out the door a few moments after him. My heart was in my throat, painfully pressing against the sides, slipping out the door only to find the streets around empty.

Already, I had lost sight of Glin.

Camillia ran into my back, so she had no clue where he went either. Just as I was about to turn around – exasperated– the gentle hum hit my ears. The look on Camillia's face told me only I heard it. But I had far more experience with the sound than my blonde counterpart did. Reglin pulled out (straddled on a lightcyc) and looked hardcore. Especially with the helmet on his head.

I didn't miss a beat, bounding down the steps and only slipping once before my feet reached the bottom. "Keep your eyes on Glin's cyc!!"

Camillia ran to the sidewalk to do as told. With

Reglin's cyc railbroken, it wasn't connected to the magnetic system that regulated speed. He could get very far, fast, while I got my cyc to start–silently praying that it would. And it took quite a bit, given its condition. I had only had a few days to work on it, and it still needed a lot more love. Luckily, there were a few slow autos (self-driving cars) and stop lights in front of Glin, still in sight when I pulled up next to Camillia.

She was so focused that she missed the second hum until it was right next to her. Cami squealed when I thrust out my extra helmet. "Hurry up!!!"

My voice muffled as I shouted through thick plastic and loud humming (that was starting to sound like a rumble).

Camillia took the helmet even in her continued confusion. "What the hell??"

"Just get on before we lose him!!"

We were supposed to follow Reglin on foot, get on a tram, or be in a Rental. And Cami had no clue about my past and experience. I wasn't offended at the blonde's obvious hesitation and fear. Or when she split her legs around the cyc behind me, refusing to ride 'side–saddle' even in a dress.

First, I caught up with Reglin, who was already ten blocks ahead of us when we left the house. Then, I kept up with him even as the streets got a little clearer and Reglin opened his cyc to the free roads. I hoped I was as covert as I thought I was, keeping my distance as best I could. The lights on the magnets still worked, lighting up with a dark blue as if still connected to the magnetic track system below–a speed control put into play just after the Reconstruction. But they were just a front, the tilting of our cycs and the speeds we were keeping made it clear that our cycs weren't connected to the track system below the concrete. If an interested (or bored) Regulator saw us, Camillia would be guilty along with me. Just being on a railbroken cyc broke the law. It was a ticket (at least) for a couple of Gilded like us. We'd probably get forced to pay a bribe.

Camillia was gripping the black windbreaker I had thrown on like a lifeline. Guilt tore at my belly, Cami in her thin summer dress while I had changed into jeans. The wind would be whipping mercilessly at Cami's skin right now, but there was nothing we could do about it. I hadn't thought this through, honestly, expecting Reglin to use his cyc but not like this. He was a good boy, upstanding, and not a lawbreaker. But the railbroken cycs in the garage should have clued me in that nothing was what it used to be.

We entered Tinsdale. Both of us got held up by swarms of pedestrians. With few Mutes owning autos, it was another sign of the kind of area we were entering. We went deeper into the city's Mute parts. The streets cracked, and pieces of the magnets below peaked through. If it weren't for the strict driving laws, I doubted areas like this would have magnets. While the Gildes got glittering sidewalks and buildings during the Reconstruction, Mutes got nothing. That's how you knew you were in a Mute area. The ancient and decrepit buildings and streets gave it away. The world wanted to forget about these people entirely.

The autos began to disappear, and soon it was just the two cycs on the street. Then, when I thought Reglin was just joyriding, I saw it. Or rather, I heard it and knew what it was before my eyes found it.

The tramway tracks were above us while high–rise apartments closed in, making me feel claustrophobic. And I was just visiting. Imagine what it was like for those forced to live here. The buildings didn't look all that safe either, with large cracks along the sides of the foundation. It didn't stop the crowd that gathered under it all.

Starting to slow, the sound of multiple compressor motors (or com-motors) dancing at once filled the air. I found myself searching for the sound as it echoed off every wall around us. I didn't have to search for long, the large huddle of vehicles coming into view. There was a variety of autos and lightcycs in various makes and models. The street was lined on both sides with a mixture of them. And hues, it was a rainbow of transports, the lights of the link magnets reflecting off the dark pavement and cement walls. Some were brightly colored with far more gadgets needed to be functional. Others almost blended into the atmosphere of the Mute community.

Bodies zig-zagged in between what little space to move there was. Based on their movements, it was a mixture of Mutes and Gildes. None too high on the chain. Cami and I were easily the highest Gildes on the street. There were a lot of colors worn by the populace here, but many matched. These people were all in gangs. I had seen this before, having been deep within this kind of community.

It was an underground racing ring.

Slowing (even more), we were barely rolling as we passed the 'entrance'. Made up of several scary-looking men who stared us down as we wound through. They didn't stray far from their cycs or autos, though, so at least there was that. However, it still had my nerves on edge, especially with Cami here. I could take care of myself. I hoped. However, Cami plus me was more than I was sure I could handle.

But Cami would get out of this unharmed, that I would guarantee.

A few people in the crowd sported blacked-out helmets like mine, walking and talking with them even while not racing. It made sense, an event as large as this one had to have Regulators in the crowd. They would need to pay some of them off to keep from getting caught. An event like this would be very lucrative. Given the Gildes mixed in, the Regulators could blackmail.

I finally stopped by pulling off to the side, but neither of us attempted to get off the cyc. Now stagnant, Cami's first move was to take off her helmet. Then try to finger-comb the mess that it was. A pointless gesture, but I thought it best not to tell her that. I left my helmet on, pink braids tucked inside. No one would so much as ask me to remove it here, an unspoken understanding that was like law.

At least, I hoped the same rules applied from my past experience.

There were many scary looks that passed our way. It didn't affect me, but Camillia's tight grip returned. I was used to this. The event was just like home. Save for the mix of hair colors and postures. This place was a mix of social standings, so Camillia didn't stand out for her obvious rich blood. Even though I was sure we were the highest Gildes out of all those here. We were new blood, which never sat well in places like these with people like them—lawbreakers. And until I saw otherwise, it would be best to keep my helmet on. They may be okay with Gilded mixing in on the sidelines, but that didn't prove that they would tolerate someone like me on my cyc.

I had lost sight of Reglin a while ago, too much to keep track of at the moment. Like the big hulking guy that kept getting closer and closer to us.

"You here to race or what?"

93

Cami jumped and grabbed me hard. I hid my shock, so focused on the colossal man who was inches from us, I had missed the guy that had come to the other side and was now talking the driver up—aka me.

Putting both feet down to balance, I sat straight and looked the guy in the eye. Cami was shaking a little behind me, so I had to do all I could to reassure her and the guy in front of us that everything was good. "I'm just checking the place out."

"You either race or go home, Gilde. We ain't a sideshow here. You have to earn your right to stay."

The guy was stern, but he didn't seem all that scary other than his height. His baggy jeans and shirt were brightly colored, making his black skin stand out even more. And his bald head was shiny, reflecting the bits of light from above.

His arms crossed, he held his ground, waiting for me to make my choice. A tiny nod, and he left while I turned slightly to speak to Cami. "Get off."

"And go where?" Cami asked with a shake in her voice.

I took a look around before turning back to her,

hoping to find someplace for Cami but honestly coming up short. "Find a clear spot and don't talk to anyone. See if you can find Reglin."

"Is he even here?!"

"He's here alright. Things are starting to make sense for once."

Carefully unwrapping her arms from me, Cami got off the cyc and stood next to it. "Are you going to race on this?"

Cami was getting a good look at my wreck of a cyc for the first time. I knew what she saw. All those around us saw the same thing. A piece of crap about to shake apart. "It'll be fine."

"Are you sure this is a good idea? Do you even know what you are doing?!"

There wasn't a doubt in my mind, but it was clear Cami had more than enough for the both of us. "It will all be okay. Just stay out of trouble while I'm gone."

Few knew this side of me, so I knew how it looked. It looked like I was crazy. Cami was about to learn another one of my big secrets. Our friendship was going to change drastically.

All I could hope was the cyc to stay in one piece until the finish and that Cami didn't cast me off after this. She was okay with my Alloyed family, but this was something else entirely, and I never knew what to expect when someone found out about my lineage. Or my skills.

Rolling carefully up to the 'line', I glanced around the place. Autos with more dressing than needed to race. Those were the ones here just for show. The women weren't even watching the race, too busy leaning into someone else, talking and rubbing against them. It was all so showy, more than I was used to. But sneaking off to race on the edge of Renize hardly measured up to this spectacle. It had me worried about my helmet again but that would have to wait until later.

On the other side of the start -the ones who were the real deal were the closest to the 'line'- I found at least one group that looked a little serious. Their cycs were in good condition, and there were two autos that (to the untrained eye) would be considered junk. But I knew that they were for racing, not looking.

My eyes crashed into gold, a man standing and staring openly back at me. Tall and toned, I quickly took in his strong arms as they wrapped around his chest. He leaned against an auto with black and red on his shoulders like the others in the group around. I knew to stay far away from that group. They were another gang. But I struggled to pull my attention away from the guy. Something about him was so familiar. His thin threads but perfect posture confused me at this distance. He was most likely a Mute and he was very much involved in illegal activities. I couldn't know him even as he stared at me as though my blacked-out helmet was see-through. Yet, I couldn't shake the feeling that I did.

There was a familiarity to his eyes that he had locked on me.

I pulled my attention hard. I was here for Reglin and was about to be in a crucial race. The first race of the night would be the worst racers, but I still needed to focus. That's how it was at the races I used to partake in a lifetime ago. This race determined who was worthy and who would be laughed at. And lucky me, my cyc choked just as I pulled up to the 'line' in front of everyone's eyes. I knew the wind combuster had a stuck pin, but I had hoped to keep that fact from everyone else.

Anyone who truly knew lightcycs knew just how out of shape the cyc was.

Getting it started up again, the guy who insisted I race appeared before me, concern dripping from him as he did. "You sure you wanna do this?" I gave him another slight nod in response. "Look, you don't have to win. Just finish the race in one piece, alright?"

I laughed softly inside my helmet. So soft, the guy that was all business before couldn't hear it. I might have been offended if I didn't expect something like this (concern for the little Gilde playing racer). But as it were, that's what I looked like to everyone here.

Another small nod, and he strapped something to the front of my cyc—a GPS set to the route. Here I had been worried I would have to stick to the back and follow the group.

My last move was to adjust my rearview mirror, finding Camillia in it, who was bouncing on her heels, watching me. She was supposed to be looking for Reglin.

Not that I could blame Cami. The second I had given myself to search, I had fallen deep into the liquid metal pools before pulling myself out harshly.

Guess we would have to look after the race.

The hot and cold guy, who appeared to be in charge of a few things, stood at the front before all the racers, getting us started. My heart was beating hard in my chest. It had been a while, and my last experience with racing was not . . . pleasant. But I let my eyes wander to the other racers–particularly their cycs. A few of them had some *Lighter*, giving them the ability to reach higher speeds, which would be interesting. I wasn't sure I could handle getting *lit* with the current condition of my lightcyc.

There was no choice now. If I failed tonight and lost, I would never find my family. Or help them when I did. By my guess, Reglin was somewhere around here and in a heap of trouble.

The 'flag' lowered, and my heart stopped as my cyc moved in its place when I hit the accelerator, the wheels tearing up on the asphalt for a few heart-wrenching seconds. My heart started again when I had to swerve hard around a racer in front of me. The idiot stalled out right at the start. Now, he was inflating his com-motor with air as he pushed to get his cyc going again. I gave the guy my attention for a few seconds, curious whether he could get his butt in gear, but he had already lost either way.

There were still four others ahead of me. My focus was on them and their movements, allowing me to follow them and save the GPS for later. If I ever got to the front of the pack, I would need it.

The guy said I didn't need to win, just finish. But I knew better. I would be an outsider if I didn't win. Outsiders didn't get information, and it was very likely that Camillia and I would get tossed out into the street. Or worse.

Honestly, if he hadn't said anything, I might have been okay with second or third place. The only reason that guy offered to let me out of the race was all because I'm Gilded. If I were a Mute, I would have been told to win or die. That fact had me more determined than before to earn my place with these strangers.

The ones ahead had cycs in much better condition. Better looking and newer insides. That said, it looked like none of them knew how to race.

They took their turns too broad, and a few had already used their Lighter a few times. Their lightcycs looked good, but they hadn't taken care of them as they should. It was like they only ever rode on the mag-rails, making this their first time racing without the magnets' support.

This race was for show, and these idiots didn't realize they only showed their incompetence.

The track took a hard turn and the others took it wide. My heart danced as I cut in, dipping my cyc, so my knee barely missed the unforgiving asphalt. This singular move gave me a significant lead. The others backed off for a moment as if surprised more than submitting. Maybe it was the first time someone had really raced against them?

The sound of their buzzing motors came from behind, telling me they had broken out of their stupor and were finally challenging me. The GPS had another hard turn, getting us to turn back the way we came, so the race was halfway over as it was.

One of them hit their Lighter, sprinting ahead right before the turn. He proved just how much of an idiot he was because he slowed down and banked high for the turn, allowing me to pass him again with ease. I would win without even trying if the race were nothing but figure eights. They were all afraid to get their knees close to the ground or something.

The track had us take two more tight turns to get us back to the start, but the last bit was a 'straightway'. All they would have to do was stay close behind me and hit their Lighter once close to the finish. I needed to get a big enough lead before we got that far.

Having been at 'tentative' speed thus far, I hit the accelerator, and the cyc bucked slightly from the strain. I had to be careful not to push too hard, too fast, or the poor thing might fall apart. Even with working on it every night, I had only had two days to fix it—the first problem. Luckily, I had set the loose muffler and the stuck stabilizer. However, there were still a few concerns, like the occasional misfire from a sticky pin. I wouldn't know what all was wrong until I took a closer look at the com-motor, but I had to just deal for now.

The others on their fancy cycs were still getting smoked by me with all my issues and concerns. I had a seven-second lead by the time they got to the final turn, which should give me a ten-second lead after the turn. The straightway was left—a few twists and turns but nothing as hard as the ones before that gave me the advantage. But now I had enough of a lead that they would have to use their Lighter just to catch up.

It must be the reason they gave up. The finish line came into sight without even the slightest buzz of a com-motor behind me. When I hit the crowd, I slowed to a crawl. It wasn't polite to show off and make fun of the other racers behind me. And at my speed, someone might see the shaking of my hands from the adrenaline, but the shocked look on all the other's faces was worth it.

Either they were shocked I was first or that I was so bold. Not sure which and I didn't care. A few laughed when I started to sway back and forth, doing a serpentine to the finish line. To them, I was a low-level Gilde sticking it to these higher jerk-off Gildes who raced for easy money and the thrill. And they were right—save for me being a low-level part.

My front wheel crossed the line, and I stopped, sitting

right on top of it -claiming it- as the sound of the others hit my ears. My heavy breath was fogging up my helmet, waiting for them, but I didn't dare take it off now. I had everyone's attention, including any possible Regulators–most likely mixed in. And I had just won the right to keep my helmet on if I wanted, new or not.

The other racers passed by at high speeds and squealed to a stop before me. The one that had stalled from the start passed several seconds later as I had predicted. In last place, his eyes were on me as he passed, the confusion clear in his body language. They all got off their cycs and took off their helmets as if ready to go to war. My experience taught me a lot in situations like this, and if they had no trouble taking their helmets off in front of everyone, they had no fear of anyone stopping them. They were the ones helping pay off Regulators mixed into this event. Getting pushed around would destroy whatever I had just built by winning, so if they were going to be sore losers, then I would handle them appropriately.

As they made their way over to me, I hit the accelerator, turning hard in front of them and sending my smoke their way–something I had a feeling none of them even knew how to do on their cycs. And I didn't stop until I was next to Camillia, only dismounting when at her side.

"Are you crazy? And how the hell did you win by so much??"

I shrugged, "They weren't very good." What else could I say at this point?

Camillia was shaking her head at me, "You have a lot of explaining to do, missy!"

I couldn't have this conversation. Not now and *definitely* not here! "Did you find Reglin?"

Camillia's grimace fell to a frown but she didn't fight my subject change as she pointed toward the group that rested near the finish line. I followed Camillia's finger but failed to find Glin, golden honey eyes cutting into me before I had a chance to look anywhere else. The guy was still right where he had been when the race started, leaning against an auto with his arms crossed, looking cocky as ever. Black hair attractively falling over his brow, I still couldn't shake the feeling of deja-vu from the sight of his molten eyes. I also couldn't get rid of the feeling that the guy was a jerk, even if I had no other proof than the smug air about him. It was the second time I had caught him staring, and it had me hesitating in removing my helmet all the more.

The guy had no problem staring or being caught at it, so I gave up and searched for Reglin instead, who I found not that far away from Gold Eyes. Glin was still in the clothes he left in, blue jeans and light blue button-up. It made him stand out painfully from the others in their dark colors and serious attitudes.

Suddenly, my view got blocked by the guy from before, the one running the races. "Here you go."

He held out a handful of credits, the metal transfer chips rattled in his hand, and it looked like a thousand. My head popped up from it to his face. "That was a cash race??!"

The guy chuckled, "I probably should have told you beforehand."

"YOU THINK??? What if I lost?? I don't have any money!"

He shrugged, "You do now. I had a good feeling about you. You just won me big girly, so thanks."

"Why did you try to get me to drop then?"

"All an act, Sweetcheeks." He coupled the endearment with a glance at my butt. "Name's Jimmy, by the way. Feel free to come by anytime you like if you need anything."

He held something else out, his card. I glanced at it, not reading the words, before shoving it and my winnings into my front pocket. "I need something right now, actually. See that guy over there?"

He followed my finger to Reglin and quickly looked back at me. "Stay away from them, Sweetcheeks. That's the Cruor, and they don't take newbies no matter how good."

Camillia stayed close to my side -listening- while I continued to pump Jimmy for information. "Isn't that guy a newbie?"

Jimmy glanced again, looking right at Reglin and quickly turning back to us. "He's just a dog for them."

"A dog?!" Camillia sounded disgusted.

"Yeah, he wanted in and wouldn't leave them alone. But he's not one of them. They just use him like a dog. Fetch this, do that."

"But…. he's a person, not a dog."

Jimmy held up his hands in defense like he was on trial. "He's really lucky they only did that. Getting on their bad side is dangerous."

"Is that so? Well, getting on my bad side is dangerous too!"

I ignored Jimmy and his protests as I stomped towards the Cruor. My heart was in my throat again, but acting tough helped. This wasn't my first race, but it was about to be my first fight. At least the first one I started and fought alone. But I couldn't expect someone else to have my back forever, and I couldn't run. Not from this.

Chapter Six

"Everybody wanted to be the hero of their own story. Nobody wanted to be comic relief."
— **Lev Grossman, _The Magician King_**

I left Cami behind as I stomped up to the gang, or I hoped she stayed back and out of the way. This was new territory for me, not handling nasty people but trying to get myself and two people out unharmed? I didn't see this going well at all. All eyes were on me, including the group or gang called Cruor. At least I was right. The matching colors were a dead giveaway. Even the girls with them wore red and black.

One girl jumped to her feet off the hood of an auto when I approached, standing at attention. She was young, with long black hair and red tips. A Mute, just like many of the members, her posture the worst I'd ever seen. Something was up with her left leg, but I ignored it for now.

Not all of them were Mutes, a few hand gestures and

clothing styles stuck out amongst the group, and that wasn't just Glin. Two were a couple; ebony and ivory. The pair's skin stood out against one another with beautiful differences. Although a naturally dyed color, their shifting weight still matched a Mute to a T. Their clothes were a high thread count too so they both probably had jobs within the Gilded community and worked on their postures to make Gildes more… comfortable.

None of them said a word to me, silently staring as I stood there awkwardly. That was to my advantage, focusing on slumping a little and hoping no one noticed my high-quality shoes. The tension was high, and I wasn't sure it was so one-sided, but the pounding in my chest was easy to ignore and hide. Wrapping my arms across hid the small jumping it did and kept my arms from shaking. It also hid my Gilde background more, copying Rene and a few other Mutes and low Gildes nearby. I was very thankful for all of the above when one Cruor pushed the others out of the way and glared down at me.

He swept a few black strands out of his face and opened his mouth to speak. But another body collided with my side, grabbing hold of my arm and squeezing it tight. I didn't have to look, I knew it was Cami, catching platinum strands as they flew past my visor and the bright color of her sundress. Camillia stood out worse than Glin did, which said a lot at the moment. I really wished she'd stayed back.

It was a massive slap in the face, keeping my helmet on, but I wasn't about to reveal my identity to anyone around here. Not yet anyway. I still needed to assess the situation first, and with how the Cruor treated Glin, I was sure I never wanted them to know me or my face. And no one would even ask me to remove it, not in this group. They were the real deal. Real racers. They didn't care what I looked like and followed the rules. At least, that's what I hoped, but they could rip it off me if they decided to. A Regulator here wouldn't stop them.

"Oh, crap…"

Glancing past the man that stood in front, Reglin looked right at the two of us. I wasn't sure if he recognized my cyc or if Cami had given me away. But, either way, he knew we were there because of him.

"You know these two?" Glin just lowered his head, a

sign of disrespect that I was sure would get the crap knocked out of him. "What the hell do you want?!"

Instead of taking it out on Glin, the guy turned his anger on me. I was fine with that. I didn't want to cause my cousin any additional trouble. "I want him."

"Why?"

A new voice shook me to my core, not only because of familiarity. I hadn't noticed when Golden Eyes joined the angry Mute. The two stood at the same height, both Mutes, but the man that arrived first was still more intimidating.

"That's my business."

I thought I caught a wisp of a smile, but the one with familiar eyes wiped it off with a frown before I could be sure. "Sorry, but he is my *Inu*. I won't give him up so easily."

"He's a person, not a dog!" I shouted, my irritation boiling over and making me bold. Of course, it was a mistake, showing my knowledge of other languages. But Golden Eyes didn't react other than to sneer as I let it slip. I knew what Inu translated to.

How Golden Eyes, a Mute through and through, knew the ancient language, I didn't know.

Meanie took a step closer to us, and my heart shot up into my throat while Cami's nails dug into my skin through the windbreaker, "Who the hell do you think you are?"

Golden Eyes shot out an arm to stop him, "Relax, Kaito." Meanie (Kaito) glared at him but backed down, making Golden Eyes the leader. Digging in my front pocket, I pulled out the pile of credits I had just won and held it out to the leader, who only chuckled in response. "If he were for sale, that wouldn't be nearly enough."

Swallowing my fear back down my throat, I kept my eyes on his golden ones. "What do you want for him then?"

This time, the leader took the step forward, and I held my ground. Cami still held onto me, but took a small step back as if to pull me with her. That gained Kaito's attention again. I didn't dare take my focus from the leader before me as he loomed over with a wicked and handsome smirk on his face. He was beautiful, but he acted as if he knew it, which aggravated me more.

"I'll tell you what. We'll talk about it if you can find us next week."

Not that it was hard to figure out, but Golden Eyes

had caught on to our evident lack of belonging. He knew we had snuck into this place. And by the look on his face, Reglin knew how we had found the site too—no more following him to the next race. The Cruor's leader had just given me one hell of a challenge, and I wasn't sure I could live up to it.

He backed up, and Cami pulled me away. We said nothing, heading straight for my cyc and motoring quickly back to our side of town.

From chasing down Reglin, facing the Cruor, taking a freaked out Camillia home, and getting home myself, tired didn't even begin to cover it. With only a few more hours till dawn, I left my helmet and windbreaker on top of my cyc and made for my bedroom, fully content with sleeping in the clothes and sweaty dirt that covered me.

Almost to my room, Reglin popped out of his, glaring. "What the hell was that, Josaline?"

"That was me making sure you were okay. And then trying to help when I found out you weren't!"

He yanked me into his room, and I whimpered as my door disappeared. Glin quickly but silently shut his door, not speaking again till it was secure. "You followed me. Invaded my privacy and put yourself at risk!"

"I didn't have a choice now, did I??" He sighed and flopped on his bed, so I dropped down next to him. "You want to tell me the whole story? Like, what the hell do you think you're doing? This isn't about money, is it?"

"Of course not!"

"Well, then what is it?!"

Glin hesitated, the silence stretching for only a second, but that was long enough for my fear to spike and warm my skin. "Rene used to hang out with someone involved in those races. The Cruor were involved with her disappearance, and I'm going to find out what they did!"

It was far worse than I feared. If Glin owed the Cruor money, that was one thing, and I could race for his freedom using the funds I won. He was there by choice and wouldn't leave without what he came for. "Are you crazy? If they're involved, then they're dangerous! You'll disappear just like she did!"

"Then I'd know what happened to her!" He growled in my face. "Do you have any clue what it's like, Jo? Always wondering and worrying? Dreaming all the terrible things being done to Rene or already done before her body was dumped off in a river somewhere...."

All this time, Glin had been holding it in. He was still trying, but some of his anger and sadness were leaking out. "You can't think like that!"

"It's all I think about, Jo!"

We were far too loud and would wake Auntie and Uncle any second if we weren't careful. "What about your parents? Huh?! They feel the same as you but worse because you're going out at all hours and scaring them to death! What if you didn't come back?!"

His hands thrust into his hair, holding his head up by his strands as he reclined over his knees. "At least they'd have you to help them. Mom is so excited to have you here."

Once again, I felt helpless. My cousin was right before my eyes, yet he was fading away. And there was nothing I could do about it. "I was excited too, but I wanted to do all of this with Rene. I miss her too, and don't you dare think you're the only one suffering for a second. I..."

I had to stop, my throat closing up with tears. Glin looked up from his self-torturing position and back at me. A shattered heartbeat later, he had his arms around me in a hug. It was comforting but not healing. I was sure I'd never recover from Rene's disappearance.

Releasing me, Glin returned to his slumped position. I wiped my face and pressed on. "What do they have you doing?"

"Stuff they don't want to do. Cleaning their cycs, taking messages to people, getting take-out...."

"That doesn't sound too bad...."

"It's just the start, Jo. Once I prove myself, I'm sure they will have me do more."

"Like what?"

"Not sure. Probably race for the Cruor." I had given Glin and Rene lessons years ago, but I knew he was far from winning races like me, "Who knows what they will do if I lose."

I shivered, remembering the menacing looks the Cruor gave me for simply standing before them. "That angry dude, Kaito, was pretty creepy."

"He's sort of the leader. Although Yuuto, the other guy that talked to you, is also essential. They don't have one

117

person in charge. They mostly just hang out together."

"Hang out together? What kind of gang is this?"

Reglin shook his irritation out of his head as best he could, "They aren't a gang, just a close-knit group. People want to join them because they win every race they're in. Anyone who dares to mess with them gets torn apart too. So it's easy to see why people want to be on their good side. I want to get on it to get information."

"If they aren't bad, why do you think they know anything?"

Glin seethed. "Because Regulations pulled in a few of them for questioning. It was bullshit, the way they handled it all, of course. Who cares about a Mute? Especially a little Plunge girl, right? But their so-called investigation led them to the Cruor, and so has mine."

Regulations didn't do anything without getting paid for it. The privatized system meant that Uncle had given what he could, and it wasn't enough. "If the investigation was bull, wouldn't it stand to reason that Regulations pulled in the Cruor for a show? Or even just to mess with them?"

Reglin laid back on the bed, his eyes hardening at the

ceiling as he thought it over. "Even if that's true, the Cruor have to know something. They're right there every night and see everything. They're deep within the underground and therefore are accomplices regardless. They may seem harmless and stupid, like Buri, but they're untouchable, which makes them dangerous."

"Wait . . . did you say . . . Buri?"

"Yeah, the blond with shaggy hair. While you talked, he was behind Kaito, so you probably didn't see him." Glim said casually.

Was it the same one I had met? Buri wasn't a widespread name, but blond hair was pretty average. What were the odds it was the same guy? It would mean the Cruor were at my school...

"Something wrong?"

Reglin was looking at me, catching me mid-thought. "No, nothing."

"You were fortunate this time, Jo."

"You know it was far more than luck. Those guys have no clue how to race...."

"I mean that the Cruor didn't challenge you to a race

right then and there. You won't be coming again."

I jumped off the bed, spinning to face him. "What?!"

"Don't worry about me, Jo. I can take care of myself. And I won't let you follow me like tonight, so there is no way you will meet Yuuto's challenge." It was just as I expected. Next week, I would have to find another way to get to that race. "Why the hell did you leave your helmet on, by the way?"

"I didn't want anyone sucking up to me. I had hoped no one would know I was a woman…."

"Cat's out of the bag on that one. Should have worn some of my clothes or a bag." Glin chuckled.

My irritation at the reminder swelled again. "Yeah, well, I didn't want anyone seeing me as a little Gilded girl, so I kept it on. Besides, there are clearly Regulators in that crowd getting a cut. And you never know who they work for or who they know. The last thing I need is my parents getting wind of all this."

"Given your skill, wouldn't the little girl look only help you make more credits?"

"I'm not in it for the credits, Glin. I'm in it to help

you!" If I weren't exhausted, I would have punched him with all my might at his stupidity.

"If your identity can't be known, then it's a place you shouldn't be."

"I don't want my identity known anywhere," I muttered.

He ignored the comment and focused on his message. "Then we agree, you don't need to be anywhere near those people ever again."

He grew silent, so I left, laying restless on my bed until the sun came up before drifting off.

Chapter Seven

"To assess the quality of thoughts of people, don't listen to their words, but watch their actions."
— **Amit Kalantri, <u>Wealth of Words</u>**

It was a night like any other. Nothing extraordinary was going on. Mostly, I tried to figure out my homework when my Holo blinked and jumped to be answered. A small rush of joy ran through my skin at the number displayed. It had been a while since I spoke to my cousin, but our conversations were relatively the same: 'What are we going to do in Career Placement together?'.

Grabbing it up after nearly tossing my now-forgotten homework, the bright smile I wore was involuntary while the hologram loaded over my Holo. It was a smile that faded a little when it was my Aunt's image instead of my cousin's. "Aunt Caroline?" I quickly adjusted. A call from my Aunt was just as lovely anyway, "How are you?"

"Josaline . . . is Rene with you?"

My heart picked up a worrying pace at the question, beating painfully with fear as I hoped I had heard Auntie wrong. "Huh?"

I watched as the figure shifted. Holograms only showed a person's face on a Holo like mine. But that was more than enough to see the worry and fear filling Caroline to the brim. "Rene. Is she with you? Have you heard from her??"

As much as I loved my cousin, we hadn't spent time together in almost four years. And it had been a few months since we talked on the phone. "No, I'm sorry, Auntie. I haven't seen or talked to her in months."

It was then that Caroline broke, a sob choking her and echoing through the phone. "Josaline . . . Rene . . . she's gone!"

Whatever hopes things weren't as bad as they seemed -that this was just a silly prank by my cousins- left me. My blood went cold as the reality sunk in, slowing from rushing to sludge. My heart struggled to pump.

Rene was missing, and no one would do a thing about

it.

If Rene didn't show up on her own, there wouldn't be a search party, no ads on the teleque or the newsreel. No one would be looking for her save for her own family. And as it stood, that meant only Rene's family. I wouldn't be allowed to join. I would be stuck waiting and wondering.

Regulators didn't care about Mutes. They couldn't afford the commission, and a Plunge was even lesser.

"I'm so sorry. Please . . . let me know if you hear anything?" It was all I could say, and it felt like nailing a coffin together with my forehead.

Waking with a start, I found myself in my borrowed room. The smells reminded me of my childhood. Spending summers here with my cousins were some of my favorite memories. And now? With one cousin still missing and the other determined to find out why it left an asterisk on the whole thing.

But Glin couldn't do this alone. He wasn't nearly as good on a lightcyc as I am, and it was clear if we were going to find anything, we would need to get deeper. Gaining respect was the only way, and I could do it far faster and easier than Glin with my skills. It wasn't hubris. It was a fact. If there was one thing I was confident in, it was my skills on a cyc. Even with my forced retirement two years ago, I'd been at the top of the races back home.

With the way Glin spoke last night, he was expecting to find a body while I still believed Rene was alive.

I decided then that I would go deep and not stop until I had the answers we all needed. Answers that would start with ones I gave to Cami–unfortunately. I had dodged her calls yesterday, but there was no way around Camillia today. The two of us had most of our classes together. Plus, Cami knew my schedule, so if I did manage to escape, the blonde knew where to find me.

As I filtered through the front gates, surrounded by fellow peers, I found Cami's eyes instantly. My pink hair stood out painfully as usual in the multitude of humanities majors, and it had Cami on me like a laser scope. Trying to move through and around the other bodies turned fruitless. Cami suddenly stood before me and blocked any further escape.

"Time to talk, Jo."

There was no escaping this, so I stopped trying. "Fine. After class."

"You better not run off because I will keep pushing till you spill."

"I get it," I said with tired irritation.

It was hard to focus the rest of the day, knowing that I was about to tell Cami more than I ever wanted anyone to know. Not here. Going to college in Orcestra was supposed to be a new start, a drastic change from my life in Renize. But that was shot to hell the moment I got here. Rene was gone, and Glin was in over his head. Any hopes of a quiet and ordinary life were long gone.

But I supposed that was boring anyway.

Classes flew by with my impending conversation and how it would forever change my friendship with Cami. This might be the end of our friendship. There was no telling how the heiress would react.

We met under our fan tree. The leaves started to turn and would soon be a beautiful gold color. But not yet. "Are you going to explain to me how you could pull all that off the other night? How do you know how to drive a lightcyc? A railbroken one at that? So well that you can race and win? And how did you know how to act? Like you knew the rules or something, you never once flinched the entire night!"

I looked around, but no one was near or paying attention. "The truth is, Camillia, that wasn't my first race."

"No, duh! I figured that out already!"

Signing, I fell back against the trunk of the tree. "What do you want to know?"

"All of it!!!"

When I looked around again, Cami looked this time as well. I expected her loud voice to draw a few curious eyes. But we were still alone in our bubble. "When I lived in the country, I did some racing. There wasn't anything else to do there. A few of us did it, and it wasn't a big deal. But it was a well-established organization, and they followed the rules just like any other street racers."

"Wait . . . how did you even get that good? If it was an established race like the one we went to last night, wouldn't you have been laughed out of the place if you showed up with no skills??" Camillia asked.

I hesitated. The very secret I'd held onto for so long

was forced out of me. I lingered in anonymity for a few more seconds before revealing myself. "My full name is Josaline Pryce," when my reveal didn't wash the confusion from Camillia's face, I continued, "I had my skills already…. my father…. he owns a few autos and lightcycs…."

"Your father? Hold on . . . are you . . . *that* Pryce? The family that owns all autos and cycs? Your family wrote a lot of the Mute regulations! Oh…my…Josaline, you're an *Untouchable*?!"

"Keep your voice down, please!" I was looking around constantly, afraid someone had heard. "It's not something I want to get out, so please keep it to yourself!"

The last thing I wanted known. My family was royalty with inheritance as far back as the fossil fuel days. And it was all over Cami's face. "Fine, but Jo, what if those others find out? What if the Cruor finds out?"

"They won't! It's not as if my face is out there! Dad was always very strict about that—worried about kidnappers and stuff. And I'm going to keep my helmet on just in case. I'm just going to get something from them, and that's it. There doesn't have to be any information shared, and it doesn't exclusively mean the Cruor."

"What's to stop them from taking your helmet off for you?!"

Terror laced her voice, all for me. So I patted her hand gently. "They won't. It's part of the code. All races need some support, or everyone would get caught right away. That means paying off some Regulators. A large race would never go unnoticed otherwise, and a Regulator wouldn't miss the chance to score big. You never know who is one and who isn't, so there's an unspoken rule to leave anyone with a helmet on alone."

Cami shook her head at me, "you have no way of knowing the Cruor will follow that code."

"They will. The Cruor are the real deal. And if no one made me remove it the other night, they never will. Not without my permission." That's what I hoped anyway, and Cami looked as sure about it as I felt.

Cami was trembling, and I wasn't sure if it was the promise of a return to the underground or of who I was that had the blonde so freaked. "Come, let's go somewhere."

"What?"

Already on her feet, Cami was pulling me to mine. "Let's go check out more of the campus."

"Cami…"

"You owe me. I feared for my life the other night, so you at least owe me this."

There was a happy thump in my heart. Because Cami still wanted to be my friend even knowing who I was, even after keeping it from her. Cami renewed the promise of a fresh start and new life in me, and I wanted to do all I could to please Camillia.

Hoping to quash some of my guilt for my omissions of truth, a silly fear now that it was out there and the response was so endearing, I gave Cami a slight nod. Standing with a weak smile and giving over my hand, I caved to Cami's every demand. Today, she wanted to check out the Medical Research part of the campus. Camillia had every hope of finding her future husband in that area, and today she might get lucky. Or rather, Cami needed something else, anything else to focus on than my ancestry. Something I needed myself almost daily!

Even with classes done for the day, many people

were on campus. It was filled with the splendid variety I had grown accustomed to. So many Mutes and Gildes of all tiers were there. It was a new world with everyone on the same standing. They were all students there trying to earn their placement for their futures. But, the Glides were still clumped together and kept away from other Mutes. Even though they were likely very close tiers, they didn't dare mix too much. It made those who did mix together stand out more.

The Research buildings were so high they blocked the setting sun. It made the world seem so much darker and almost creepy. But not dark enough to hide the golden eyes that were dangerously close to landing on me. From the angle I caught them, they glinted like fire. After hearing about Buri with the Cruor, I had suspicions about them being at Utirius. I didn't expect to run into them, though, especially not now or on this campus. And I wasn't prepared for Yuuto's golden stare to be on me again without my helmet to spare me.

I didn't think. I ran, fearing those eyes landing on mine and seeing through me. Cami's hand slipped away, but I thought for sure the blonde was right behind me. When I turned the corner to hide, I realized that I had left my friend confused and behind.

"Well, well. Look who we have here?"

Cami's eyes, which had been watching my retreating form in confusion, snapped back to the front, and my heart stopped. Before Cami was the two Cruor that had chatted me up the other night.

"Wha....what are you doing here?"

I was still in earshot. I shifted my weight on my feet, figuring out what to do.

"We were about to ask you the same thing." The tall, scary, square-jawed one, Kaito, stood over Cami as he spoke, just as intimidating as he had been the other night.

Caught off guard, I watched as Cami did the best she could to rein herself back in and take control of the situation. Cami played it cool, crossing her arms over her chest and popping out a hip in irritation. "I go here. What about you two?"

They chuckled at her, looking at her like a small child. "That's cute. What campus do you belong to?"

"Humanities."

Cami nor I had been ashamed. Getting into Utirius Omega was an outstanding achievement, even if we only made it into Humanities. However, these two looked down on Cami even more than they had before. "Of course, you do."

On the bright side, I lost all fear of the dark-eyed Kaito. Now I wanted to punch him. And I could tell Cami felt the same way. "What about you? What are you in?!"

The smirk on his face remained as Kaito gestured to a building behind him. "Medical, of course."

"It's not like it's a dumb question. I don't go here, but I'm on the Medical campus!"

"Yeah, but it's clear you don't belong." The bright-eyed Yuuto sneered. And I had thought he was the nicer of the two, but he was just as big a jerk.

Cami finally turned on her heel to leave, but Kaito stopped her–oddly. "Wait! We're sorry. We were just joking with you."

Kaito grabbed Cami from behind and spun her back around with a hand on her arm. She ripped herself from his hold and glared back at him. "You're bullies, and I don't associate with rude jerks like you."

"You associated with us the other night." Cami turned her glare on Yuuto, and he met her with a grin.

"How about we start again. I'm Kaito. Kaito Maki and this is Yuuto Himura." They both bowed like Mutes showing respect, and Cami's shock was obvious. "And you are....?"

"Camillia Trevor."

"And your friend? What's her name?"

My heart leaped into my throat. Not out of fear that Cami would reveal me, I knew her better than that. But the fact that Yuuto was asking about me made me feel nervous without a good reason. I had expected him not to think twice about the new racer who was terribly out of place the other night. And that was all, nothing more, I told myself.

Cami's glare returned, looking Yuuto right in the eyes. "Nice try, but I'll let her be the one to tell you."

He chuckled and relented, not pressing it like I feared he might. They both were a bit less creepy than when I first met them. Probably because it was daylight and far from an underground racing ring. But only a little less eerie, and I had no clue how I would get back to Cami now.

It hit me then. The Cruor didn't know who I was or what I looked like. So, what was I anxious about?

It's not like I was used to living a double life like this. I had forgotten the benefits of hiding your identity. I smacked my forehead for neglecting the details like a fool. Then I got to full speed on my return. I hoped to crash into Cami and pull her away before they noticed. Plus, it helped with my nervous fear to just make a run for it, racing up to Camillia and wrapping my arms around her neck to hide my face. "There you are, Camillia! I have been looking for you! Come on. We are running late!"

Before Camillia could regain her wits, I had her hand in my grip and tried to drag the blonde to safety. "Hold on!"

But I didn't stop, not until Yuuto raced around to stand in front of me. His longer legs gave him an advantage. I kept my head down. Irrational fear of recognition had my chest close to exploding. I watched my feet and turned to go around him. But then Kaito swept in beside Yuuto to stop me as well. Cami yanked me back to stand by her side as if - somehow- the distance would help me. Looking at her, Cami didn't understand why I had come back for her. No way I would ever leave Cami behind with these guys. Now we were stuck. The Cruor weren't letting either of us go.

"I'm so sorry. My friend and I have Digiflix tickets and are in a hurry."

Cami tried her best to lie, but she was never considered a quick thinker. "You weren't in much of a rush a second ago."

Stupid smart people. Couldn't they just continue to be polite and let us lie our way free? A true gentleman would have accepted the excuse regardless. But these guys were far from gentlemen.

That thought had it all crashing in my brain, the realization making me gasp. "It's you!"

My finger flew into Yuuto's face while my fear flew out the window. Cami grabbed my hand and pulled it back down, but Yuuto's attention was already on me. "You know me?"

Pushing a scowl onto my face hard, I went for as menacing as possible "You're the jerk on the Magtram!"

When Yuuto grinned slightly, my heart started to beat wildly in my chest. This time it wasn't in fear, though. "I think you mean the guy who saved your ass. Literally."

Leaving Cami and Kaito out and behind the conversation, I continued even as my heart threatened to burst. Yuuto was the guy that had insulted me when I first moved here. Sure, he had saved me, but he was such a jerk, and this guy was in the Cruor?! "You accused me of asking for it!"

"What girl wears a skirt that short on the tram? Oh wait, let me guess, you're in Humanities too?"

In an irritated rage, I lost myself. I reached over and slapped Yuuto's arm. I no longer worried about Yuuto or his friend. I was too peeved. "What the hell is that supposed to mean?"

Yuuto only chuckled, "Am I right?"

"That's beside the point!"

"Is it? Is it, Flamingo?"

I slapped him again, more brutal, and Kaito even flinched. "The name is Josaline!!"

Yuuto pulled out his hand from his crossed arms that sat on his broad chest, and Cami quivered as if he was about to smack the crap out of me. Instead, he held it out to me.

"Yuuto Himura. Nice to meet you."

Looking at Cami, I saw her mouth drop open. I was a little surprised too. Just what were people so afraid of with the Cruor? That said, Kaito didn't nearly look as amused as Yuuto. Kaito looked more like he was bored–borderline pissed.

"Yuuto, we're going to be late."

Yuuto still had his hand out for me, and I adamantly refused to take it. In a swift move that took my breath away, Yuuto grabbed my hand in his and pulled me closer. "You're not a very cautious person, are you?"

He was gently pulling me away from Cami and Kaito, but I felt far from scared with his proximity and the loss of the others. "I have no reason to be."

"Just like on the tram," he said, clucking his tongue, "I can't decide if you're naïve, stupid, or careless?"

Wrenching from his hold, I took a step closer and got up on my toes, putting my face as close to him as our height difference allowed. "None of the above. Just not afraid of jerks like you."

Yuuto wore a lopsided grin and drifted a little closer

138

to me. My breath hitched in my throat, trying and failing not to take in the rugged line of his jaw. "You should be." Pulling away completely, I fell back to my heels while Yuuto went back to Kaito. "Let's go."

Cami was dangerously close to Kaito for some reason but had all her limbs. The blonde looked me over, checking to see if I had all of mine before grabbing my arm and briskly pulling us away. "What the hell, Jo?"

"Sorry, I thought you were right behind me. I did tell you to run."

"You did not!!"

A giggle that was more out of relief as the distance from Yuuto got larger rushed out of my chest. A flush burned my face, and I shrugged it off as best I could. "I guess I only thought I did."

"Why did you come back? They didn't see you. You could have gotten away!"

"I couldn't just leave you behind!"

Cami grabbed my shoulders, trying to scare me or emphasize her fears. "What if they recognized you?"

A sheepish grin formed on my lips. "Yeah, I figured,

since I kept my helmet on, they wouldn't be able to."

"They're smart guys, Jo. They could have figured it out. And what was all that with Yuuto? Are you completely crazy?!"

"Oh, that. I knew Yuuto looked familiar, but I couldn't figure it out the other night. But now that I saw him in the light and without my helmet, I realized he was the guy that saved me from the pervert on the train."

"….What? Josaline, you are too much. I don't think I can keep up."

"Excuse me…"

We both jumped, the small, sweet voice coming out of nowhere as it popped our bubble. A petite girl with dark hair and beautiful brown skin stood next to us. Her large brown eyes covered most of her face and drew you in. She was a stranger but smiling warmly at us and looked utterly harmless.

"Did I see the two of you speaking with Maki and Himura?"

She was so formal and polite. It was adorable. "Uh . . . yes?"

The girl then bowed her head perfectly before us. "I am Mia Bunnag. You can call me Mia."

Glancing at Camillia, I saw that she was just as surprised as I was. "Josaline. And this is my friend Camillia Trevor."

"You can call me Cami."

Mia smiled brightly at both of us. "Josaline, do you know Mr. Himura?"

Cami looked taken aback, probably due to Mia's formalities. "No, not really."

Now it was Mia's turn to look confused. "Oh, you two looked so… familiar. I thought that was how Mr. Himura is with those he knows?"

"I… I wouldn't know. Do you?"

Mia continued to smile even as sadness crept into her eyes. "No one does outside the Cruor."

"You know about that??!" Cami yelled but quickly calmed herself.

"Everyone knows. It's Himura and Mika's cliche. And no one is allowed in. You two are the first people I have seen them have beyond polite conversation with before."

141

"Forgive me, but why do you care, Mia?"

I tried to say it so that it wasn't offensive, and Mia seemed to take it at face value. "It's expected that I… *excel* as a Bunnag. Himura and Mika are the only ones who surpass me in this school."

"Wait," Cami squeaked, her face pale, "you're telling me we are speaking with the third in her class at Utirius Omega??!!"

Mia's smile still reeked of sorrow, and I didn't pretend to understand why. "Yes. And third in my graduating class in Fundamentals, I'm afraid. Everyone said I should go somewhere else, so I no longer had to compete with those two and take first. But it would be pointless. They would still be ahead of me no matter where I went."

I was amazed with this girl. "Wow, Mia, that's brave. You're amazing!"

"That's too kind, Josaline."

"No, it's not," Cami shrugged, "I know I wouldn't do it!"

Mia blushed as if she wasn't used to the admiration. "I admit I have become a bit obsessed with those two. They are my rivals."

"They are our rivals as well, right Camillia?"

We both giggled while Mia looked confused but interested.

"Who knew we would have so much in common with one of the smartest people in Ocresta?!" Cami cheered.

I doubted I had much in common with Kaito, Mia, or Yuuto, but it was nice to pretend. However, something told me that none of them had to deal with the issue I now faced as it was splayed out before me and all over the garage. Mia made it clear she didn't touch lightcycs when Cami slipped into the conversation yesterday, and Yuuto and Kaito had a whole crew to help them with something like this. Or the funds to hire someone else to do it.

It was all a big mess, metal and lubricant everywhere. I should be overwhelmed with a race that I still had no clue how to find in a few days. But I found all this relaxing. It reminded me of my childhood which was a happy one for the most part. It was when I got older that things went wrong.

There was a knock at the garage door, so I got off my hands and knees, wiped the grease off my palms, and adjusted the bandana wrapped around my head, hiding braided cords of pink hair. It was a pleasant surprise finding Camillia and Mia on the other side of the door. The dark beauty looked overly nervous about being there, but I was sure the girl was not used to social situations much. It only endeared Mia to me more.

"Hey, guys! What are you doing here?"

Other than the box of pastries and coffee they carried, I didn't have a clue. As far as I knew, neither of them knew a thing about cycs or mechanical engineering.

"You've lost your mind, and Mia is here to help me find it for you!!"

An awkward laugh bubbled out of me. It was one thing to have Cami here, she already met my family. But Mia? We'd exchanged digits and met once off campus. That wasn't enough for me to trust her but Cami clearly did. Mia looked around, taking in the disaster. "Josaline . . . what are you doing?"

Bits and pieces of metal were everywhere, and the skeleton of a lightcyc was in the middle. It seemed pretty obvious to me just what I was doing. Mia was either ignoring our location or hoping to skip over that part. "I'm fixing my cyc."

Taking a small step forward, Mia entered the shade of the garage. The smell of lubricant permeated the air and covered up whatever was in the box they brought. "I can see that. What have you done to it?"

Camillia took the box from Mia's possession, setting it down next to the drinks on a small empty spot she found on a workbench. "Jo took the com-motor apart and is now putting it back together!"

Cami only knew that because I had told her, causing a chuckle to bloom out of me at the thought, as did the palpable shock on Mia's face. "You know how to do that??"

Mia had barely taken her eyes off the mess but did when I laughed. She was surprised at the task I was taking on. Even with knowing who I was, Cami had no faith in me. Mia had no clue what life I'd led. I guess neither of them did. It was a lifetime ago but I used to get to play all the time like this. Before Mother intervened. "I sort of know. I watched it happen several times. But it's a lot of work, and now I'm not sure I will get it back together in time."

"In time for what?"

"This weekend."

Mia's mouth popped open at that, the mess looking insurmountable at the moment. "Let me help you."

Chapter Eight

"To all those women — strong enough to be heroes. fair enough to be ladies. This song is for you." — **Robert Fanney**

The most Cami could do was make sure the two of us (Mia and I) ate. She had no skills with any tools or mechanics. However, with the race tomorrow and us at it for the past three days, ensuring we ate was an essential task that Mia and I would have failed if not for Cami. We stood a chance to get my cyc in working order at this rate. Whether it was in better or worse condition since we started... only time would tell.

Mia was busy putting a few bolts in place with a monkey wrench, and it had Cami intrigued. "Mia . . . I have to admit. I'm impressed with your skills. How do you know mechanics?"

The dark beauty shrugged, keeping her focus on her task. "I don't really. Biometrics are different than any type of auto. But it is so similar to the body."

Cami swung around on the chair I had put in just for her, "wait, I thought you were in medical research?"

"I am. My specialty is Biometrics."

I gawked at Mia, "isn't that like two majors in one? Engineering and Medical? Plus all the holo programming…how smart are you, Mia??"

Mia sighed, "just a little less smart than Yuuto Himura. He's Biometrics too, but he has a better reason." Mia stopped there while I wanted to know more. Then, she pointed at parts and tubes, "This is good practice. See here?" Mia pointed to the pipes that exchanged the heat for energy, "these compress the air and cause it to heat up. Then the converter turns that heat into power. It would all work well in the human body, and many Biometrical MDs use something similar these days."

"Have you checked the brakes?" I asked while Cami's eyes glazed over. "Their regenerative process might work in legs?"

"That's a great idea!" Mia squealed but then looked as if she regretted her reaction.

". . . Oh . . . okay, sure . . ." Cami studdered, not following our conversation and probably regretting asking. It was already hard to imagine our little group without the girl genus. "It looks like you two will get this done in time."

I smiled, but it quickly turned to a frown. "Yeah, thanks to you two. But that doesn't solve my bigger issue at the moment. Reglin is still adamant about me staying away. Since he knows I followed him last time, he will ensure I can't follow him this weekend."

"I've been giving that a lot of thought, actually." Cami pulled out her Holo for the two of us to see. "Although I agree with Reglin about you going, it's too bad for him that he doesn't pay attention to what he shares with his connectors on Aimless."

"He put the race location on social media???" I squealed.

Mia giggled, figuring it out quickly. "He has his 'follow me' function turned on."

"And he and I happen to be connectors."

149

"So you can track him??!!"

I jumped up to grab Cami's Holo, but the blonde pulled it out of reach at the last second. "Yes, but it comes with a price. You have to take me with you this weekend."

"Camillia, it's too dangerous," I answered, shaking my head.

"If it's that dangerous, you shouldn't be going either." Cami countered.

I frowned while Mia remained silent, watching the two of us. "Fine. You can come with me. But I draw the line at you. Mia, I'm sorry, but you can't come with us. Not to this."

Mia waved her hands, her practiced polite tendencies showing again. "That's alright. I don't want to intrude."

"You should tell her. If anything happens, we have someone looking out for us."

I nodded, telling Mia everything she needed to know. Save for the part about Rene. I hadn't told Cami about that either. It was my cross to bear, and I worried about what they might do if they found out. Or rather what they would do *for* me.

"So your cousin Reglin wants in the… group? I didn't think they took new members ever?"

"He's in… in a way. Yuuto seems intent on having his 'dog'," Cami muttered loudly.

Mia looked a little in shock, "Wow. I didn't know the Cruor were so . . . *rough*. They're so reserved in class, and they seemed like friends of yours the other day!"

"They don't know who Josaline is as the racer. And I was just on the side watching. I'm sure they just wanted to pump information out of me, which is why they were so… polished."

Now I felt guilty. Mia looked disappointed. It would appear that we had broken whatever image she had of her two rivals. "I guess that makes more sense. There had to be something that tied them all together. It wasn't logical that they were so close, coming from different interests and backgrounds."

"Backgrounds?" I set down my socket wrench and gave Mia my full attention.

"I suppose it's public knowledge, Yuuto and Kaito's backstory," Mia spoke to herself at first, permitting herself to tell their story. "Kaito's parents left him at an orphanage when he was five. He grew up taking care of himself but was always close friends with Yuuto. Yuuto's mother died, and their father left them. He was twelve while his sister, Nori, was seven, leaving him to care for her. After that, Yuuto disappeared for a while and showed back up when we were sixteen, Kaito in tow. The two were always like brothers but even more so when they started Fundamentals together. And Kaito helped Yuuto take care of himself and Nori. I have only seen the others of their group in passing, but they all act like family. Everyone just assumed that Yuuto and Kaito built themselves a family to replace their lost ones."

"Wow . . . " Cami looked down at me. My eyes were dancing around while looking at nothing.

"Josaline?"

My head popped up like bread in a toaster, the idea hot on my brain. "They started racing to support themselves."

"That makes sense. Utirius Omega isn't cheap, and I know they sent Nori to a private, all-girls Fundamental and that she starts Utirius next year. She will be at the South campus studying cosmic rays." Mia added. "And there are all her medical bills."

"Medical bills?" I asked, but Mia kept silent.

Cami squeezed her head as if trying to make her brain understand it all. "So one sibling is studying…. star stuff, and the other is studying to be a Biomechanic?! Yet they both do illegal street racing? What the hell is this?!"

I started back on my work, keeping my eyes on my tool as I twisted it. "I guess you could call it making the best out of a bad situation. That's the life of a Mute, Cami."

My thoughts raged in my head. All about Yuuto and his situation. It wasn't that different. Reglin joined the underground to discover what happened to Rene, and Yuuto did it to support his family. It made me wonder if the two had any clue just how similar they were?

Either way, I doubted even more that the Cruor were involved in Rene's disappearance. But, I had never been very good at reading people and was far too trusting.

It had all of my thoughts and feelings confused, unsure of what my next move should be. So I focused on my cyc, knowing that I would need my cyc working and winning to make any other decisions.

When the race day arrived, my cyc was in much better condition, even if it didn't look like much and still needed some love and attention. Reglin hadn't even come home all day. I wasn't surprised as I expected him to leave from some obscure area to get to the race. It gave me more time to prep anyway.

Auntie and Uncle, safely tucked in bed, I dug my riding jacket out from under my bed. Black leather and hot pink zippers went well with my skinny black jeans. I zipped it up, the collarless jacket covering the white tank I wore underneath as it stopped right at my collar bone. My braided hair was already wrapped around my head, ready for my helmet to be slapped on. I just waited for Camillia.

Time ticked away, getting dangerously close to midnight as I sat on the front steps looking for Camillia's rental. Finally, the flashing yellow auto showed up, and Camillia hopped out. Before greeting her, I sent a Digi-note to Mia, letting her know we were heading to the race.

I didn't give Camillia much attention until we were standing in the garage. Her outfit had me snorting as I tried to hold in my laughter.

Camillia put her hands on her hips, her leather pants barely covering them, which had her hands on her skin. "What?!"

Not saying a word, I handed Camillia a black windbreaker. She didn't hesitate to zip it closed over her dark blue halter top. "You know, you don't have to 'try' so hard, Cami."

She shook her head, the short braid down her back scraping against the material of the windbreaker. "I'm not about to show up looking so out of place two times in a row. Besides, you don't look like yourself either! I want to look as cool as you!"

Camillia took the helmet I offered while I picked up my blackout one again. "Whatever you say, dear."

Before we took off, Camillia pulled out her Holo, showing the dot that represented Reglin. He was still in the Tinsdale area but on the other side. Still on the outskirts as to be expected. And in a less populated place, too, no businesses or homes, just factories and forgotten office buildings that would be closed this time of night.

"Is this thing going to run?"

We were already straddling it, and Camillia was only now asking such a question. "Yeah, it runs great now. I took it for a test drive last night after Mia left."

"If you say so."

Even I had to admit, it still looked a bit rough, but all of that was cosmetic. It lacked spoilers and color. For now, it was roughed up silver metal that light didn't reflect off, but it didn't need those things to be a winning machine. Even though I knew I would pay for it later, I decided to make Camillia eat her words and never question my cyc again.

We arrived at the spot, autos, and lightcycs lining the start point of the track. Just like before, many gave us mean looks. But this time, I was more focused on my surroundings and finding the Cruor. Like the race I used to run, the more important you were, the closer you were to the 'line'. The best racers and the highest payers got those spots. So it took me no time at all to locate the Cruor.

The beat-up auto was joined by a sleek–looking M3 GT 2173 model auto. Painted blood red, the divider on the back told me it was an auto for racing and not just for show.

A couple, a black male with bright white tattoos and a white female with long, chocolate hair, sat on the hood of the lesser auto. They were married given how very friendly with one another. Paid or not, Regulations would never ignore an unsanctioned couple.

The girl with long, black hair and red tips stood beside them, not bothered at their public displays but looking bored with it all. All three of them had been there last week, standing and staring at me as I rolled up. Cami squeezed me a little tighter but not as bad as last time.

This time, I found Buri. He was chatting up a group of scantily dressed women fawning over him. Kaito and Yuuto talked over their cycs while Reglin sat next to them on his. When I pulled up with Camillia, Reglin almost fell off his seat. This, of course, gained Yuuto's and Kaito's attention; the two of them looked at what had him choked up. Yuuto smiled (making my heart skip) while Kaito looked indifferent, they both met my cyc hallway to their 'spot'.

"You made it."

Yuuto had a hand on my handlebar, helping to hold it steady while Camillia got off. "You sound surprised. Wasn't that the deal? I find this race, and you give up Reglin?"

He shook his head, golden eyes glowing with delight. "Nope. I never agreed to give you Inu. Besides, no one forced him to be here. He came to us."

I wasn't surprised. No way the guy would make it that easy for me. "Fine. What do I have to do now?"

"Race, of course."

"Who am I racing?"

"Inu."

"Excuse me?"

Yuuto gestured, and Reglin came over to us as called. "Inu, you will race your buddy here, and if you win, I'll remove your Inu status."

Reglin tried to hide his smile, looking over at me expectantly. But no way it was that easy. "What's the catch?"

Yuuto was grinning too broadly to be a good thing, and Reglin paled. "He's in, and you take his place. An eye for an eye, as it were. Or, in this case, a dog for a dog."

"What do I get if I win?" I dared to ask.

Yuuto shrugged, "You get money. What more do you want?"

What little enthusiasm Reglin had drained away instantly, and he left to retrieve his cyc. Even though he couldn't see it, I glared back at Yuuto, who took it in stride. But the grin on his face fell quickly, his eyes on something or someone behind me.

Finding what he was now staring at, I faced two pissed, skinny, mid-tier Gildes. The weird part was they were looking right at me. "You. We want a rematch!"

"Rematch?" I looked behind them and found their cycs not far away. I recognized the machines. "Oooohhhh, you mean from last week? Fine, I'll race you again. If that's what you want."

"Good. We'll set it up with Jimmy…."

"She is racing for me first."

Yuuto had gotten close, his hand on my handlebar again as if to claim me. Any trace of his smile was long gone, and the two guys struggled to hide their tension. "Fine, then she races with us."

They walked away, off to find Jimmy–I was sure. Yuuto still had his hold on my cyc and his grimace on their retreating shapes. "You're going to have to let go, you know."

159

He glanced at me with his eyes simmering with animosity. Then at his hand before letting go quickly, as if he had forgotten. "You should be careful who you piss off around here."

"You mean you? Is that a warning?"

He smirked, but it held none of the light his earlier smile did. "Me. And almost everyone here."

"I can take care of myself."

"We noticed!!"

Out of nowhere, Buri wrapped an arm around Yuuto's neck. The same greeting I had seen him give Jeb the first time we met. I couldn't help but stiffen at his nearness; the dread of being recognized coming over me. The need to find Camillia hit me hard, searching desperately for the blonde. But she was only a few feet away with Kaito talking to her as he stood a respectable distance.

"Don't worry about your friend. We'll take care of her while you're busy."

Yuuto watched me the whole time, and Buri practically bounced as he called out to Camillia, getting her to return to our sides. "Hey! Remember me? Where's your friend Josaline?"

Buri was already looking around, and Yuuto took a second to look. At first, Camillia looked at me -terror obvious on her face- but she quickly turned it to anger. "We're not tied at the hip! We have our own lives, and Josaline is currently living hers!!"

Buri released Yuuto, holding up his hands in defense. "Alright, lighten up. Just asking!" Buri looked back at me, a smirk on his face. "Then who's this?"

Camillia got flustered again, but I kept my eyes on the duo before me. "Just call me . . . *Mōtāgāru*."

They stared at me blankly before Yuuto burst into laughter, making me worry that I had messed up the ancient language and said something other than 'Motor Girl' as I intended. But I had heard it so many times. Uncle Haru and Rene called me it for years before. Yuuto recovered a few troubled heartbeats later. "Alright then, Moto. You and Inu are up next. Good luck."

They left, leaving Camillia and me alone. "Are you okay?"

Camillia brushed her long braid off her shoulder and

to her back, full of bravado that I wasn't sure was real or faked. "I'm just fine, of course."

Reglin popped up next to Camillia, glaring down at me. "How the hell did you find me again?!"

"Not telling."

Reglin growled, howling up at the night before returning his glare to me. "You're winning this race."

"NO! You should win! I can handle the Cruor far better than you can, and you would be in! Getting what we need would be easy!"

Reglin was shaking as I spoke. "Not like this. And it's what I'm after, not you. Plus, you're a woman. I'm not about to hand you over to them. What kind of man would I be if I did that?"

"A smart one!" I hopped off my cyc and stood face to face with him as best I could. "You and I know I am a far better racer than you. I can move up the ranks and out of Dog faster and easier than you can. I'd be fine!"

He glanced behind me, looking at the refurbished cyc and returning to me with a small smile. "You've been busy?"

"Yes. And now I am sure I can beat anyone. So no

matter what the Cruor throws at me, I will win."

Reglin sighed, his shoulders dropping as he gave in. "You aren't going to let this go are you?"

"No." I was winning, and I knew it.

Without another word, we both moved up to the start line. There was no flourish to the start. This race was just a quick filler while the rest set up their bets for the next race. No one watched as Glin and I took off.

I was more than ready to face the Cruor head-on.

The track wasn't anything special, similar to last week. Just empty streets lit only by the lamps above. It was nice riding alongside Reglin as if just the two of us were playing around. That was how it should be; us fixing cycs up together only to test them out with a race while Rene cheered us on from the sidewalk.

There wasn't a chance I would ever let the same thing happen to Reglin. He was older than me, and he had lost his sister, but I was determined not to allow him to disappear as Rene had. If that meant keeping close to him and the Cruor, then that's what I would do, keeping a slow pace beside him as we burned through the night.

The air was crisp. The start of fall was upon us. It meant cooler nights and hot days, but the cooler air was great for the com-motor, keeping it from getting too hot as it pushed the air through the cyc to move.

Everyone was on their feet near the edge of the track, watching as we returned. Glin was in front with me right behind him. I was letting him win, slowing every time he dared to do so, but I didn't care. It wasn't in the rules that I couldn't rig the race. Every attempt he made to force me ahead of him failed, so instead, he sped up.

The finish line was his. His crossing was coming in a few seconds while I kept a short distance behind him. Reglin was going to take first as we planned.

Inches from the line, Glin sped up even more but pulled a hard turn. His foot went out to steady himself, pulling a u-turn right in front of the finish. It left me in such a state of shock that all I could do was watch as he passed by me, going the other way. Hitting my brakes did nothing, in large part because I hadn't replaced the pads as I should have–it seemed. Glin had given me the confidence to speed up enough that a hard stop would be dangerous. I had no way of keeping myself from rolling over the finish line, pulling a turn just like Glin too late as my back wheel crossed the line with my efforts.

My lungs burned with rage, my heart in my shoes at the betrayal. Glin was already back with the Cruor, and I lacked apprehension as I stomped over to them. Too pissed to care.

Chapter Nine

"Quite, quite,' she thought with a little sigh. 'It's always like this in their adventures. To save and be saved. I wish somebody would write a story sometime about the people who warm up the heroes afterward."
— **Tove Jansson, <u>Moominland Midwinter</u>**

I chased Glin, hopping off my cyc as soon as I had it propped while he returned to the Cruor. He finally stopped, deep within the group, and I took one step into their 'territory' only to get blocked.

With a hand on my stomach, Yuuto held me back, keeping me from getting to Reglin. I pushed his hand away, fully intent on slapping some sense into my cousin, but his hand returned, stopping me again.

This time I shoved Yuuto. The result was me going back more than he did. "What's your problem?!"

His grin had returned, and it pissed me off -even more- this time. "You won."

"Yeah, I know. I was there!"

"Which means you're not my dog. Glin is." I tried to step around Yuuto, but he stopped me again, stepping in front. "So you don't belong here. This area is for Cruor." He gave me a gentle but firm push away from his crew and Reglin. Then Yuuto grabbed Camillia, pulled her over, and shoved her into my arms. "And here is your girl back, safe and sound as promised."

Those near enough to hear and see chuckled loudly, and I was glad for my helmet as it hid my embarrassment. Yuuto continued to wear his stupid grin. Never had I wanted to slap someone until this moment.

Holding a finger as close as I could to his face, Moto warned Yuuto. "This isn't over."

Kaito appeared behind Yuuto -as if I was some kind of threat- but kept his eyes on Camillia for some reason. "I hope not."

I gave one last glare to Yuuto for my benefit before turning away and pulling Camillia with me. "I thought for sure he would rip your helmet off or something! What just happened?"

Going back to my cyc, I settled on pushing it to the back where 'no-name newbies' belonged. "I told you they wouldn't. I just got put in my place. That's what happened."

"What do you mean? I thought that the Yuuto guy liked you, but now he won't let us sit with him? What is this, Primaries??"

"No, Camillia, it's racing. And we don't belong at the front. I'm going to have to work my way up."

"Soooo . . . more racing?"

I looked back to give Camillia a nod when I saw the two cycs advancing way too fast for my liking behind us.

Dropping my cyc and letting it fall to the ground hard, I grabbed Camillia and pulled her to safety while facing their wheels head-on. It was the two Gildes that challenged me earlier. A few onlookers shouted at the two racers, giving them a scolding like you would a small child and not the two grown men they were, like adults who had just tried to hurt my friend.

"You better not be leaving!"

The sudden drop of my cyc had caused a few scratches, but nothing more. My nerves took the harder hit, swallowing my heart down from my throat and back to my chest. "No, I'm not."

"Good, 'cause you're racing us next!"

Looking past them, I saw a few autos take off from the start line. I had until they returned before having to face these jerks. "Fine, I'll be there."

They buzzed away, and I pulled Camillia quickly along, my heart settling back to normal with her safe. "I think this needs to be the last time you come with me, Cami."

"What? No way, I'm with you till the end!!"

The wait was probably longer than it felt, but it didn't seem long. The racers were flying by and signaling the end of my rest. The other two were already at the line–waiting. They were far too enthusiastic about this for my liking, especially knowing their 'abilities'. If those racers thought they could beat me using the same skills they had last week, they were idiots.

An auto rumbled loudly across the street, gaining my attention as I mounted my cyc again. Which was what they wanted, it seemed, all eyes on me. They were either Mutes or trying hard to look like they were, the 'group' three times larger than Cruor and rougher looking than the others around them. And they all looked mean, which was quite an accomplishment given the mix of gangster-looking guys and gals of this establishment. The racing in the country had a few tough guys, but they were more bark than bite, taking me in after a few runs. But then again, I hadn't been alone back then, and Camillia was hardly intimidating.

Breaking my attention from the large and menacing gang, I focused on the task at hand—my race. Camillia was still hovering close to me, so I gave the blonde a gentle shove back, hoping to keep her hidden a little longer with the gang across from us zeroed in on me. They were probably poaching, wanting me to join their 'team' or something. But they looked like the type that didn't take Gildes, no matter how polished or not. They also seemed the kind that liked more illegal things than street racing. This was as far as I went on the criminal spectrum.

Jimmy met me at the line, the others glaring at me. "Alright, Sweetcheeks, I need a name this time."

"Moto."

He smirked, "Okay. The entry fee is one-k." I fished

out the money I won last time and handed it over. "You want to add a wager on yourself?"

"No thanks."

The shock was clear on his face. "No confidence??"

"No interest. I'm not a gambler." I answered plainly and honestly.

His smirk returned, "Yet you come to this place again and again?"

I left his question unanswered, and he left soon enough to collect more bets. I kept my attention anywhere but on Jimmy, not wanting to see money going around on this race.

Time ticked by slowly. Sitting up, I flexed my fingers inside my gloves. An old habit, threading my fingers through one another to tighten the grasp they had on my hands.

Another place I refused to look was over at the Cruor, which I soon found impossible. I didn't want to know if Yuuto was watching because I didn't care. But I also needed him to watch so I could gain the respect required to get anything from all this. Not that racing these guys would get me anything. Still, I slowly turned to glance back even as I

171

begged myself not to. Curiosity over golden eyes had me losing control.

I wasn't sure if I was lucky or not, but I was still silently thankful when another racer joined. Putting themselves between the Cruor and me was a blessing in disguise, no matter the outcome. Blond hair that stuck out the back of their helmet and a jacket that could be a low-tier Gildes or high-tier Mute were the only clues to who they were, but it didn't matter. My focus was on winning. If I didn't, I would never get a chance to get Reglin out safe or ever find Rene.

Jimmy appeared in front of us again as the race was about to start. The crowd was getting restless, and I wasn't sure if they were rooting for or against me, but it hardly mattered. Hearing 'Moto' getting screamed out by more than one voice near the line caused my attention to split.

I had promised not to look, but it came from the direction of the Cruor, so I had to. Finding Camillia once again standing within their group was shocking (to say the least). How had she even gotten up here so quickly? The female half of the amorous couple and the girl, whom I assumed was Yuuto's sister, Nori, stood on either side of her, all three of them cheering and rooting Moto on wildly. It warmed me up, a smile spreading on my face, giving them a 'fingers up' in response, making Camillia and the brunette act a little wilder while Nori just blushed with a smirk. A strange reaction.

Jimmy was counting down, time to focus. It was a real race, so I revved my com-motor, accepting the challenge from the two idiots next to me. They glared over at me while the mystery rider on my other side responded, revving their com-motor as was expected. They held a fist up to me when I looked back at them, waiting until I bumped my knuckles with theirs before lowering it. At least one person liked me in this race.

With Jimmy dropping his arms, we all took off. The track for this race was different from the one I had with Reglin a few minutes ago. It was open, with light traffic adding to the challenge. The mystery rider kept to the back, gliding around behind the three of us. They weren't here to win. They were here to watch.

For now, I was in the lead, the two others hanging

back behind me. The bad feeling I had from the start was slowly becoming a reality. Whatever these guys wanted, it wasn't to race or watch.

A tight turn was coming up according to GPS, and it was then that they made their move. The amateur Gildes came up on either side of me. I was just about to dip into the turn when they closed in. The racers' proximity ruined my plans to sink low into the turn. They blocked me in and forced me to take the route they wanted.

They were so close that the colors of their magnets mixed with mine on the pavement, making a sick green color. I could barely hear another com-motor as it got close. The mystery rider quickly caught up even as the duo picked up their pace, forcing me along. This was not the time to freak out, that would get me hurt, and these guys wanted me to lose it all over the asphalt.

The turn was over. All I had to do was hit the brake and get out from between the two bruisers. But the racer to my right grabbed my hand and kept me from letting go of my accelerator.

Now I was truly trapped.

These guys were playing rough, more than I had ever experienced personally. No way these guys would be stupid enough to try and kill me, so I kept calm and let them have their moment.

It was then that the mystery rider went around them, got in front of the one that wasn't holding onto me, and hit the brakes. Their plan worked. The rider was braking as well and going around them. Now Mystery Rider was next to me. The other guy glanced their way but didn't let go.

Quickly, I shook my head at the Mystery Rider to stop anything else they might try to help me and then accelerated–taking the other racer with me. Mystery Rider followed along, sticking as close behind as they dared. Faster and faster, more than the cheater was used to. He held on even as he started to wobble. The mystery rider looked nervous, the tension in their shoulders visible even as they shrank in my rear reflectors, probably because the rider that held me tight had Lighter while I didn't.

As if reading my thoughts, my captor sprayed, holding on tight to me as he did, and he expected me to lose it. A tumble at this speed would be fatal. As the Lighter wore off, he was confused that I was still up and running. While I used the momentum to my advantage, the other guy didn't know how to keep himself steady at such a speed on a turn. So he finally let go before he dragged us both down. My two attackers were behind me with the mystery rider, slowing just as they had the first time we raced for the sharp turn.

Now I slowed slightly, allowing the mystery rider to catch up. But they remained on my tail, not allowing the other two to have the advantage again. The cheaters hit their Lighter a few more times, gaining a little lead way, but the race was over.

I slowed more and raced beside the mystery rider. They couldn't see how I felt, the downside to my blacked-out helmet. But I was worried because the mystery rider was shaking. Hard.

I was worried they would make themselves tumble. So I stuck by them until they waved me on. I hesitated but took the lead to the finish. Even with my quick stop, my faulty brakes didn't allow me to be fast enough as the mystery racer was up and off their cyc before I could turn around. They were heading straight for the other two. Both the cheaters were sitting on their cycs and taking their helmets off like it was nothing. But then they saw my helper, both stiffening and paling instantly. They didn't wait for the other two to dismount, just till they had their helmets off.

He took his helmet off and threw it at one, hitting the guy in the face and knocking him off his cyc. The one closer to the mystery racer got a fist to the jaw. I started running when the first guy hit the ground, going as fast as my shocked mind would let me try and stop a raging Buri–my mystery racer.

Hitting the one that held my handlebar repeatedly, I grabbed Buri's arm and tried to pull him off. In his anger, he flung me off, and I nearly hit the asphalt but was caught and set back on my feet by strong hands. With the cheating racer's face getting turned to mush, I didn't even take the time to look or thank whoever saved me from a magtrak burn.

"Buri, stop!! It's okay!!!" I screamed to deaf ears.

Kaito and the male from the couple came around me, grabbing Buri up and off the guy. "You assholes!!!"

The one who got the helmet in the face held his nose, blood dripping from his fingers. "We were just trying to teach

Moto a lesson!"

"You almost killed her!!!"

I sucked in a breath, and then it refused to come back out. Had I been in that much danger? Not once did I feel out of control like the two bleeding before me wanted. It wasn't the first time I had my 'cool' tested. This time it seemed it had blinded me to the reality of the situation.

Someone nudged me, and I found Jimmy sadly smiling down at me. "Here you go."

He held out a large cup of credits to me. "What's this? I didn't place any bets."

"Your winnings. These two betted a lot against you."

It was like the floor was knocked out from under me. ". . . What?"

"Twenty-k is your cut!"

I looked down at the money I held, and every bit of me felt hot. Kaito and the other male Cruor still had Buri, but they grew still as I stomped over to the two men. One was quivering on the ground. A few called out to Moto, but I ignored them, focusing on the one on the magtrak, the one that held my brake hand hostage. Stopping short of stomping on him, I threw the money into his bloody face, the metal transfer chips clanging loudly on the hard floor.

"You want it so much? Take it! I don't want your dirty credits!!"

The entire raceway was silent, my words ringing out over the crowd as everyone seemed to hold their breath. It was all in vain. I had nothing more to say to those who had put a price on my life. I wasn't sure I could come back from this. All I wanted was to help my cousins–keep Reglin safe and find Rene alive. It was a childish dream, but it was one I wanted more than anything. All I was doing was putting myself at risk, making a fool of myself, and putting Glin at risk because my death wouldn't help the situation.

When I turned, thoughts of running filled my head. But I met a chest, its broad expanse blocking my view completely. "I hope it was worth it. You both just lost your ticket. If you show your face around Moto or this race again, you will have the Cruor to deal with."

It was the same tone Yuuto used on the pervert, so dark and full of malice it had me shivering even without it directed towards me at all—the power of the Cruor. Yuuto had just permanently kicked the two racers out, and no one stood up for them. Guess this was what I faced if I ever got on Yuuto's bad side.

I peeked behind me, the two slowly scraping each other and the money up and leaving as quietly as possible. The rest of the crowd started to wake up, heckling the two cheaters as they left for good.

"That was a lot of money."

Yuuto was talking to me in soft tones. Only I would hear him now. "I didn't want it."

He sighed while I kept my eyes to the spot behind me where the two bodies had once been. "It was pretty badass, tossing it at them like that."

That had me turning my head and popping it up to look at his face. It lacked a grin or smirk. He was completely serious. "Enough to take me in?"

Running a hand through his hair, I noticed how messier it looked compared to usual. Like he had run a hand through it over and over again. "Guess I'm feeling a bit sorry for you. Too bad, too, cause it won't last. If you had those credits, I would have let you push me over and buy your way in."

"How about I just give you a transfer IOU?"

His smirk returned, "I don't feel that sorry for you. Besides, you already owe me. Hate for you to be in any more debt." Disoriented by his words and the stress, I struggled to get the questions I needed to come out of my mouth. "You know, I can't see your face, but I can still imagine what kind of expression you're making."

I struggled again to follow along, "Is that a compliment?"

"Let's say it is."

Arms wrapped around me, a body on either side. My first reaction was to push and shove them away. Looking, I found the flustered faces of Camillia and Reglin. "Sorry . . . I just . . . I don't want to be touched right now."

Yuuto backed away, and the two of them followed me to my cyc. "Josaline, are you okay?"

Reglin was whispering, but it still irked me that he used my real name. "Moto, and yes, I'm fine."

"No, you're not. You're still shaking!" Camillia stood dangerously close since I wouldn't let them touch me.

"It was a close call. I just need a minute." I needed a distraction. "What were you doing with the Cruor?"

We all glanced back over at the group at their name, and none of them were paying attention to us. "Buri came over and got me. He asked me to wait with the others. Roxana and Nori stood with me to watch you."

Cami pointed as she said names, teaching me the pretty brunette's name and confirming my theory on Nori. "Oh . . . I . . . I should go, thank Buri."

"Make sure you thank Yuuto too."

Reglin cringed hard at the look I gave him, knowing what kind it was. "Excuse me?"

"He had Buri join the race to keep an eye on you," Camillia whispered even with no one around.

Yuuto stood with Buri. He and Kaito were still trying to calm the guy down. Although, with what little I knew of Yuuto, he looked almost as agitated as Buri. Now I knew what it looked like to be on the Cruor's wrong side . . . and what it looked like on their good side.

Chapter Ten

"I know, better than anyone else, that there are no heroes coming to save us. There are no good Epics. None of them protect us. Power corrupts, and absolute power corrupts absolutely."
— Brandon Sanderson, <u>Steelheart</u>

My back ached from the chair I had been sitting in for too long. Camillia was probably done handing out the gifts by now. 'Thank you' tins full of homemade cookies for all of the Cruor. I knew it was stupid, but Camillia insisted that it couldn't hurt all in all. If anything, it would remind the Cruor that we were girls and offer their protection again later. And with most of them Mutes like Yuuto and Buri, it would be a gesture they were likely to appreciate and understand. Poor Camillia was surely getting laughed at for it, such an old custom. But I couldn't go with her, it was too much of a risk, and I wasn't ready for it yet. That last race still had me shaken, and seeing the Cruor now would make it worse, forcing me to reveal myself.

Exams were coming, and the Library was full of people. I left as the sun began to set, most staying behind and continuing the fight. I waved my white flag with a few books in my arms and headed for the tram station. Auntie and Uncle lived reasonably close to Utirius, but it was still a long journey home. It had me questioning the cost of taking my cyc to school instead. But no matter my exhaustion and irritation, I couldn't rationalize it. Besides, it would be too cold soon.

The tramway doors swished open, breaking me from my thoughts. I had learned over the last three months how to time my travels. Now I knew when to go, so I wasn't stuck on an overcrowded train. Cooling with the night, I still wore a short skirt to battle the day's heat and felt brave alone on the tube. But as the sun set, I had to pull my knee socks up a little higher and put on the sweater I packed. I would never admit it, especially to Yuuto, but I felt a slight ounce of relief covered even a little bit more.

Several stops to go, a majority got off, and only a few got on. The Magtram got back into motion, humming as its magnets held onto the tracks below. Standing by the door, I watched Ocresa fly by, thick with colors and bodies even at the late hour.

"I see you have learned nothing." The edge to his voice made me jump more than average—no matter how much I wished it didn't. So lost in watching the world fly by, I missed Yuuto getting on and standing on the other side of the doorway from me. "And now you are even spacing out. Completely unaware of your surroundings. That is even more dangerous."

His back was against the seat rail and one hand held onto the strap of his book bag while the other was in his pant pocket. Add in his straight jeans, the thin t-shirt that was tight in a few lovely places, and how his hair fell messily over his brow, and Yuuto was far too good looking to be legal. If Yuuto weren't frowning heavily at me, my heart would be in trouble.

"I think I'm safe today."

I was gesturing around us, the tram only holding four or five others at the moment. "You never know when that might change. You should be paying attention."

Shifting my weight, I let my fatigue and irritability show. "The only person that is a threat to me now is you."

He chuckled, and my knee weakened, "That's true."

Rolling my eyes at him only caused him to chuckle louder, and as much as I enjoyed 'light Yuuto', he made me feel . . . foolish. "If that is all you have to say to me, can you just leave me alone now?"

"I came over to offer you some cookies."

He was already reaching into his bag for what I assumed was the cookies. "What?"

"Your stomach is growling so loud the entire tube is staring at you."

"That's a lie!"

"I couldn't read. You were making so much noise!"

He was trying to contain his amusement, but it showed clearly on his face, his golden eyes glowing again as he held out the box of cookies Camillia and I had put together for the Cruor. Looking from him to the box, I hesitated. "Don't worry. They aren't poisoned." I still didn't move, but not out of fear. It felt weird eating the cookies I had given him while Yuuto thought he was just sharing.

"Actually, I don't know if they're poisoned."

Yuuto retracted the box, took a cookie, and ate it in front of me. After a few seconds, he felt he had 'proved it' and offered them to me again. "Why don't you know if they're poisoned or not?"

I hoped my offense at his accusation didn't show in my tone. After all, he didn't know that the cookies were from me. "They were a gift."

"A gift? From some girl, I'm assuming?"

He smirked, taking a small step closer and pushing the box under my nose. "Jealous?" I answered him by taking and eating a cookie before his eyes. "They're just a thank you."

"Who would thank you?"

"Someone polite! It's what you are supposed to do when someone helps you. Still waiting for my cookies from you, by the way."

"From me? Why would I give you cookies?" I tried to get my heart to stop racing, telling myself repeatedly that he didn't know it was me under Moto's helmet.

"For saving you from getting molested!"

I sighed in relief but tried to play it off as anger. "You told me I asked for it! Saying I was lonely!!"

"So, you're not? Lonely?"

"It's none of your business!" I stomped my foot as I spoke but found it did nothing for me, a smirk still firmly planted on his face. "And a woman should be allowed to dress as she pleases. Just because I wear a short skirt doesn't make it okay for someone to touch me!"

"I'm not saying that. I'm saying that you make it too easy for them to do it!"

"Well, they should learn to control themselves!"

"I agree, but that is not the case, and you should protect yourself!"

"I can protect myself just fine without you or anyone else's help!"

"Oh yeah, I saw how good you were at that the other day."

"The other day? I was just fine! I didn't need you or anyone else's help. I made it back in one piece."

So busy yelling at one another, I didn't notice that we had gotten closer till his hand was on my arm. I also didn't realize I was shaking. "Hey, are you okay?"

This was why I wanted to stay away from Cruor. Here we were talking about an incident that I had barely thought of since, but in my mind, I was reliving the night I almost died. Or rather, Moto was nearly killed. I quickly shrugged off his touch, the thought of anyone's hands on me making my stomach twist. "I'm fine."

Reading me, Yuuto took a step back. "If I had known the perv had upset you that much, I would have punched him for good measure."

"Please, you don't have to do that for me."

"It wouldn't be for you," he was smirking again, "it would be in public service to all who braved the tramways with a short skirt."

No matter how hard I tried, I couldn't keep the smile off my face. So, I turned away to the window, only to find Yuuto's reflection. "Can I have another cookie?"

With a wide grin, he held the tin out to me again. The cookie crunched loudly in my mouth on the silent tube, causing me to glance around and find it almost empty. "I thought you were sick?"

"Huh?" The story Cami and I had agreed on clicked in my brain. If anyone asked where I was, Cami was to tell them I was sick. So now, I felt caught. "Oh uh, yeah, I was. But I needed to study."

I held up the books in my arms as proof, and his attention went to reading the spines. "A Humanities major that also has to study? You really must be one dull bulb."

"There is nothing wrong with wanting to excel!!"

"Which doesn't take much in your case."

I was done. One minute Yuuto was friendly, and we were laughing, then he bullied me the next. "What's your problem . . ."

"You want to come to my house?" He cut into my rant, asking me like he hadn't just insulted me.

". . . Excuse me?!"

"Yeah, a bunch of us are hanging out there. You could get some help with your studying."

He was earnest, inviting me out of the blue yet acting like it was nothing. It made me curious about the truth that was Yuuto and the Cruor once again. "Is . . . is that allowed? Your 'friends' the Cruor won't cut me up into little pieces for showing my face, will they?"

His eyes went wide, looking me straight in the face. Then he doubled over, laughing hard and filling the tram with the sound. "No . . . no, they won't. . . cut you up?!!"

"I don't know! They are your 'gang' or 'club', or whatever! I was told no one was allowed!"

"I'm asking you to come over and study, not take a blood oath!"

"You mean you don't require those at the door?"

"No, that's Thursdays," he said wickedly.

Regardless of what I felt for Yuuto's hot and cold demeanor, this was my chance, an 'in' with the Cruor. And a step closer to finding out more about Rene. The tram slowed and stopped, the door opening before us, my home just a few blocks away. But I couldn't take my eyes off Yuuto or make my feet move from their spot. The doors closed again, with both of us standing completely still and silent. It wasn't till the tramway started moving again that he dared to open his mouth.

"Wow, she goes home with strangers too."

I didn't say anything. I just stepped over and hit

Yuuto's shoulder as hard as I could. He laughed at me and my weak punch. We arrived at Yuuto's stop and walked from the tram stop to his place in silence. The area was clean but had tell-tale signs of being a Mute neighborhood. The buildings were old and had a lot of holographic ads dancing on the front of them. City officials didn't spend money cleaning up and updating areas like this one, but they didn't allow wealthy developers to buy homes right out from under the residents. Instead, they were left alone, untouchable.

The heavy light displays helped pay the fees the City refused to pay and cut down on rent costs. I knew all of this thanks to my Uncle's stories growing up, taking all of us to the old place he had lived before meeting Aunt Caroline. He had lived a small but nice life before then, undeserving of the discrimination against him and his family.

The inside of the building showed more age than the outside. Worn carpet and faded paint had a faint smell of spices that got stronger when we passed particular doors in his hall. Mutes used a lot of favoring to cover the age of their meat. Fresh food was a luxury most Mutes didn't have. It wasn't an unpleasant smell, reminding me of Uncle's and my great Aunt's cooking—Uncle Haru's mother. My stomach growled, and Yuuto chuckled softly at the sound, much to my embarrassment.

I could hear voices inside the apartment we came to a halt in front of. Giving a quick knock before swinging the door open wide, Yuuto let me go first. It sounded like the whole gang was there, if I was guessing. Yuuto quickly took his shoes off while I was careful and slow, trying to buy myself some time. It was too late to back out, so I swallowed my nerves while placing my shoes next to the rest— something most Gildes would find weird and freak out about. But I wasn't like most Gildes. I knew most Mutes cleaned their own homes and how much removing your shoes cut that down.

Leaving me behind, Yuuto went first this time, and I followed soon enough. His living room was littered with bodies, empty soda cans, and books, but no one read them anymore. I wasn't sure what the conversation was before we got there because everyone shut up when I entered. Buri and -to my shock- Jeb jumped to their feet, causing Yuuto to turn and find me right behind him.

"Josaline!" Buri jumped over a few legs and mess to grab me and pull me from behind Yuuto.

"Buri, long time no see. Jeb? You're a part of this gang too?"

"Gang? I guess so," Jeb answered with a shrug and a smirk.

Buri pulled me to sit next to him, leaving Yuuto still standing and in what looked like shock. I was shaking my head at Jeb. "Of course, you are. I can't seem to get away from you Cruor!"

"Are you trying?" Buri looked offended, playing the wounded bird

I patted his leg in mock sympathy, hoping to rid him of any offense even though I was sure he was playing around. "I'm not *trying* to do anything!"

"Are we really so bad?"

Now Kaito was playing into it, genuinely sounding hurt. "Not all of you. But some of you could use a few lessons in manners!"

I turned a glare towards Yuuto, everyone else following. It was as if they only now noticed him. The man with dark skin and white tattoos snaking up his arms, Cami called Clyd, was shaking his head at him. "Some people just never learn." The way Clyd looked at Yuuto, I wasn't sure if he meant Yuuto's rudeness or posture. "Are you going to stand there all night or join us?"

"Hey!" Yuuto cried like the kid kicked out of his' club'.

Now thick in conversation, none of them so much as glanced Yuuto's way. I was aware he left but tried not to focus on Yuuto. Instead, I focused on the rest of the Cruor. Maybe they could get me in or get me some information?

After a quick round of introductions, while I pretended they were all 'new' people to me, I pressed on to make friends. "So, Roxana, what do you race?"

The brunette attached to Clyd shook her head quickly, "I don't race."

"Oh, I'm sorry, I thought…."

"How do you know about that?" Buri turned, looking at me even as I sat next to him.

Swallowing thickly, I quickly spun it around as best as I could. "Isn't it common knowledge?"

"No!" Jeb, Buri, Roxana, and Clyd answered at once, causing me to jump a little.

"Sorry. I guess Camillia told me. Didn't realize it was a secret."

"Where is Camillia?"

Kaito blurted but tried to look cool, even with everyone catching him. Especially me as I grinned at the poor man. "I can call her if you like?"

He cleared his throat, adjusting his seat and showing us how hard he was trying to hide and failing. "It's not my house."

When Yuuto had returned, I had done all I could not to notice. But now, I turned right to him and put on my best and pleading smile. "Yuuto?"

I hoped I came off as innocent when I just wanted another friend here. It would make gaining trust easier. "You can invite whomever you like here. I don't care."

I hopped off the couch, my Holo already in my hands. Going for the small balcony just off the 'dining room', Cami answered quickly, her face glowing in the air over my Holo. "Hey, what's up?"

"Guess where I am?"

Cami tried to look behind me for a clue but came back to me with a frown. "Not the library, I hope? It's dark outside."

"Nope! I'm at Yuuto's with the Cruor."

Cami was silent for a moment. "Jo, I don't think you should be there."

"What?" All thoughts of inviting my friend over flew off into the night. "Why?"

"Well . . . " Cami was hesitating again, and the voices behind me were bleeding through the glass door. "When I gave them the cookies today, they tried again to grill me on Moto. Even Yuuto's sister. If he invited you over, Yuuto might be trying to get information out of you too."

Carefully, I opened the door behind me just an inch, but it was like turning up the volume on pods.

"What the hell Yuuto? You bring a girl here on our night, and then you tell her to invite a friend over?"

"If you have a problem with her being here, Jeb, tell her to leave."

"I don't have a problem. I like Josaline."

I watched, unnoticed, as Nori appeared before Jeb, placing the tray down hard and nearly breaking the glasses on it. "Dinner is ready."

Nori didn't seem to like me at all, and it caused Jeb to sputter a response. "I mean, she is a nice girl, that's all. I'm not going to tell her to leave. It's not my house!"

"I have to go, Cami," Cami said something else, but I cut her off, returning to the silent living room. They all knew they'd been caught and had the decency to look guilty about it. "I should . . . I should get going . . ."

I was making for the door even with everyone else protesting. Not slowing in the least, Yuuto had to jump out of his seat to keep me from leaving entirely alone. "Josaline, wait, I'll take you home."

The last thing I wanted was to listen to anything more Yuuto had to say, leaving him behind in my hasty escape from the apartment. Standing before the elevator, I bounced on my toes, barely able to wait for its arrival as my desire to get away suddenly overwhelmed me.

The doors opened just as Yuuto made it into the hall, taking longer to get his laced-up shoes on than my slip-on flats, and I tried to shut the doors on him. "What's your problem, Josaline?"

"If you didn't want me here, why did you invite me?"

It was pointless, and I was making a bad show since I wanted in with Yuu . . . these people. I begged my mouth to stop and my chest to let it go. But then Yuuto said, "I don't know. I felt bad."

My chest ached at that, anger swelling in the place of my hurt. I refused to look at Yuuto, watching the numbers on display above the door. "You felt bad? I don't need any pity, Yuuto. I am perfectly fine."

"You had a meltdown on the Magtram!"

"I did not!!" I ripped my eyes from the count down to glare at him, only to fall silent again and return my stare to the numbers again. "I don't know who Moto is, in case you were wondering . . ."

"I didn't ask . . ."

I huffed a sad laugh, unsure why, but the idea that I was invited over to serve his purposes irked me even though my reasons for coming weren't entirely pure. "Yeah, but you asked Camillia, didn't you? And you invited me over here to try and get it out of me!"

"That's not why . . ."

"Well, jokes on you cause I have no clue who she is. I don't even know what the deal is with her name . . ."

"It's short for Mōtāgāru, which means Motor Girl . . ."

"It's stupid, is what it is." That's not what I should have said. I should have asked how he knew that. The chime rang out, calling the arrival of the bottom floor. "I don't want you to take me home. I'd rather not have you know where I live."

I stomped out, broken a little more when Yuuto lacked the courage or desire to follow after me.

Chapter Eleven

"What I wanted to express very clearly and intensely was that the reason these people had to invent or imagine heroes and gods is pure fear. Fear of life and fear of death."
— ***Frida Kahlo***

It had been raining all day, so I was surprised when Camillia still wanted to go with me even with the meeting place for the races on the other side of town. At least it had stopped for the moment. Camillia still hung on to me for dear life as I took us at a safe speed. Still faster than the tracks allowed, passing autos, massive sixteen-wheels carrying goods to stores, and cycs the whole way.

We got a little wet from our ankles to our knees from runoff and sprayed from passing vehicles. But the rest of us remained dry thanks to my leather racing jacket, Camillia's windbreaker, and our helmets. And the gathering was under a tangle of bridges. The sound of autos passing overhead echoing off the columns kept any additional rain from hitting us while we waited to race.

All the rain had run under the bridges, mixing with the dust and dirt to create a few muddy puddles in the dips within the damaged and missing pavement. Another Mute community, it created lakes of brown water that one would never find in a Gilde community. Or in my hometown in the country. Of course, this meant mud battles with people racing through them at high speeds, while the deeper ones were used by a few 'hardcore chicks' to wrestle in. Camillia showed her appreciation in the form of a tight squeeze when I went around them. A Glided girl like Camillia wouldn't dare get close to the mud.

Looking around for a spot (not quite the back but more the middle), a few moved out of the way and made room. It was surprising since I knew how hard it was for people to give up their 'spots'. My run-in two weeks ago and my return had given me some pull. It would seem. That or it was all thanks to the Cruor.

I had just propped my cyc up and settled in next to Camillia when Nori appeared before us. "I want a race. With you."

"Why?"

Nori shrugged, looking away to hide her face for some reason. "Why not? Two women cyclers would bring the house down."

"Is that the only reason? Cause that's not why I'm here, I'm not entertainment."

"Brother says he will put the winnings towards your tab."

Now I owed a tab? What was this guy's problem? I hadn't seen Yuuto since I took his invitation to his house as sincere. I got the hell out of his spectrum with it clear he didn't want me around. Whenever I saw a hint of black hair popping up over the crowd, I went in the other direction. Which I realized was crazy because there was no way the Himura Yuuto would come to the Humanities campus—especially looking for me.

Nor would any Mute, since most wanted to stay far away from Gildes. Humanities was nothing but Gildes, and someone like Yuuto would want to save face. I wouldn't put it past Yuuto to send someone else my way to fix his mess if he cared even that much. Today would be the first time I was this close, and now his sister asked me to get closer. But I was here for a reason, and I couldn't chicken out now.

"Alright. When?"

"Tenth race, we're up."

Camillia leaned up against my cyc once Nori was out of sight. "That's going to be a long wait."

"Yep."

I stood at the edge of the track, watching race after race. Maybe it was the rain or just the first time I had been around for them, but more four-wheel races were mixed in—the most recent taking off and disappearing. Camillia chatted with a few people near us during the wait. While I waited, I people watched, taking in the crowd across from me. I was trying to understand who might know something -anything- about Rene. They all gathered in clumps, chatting, laughing, listening to music, dancing badly, and drinking liquids I was confident weren't water. I silently hoped none of them were racing today. A few looked like they might fall over any second now. Camillia must have taken a good look around the first night; since she hadn't worn a single dress, sticking to tight pants and tighter tops. Cami looked like she belonged. Not that I had any room to talk.

My riding jacket was tight to my shape, but that was the point. And, given the rain, I wore black tights that stopped a few inches from my ankles. But I regretted not wearing my boots. My pink sneakers are already wet, and my feet are cold. The nights were starting to get arctic, with winter almost here.

My wandering eyes landed on the strange group again. They were farther away this time, closer to the back than we were. A chill ran up my spine just before locking on the cause, my eyes meeting a pair of dark irises. He said nothing and made no attempts to approach either of us. What harm was the guy doing? Other than being eerie. That had to be the cause of my creeping spine, the guy looked wicked in a bad way.

He was tall and thin, wearing dark baggy clothes that made him look smaller. His long black hair was in a ponytail and pulled over his shoulder. The length had it down past his chest. And his eyes. Pure black, like pools of ink, not looking away as I stared back at him. He just stood there, watching me with his arms crossed over his chest and a spooky grin on his slim face.

I was thankful when Camillia jumped between us. I struggled to take my eyes off him. It was all in fear, afraid that he would appear next to me like a Vampire if I let him out of sight for even a second.

"Stop making eye contact with that guy!"

I shrugged her off even though I already agreed, "He's harmless."

"Not according to the Cruor." Camilla fussed.

"What?" I asked, shaking my head.

Camilla didn't move other than to cross her arms over her chest. "That guy, the harmless one, was staring at you last time. So I asked Kaito and Yuuto. They didn't like it. Even Nori freaked out a little. Anyone that gets under the Cruor's skin is bad news. And he creeps me OUT! So stay away!!"

She put her foot down on the subject and I had little choice but to agree. "Sorry."

Camillia grabbed my shoulders and turned me towards my cyc. "It's time anyway."

A chill ran up my spine again, and I forced myself not

to look back, focusing on the starting line instead.

Moto pulled up next to Nori, who sat, waiting at the start. Camillia was on the back of my cyc. She jumped off as soon as I came to a stop and stood next to Kaito. The cool-hearted man was strangely warm to Cami as she came to his side. The whole scene was just too weird for me, knowing Kaito only a little, and that little had him as a cold fish with a raging temper. That is unless he talked about Cami. Kaito's floundering when I mentioned her the other night came to my mind.

Looking Nori over, the girl wearing nothing more than a dark red tank and black jeans, I quickly called out to Cami. Taking her time and care as she crossed the 'track', Camillia soon stood at my side. "Let me borrow your jacket?"

After a strange look my way, Cami stripped off the jacket. The crowd whistled at the show, and Camillia turned a little pink before bravely waving and blowing a kiss to the masses. Kaito stepped off the side a little when Cami got close, pulling her back into the protection of the Cruor a little fast and harsh.

With the show over, I held out the jacket to Nori. "Here."

Taking it out of curiosity, Nori held it by her fingertips. "Are you serious? You want me to wear this?"

I cocked my helmet to the side and then ripped the jacket from her a second later. Nori dressed as well as a Mute could, and the windbreaker was of good quality. But not as nice as my jacket. I wasn't sure if Nori balked out of confusion or general dislike, but I didn't want her riding the way she was. Whistles and howls filled the air when I stripped off my coat as Cami had. However, I did it a little faster and not as flawlessly. The windbreaker was just as effective as my riding jacket. A drizzle would feel like our skin was peeling off, and rain would hit our skin like pebbles.

Holding out my jacket, I hoped Nori would hurry up and take it. There were far too many eyes on my naked skin right now. "Even just a sprinkle will hurt like hell on your skin. That tank top isn't going to cut it tonight."

This time, Nori carefully took the offered clothing and slowly put it on. "Thanks."

Hands now free, I quickly pulled the windbreaker on

in place of my jacket, ignoring the 'boos' as much as I ignored the whistles.

Jimmy stood before us, a sheepish grin on his face. The first-ever girl lightcycs race that I knew of. And by the looks of it, Jimmy was ecstatic.

A quick twist of her locks and Nori had her helmet on, hair secured inside. One last glance, and Nori took in Moto, assessing me again. I watched her out of the corner of my helmet as Nori looked me over. Wonder what she saw? A Gilde, playing around? Someone desperate? It was hard to feel like either wasn't the truth. I was a desperate Gilde, but the line constantly blurred between needed clout for information and enjoying myself.

With our jackets on and matching black helmets, it was hard to tell the difference between us. The sound of Camillia and Roxana's cheers made it over the fray. Both of them took turns cheering for Moto and Nori. I hastily blocked out all other sounds and readied for the race. If I beat Nori, Yuuto's little sister, where did that put me in their book? What part of my 'debt' would get knocked off exactly?

Jimmy's arms lowered, and we took off, Nori's back

wheel slipping for a few seconds, and (even though I couldn't help it) I was glad she couldn't hear my chuckle inside my helmet. Moto got a head start thanks to Nori's slip. It didn't matter who won. It wasn't a money race. That didn't mean others weren't betting on us, and I wondered who had the lead in that too. Nori was more known than me and was Cruor. Odds were in her favor already.

It was a closed course, thanks to someone putting up a fake roadblock. And given the dark, wet weather while in another Mute neighborhood, I was sure no one would challenge it.

I was alone on the road with Nori, the girl moving with a bit of caution. Coming to my side, I gently encouraged her. I glanced at her. Too dangerous to do more. We were neck and neck. Together, we took it up a notch but didn't stray far from one another. Nori struck me as a kind person who just wanted to make her mark. And for some reason, that included racing me.

Light glistened on the road. And then it blinded. Nori dared to look back. There was an auto gaining on us from behind. I was looking back with her and then at her, the two of us silently agreeing to split so they would pass. Nori went left, and Moto went right. But the auto didn't pass by. It stayed right behind Nori.

The com-motor roared right behind Nori as the front bumper tapped her back wheel.

Chapter Twelve

"Real heroes are men who fall and fail and are flawed, but win out in the end because they've stayed true to their ideals and beliefs and commitments."
— Kevin Costner

The tap sent Nori flying, the cyc tumbling on without her. It made a sick sound as it bounced on the pavement.

I put a foot down to turn hard after her, the auto doing the same, but my size gave me the advantage.

They were going to run Nori down.

When I got to Nori, they suddenly veered off, placing me between her and the auto's path. It was weird, but I didn't have the time to think it over, pulling Nori off the ground. My heart was in my toes while fear rattled around like a ghost in my chest. There was no time to think or hesitate, throwing Nori on the cyc before me. Nori's arm was limp, and she had to hold it to her chest tightly. I could see the pained look on Nori's face through my visor and took off as fast as I dared with two on my cyc like this.

We didn't get far before the auto returned to our side. Now the rouge auto was trying to run the two of us off the road. I couldn't determine who was driving with the darkened windows and night. But it didn't matter because they were attacking an unarmed person without cause or reason. With Nori in my arms quivering, I didn't care if they did have a good reason.

They weren't giving up, their com-motor humming so loud it felt like my ears would pop. The auto swerved, trying to bump us, and I had *enough*. Nori was shaking in my arms, and these jerks were still at it? It was silly and pointless because what could I do? But still, I couldn't stop my anger as I slammed my fist as hard as I could against the window closest to me. It must have been an old auto or already damaged because the window shattered, glass spraying over the driver and the passenger. Pain seared through my arm and up my shoulder, but the auto slowed, so I took off. There was no more feeling in my body anyway. Whatever pain and fear there had been was gone.

I headed as fast as I could back to the start line. Not to finish the race but to get us somewhere safe. The roar started at the back as I carefully moved towards the 'line'. In the distance, I could see Cami leaning over the guardrail between her and the road to try and see. It took far too long to reach this point, but any faster, and I risked Nori bouncing off or jostling her injured arm. The auto hadn't returned, and now we were within sight of the other people. That brought me comfort even if none of them cared about me. Having witnesses just made me feel a lot better.

I pulled up to the 'line', the Cruor, Glin, and Cami just a short distance from us, and the whole place was a buzz of white noise. The group was all in shock, no one moving until we came to a stop before the gang. Then everyone moved double-time to make up the difference. Yuuto flew over the guard rail in a swift and graceful leap. The others followed, some stepping over it one foot at a time. I just watched on in a daze, my eyes drifting back to Nori, who hadn't moved in a while.

Nori's jeans were torn up all over, but she wasn't bleeding anywhere I could see save for some shallow scrapes. My brain barely registered the flash of silver under the rips of Nori's jeans. One of her legs was Biomed.

Yuuto took Nori from Moto, glaring down at me on my cyc while I couldn't understand anything. Even his furious look. Everyone was shouting except for Cami, Glin, and myself, but none of it made any sense.

"What the hell happened?" "Nori, are you okay?" "It was a closed course. Only the two of them were on it!" and other shouts I couldn't hear as they surrounded Nori, leaving me to Cami and Glin.

"Are you okay?"

My attention was still on Nori, even as Cami asked me gently. "Yeah, I'm fine."

I forced the words out of my mouth, and even then, it was a whisper. And Cami and Glin passed a worried look between one another. Glin's mouth opened to say something, but he got cut off by more yelling coming from behind them.

"Yuuto . . . YUUTO . . ." Nori's shouts could be heard over the crowd as she came back into view, pushing people away. "She saved my life, you dumbasses!!"

I realized then. The Cruor thought I had done

something to Nori on the track. I probably should have been upset or offended, but all I felt was . . . numb. "Moto! Your arm!!!"

Glin was at my side, staring intently at my limb. I held it up and looked at it for the first time. The black windbreaker was split in two, as was the skin below it, blood oozing down. That explained my pain, but now I struggled to feel anything. I hadn't noticed until Glin did.

Glin's hands were around it, squeezing it tight to try and stop the blood. "Yeah, I clipped it. I . . . I thought I felt something . . ."

"You're in shock," Yuuto explained, a strange tone to his voice sounding like guilt.

Nori had pushed her way back to me, Yuuto right behind her. Nori still held her arm tight, making me worry that Nori's arm was broken. "Somebody went through the roadblock."

"We moved out of the way . . . but they stayed behind Nori for some reason," I added in autopilot.

"Then they bumped my wheel, and I went flying. When they tried to run me over, Moto got in between them,

216

and they turned away. But they came back after Moto got me off the road, ramming into us like they were trying to knock us off. Then Moto hit their window with her fist, breaking the glass, and they drove away after that. I don't know why but I'm glad they gave up." Nori rambled, in shock as well.

Glin still held my arm tight, but I struggled in my pocket with the other one, finally getting off my lightcyc. "Moto . . . what are you doing?"

"I got their magnet ID . . ."

Before I could do anything else, Yuuto swiped my Holo away. "Think it through."

He spoke gently, and what little fight I had drained away from me. Yuuto handed me back my Holo, fully trusting my decisions. His fingers grazed mine and slowly pulled away, wiping his pads along the back of my gloved hand. I was staring, watching him and the soft look on his face but movement drew my attention elsewhere.

Cami was shifting on her feet, struggling with her hand inching towards her Holo. "We have to do something. We need to get them to a hospital."

"Nori's cyc. It's still on the side of the road." I offered, my thoughts still scattered.

Kaito carefully pushed Cami back and took a glance at my arm. "We'll handle that. And your arm."

"Nori, your arm?"

The girl grinned back at my concern, even with her pale face. "Just dislocated. I'm alright."

"You're lucky is what you are. Both of you." Roxanna said, sounding like a mother instead of a gangster. "If it weren't for Moto's jacket, you would be torn up too."

"This is all very nice, but I don't want Moto to bleed to death here."

Reglin held my arm tight, stopping a little over half the flow. Kaito took over, taking the spot on my arm Glin held in his hands and pulling me to some unknown destination. "It's doubtful she will, with such a shallow cut."

Glin glared back at the man, "Let's not find out!"

Cami stuck close to me, following as Kaito led us to one of their autos and sat me down in the back seat. Then he pulled a first aid kit out of his trunk—a big one.

"Why the hell do you have that?" Cami asked.

Kaito focused on me instead of Cami's question, a

pair of scissors in his hand. "I'm going to cut away some of your jacket."

"Go ahead. It's ruined anyway."

"And you need to remove your helmet."

Everything seemed to stop, and Cami was the first to come back to life, swiveling to me with terror on her face. "You said they wouldn't make you!"

Kaito sighed loudly behind the blonde's head. "I'm not going to make you do anything. But as the medical professional here, I'd like to check Moto's head for any damage. She did go against an auto on her cyc."

"My body never left my cyc," I stated firmly as my answer.

Kaito looked closely at my helmet, assessing my words or the plastic's lack of marks before giving a nod and moving on. "Fine. But know it goes against protocol."

"We're not exactly in a place where protocol wins out," Glin muttered loudly.

Cami kept close watch over me as Kaito cleaned and wrapped the cut. It wasn't as deep as it initially looked. It didn't even need stitches. I turned my attention back to Nori as Yuuto popped her arm back into place. Kaito had to push me back into my seat a few times when I tried to get up to see, huffing in irritation at me, but I didn't care. I was worried about Nori, who had her life threatened tonight. After my run-in with death, I worried if it would affect Nori the same.

Kaito put the last pad in place and wrapped me up, stopping me before I jumped back to my feet with a small bottle of pills that he shook in my face. "Take two."

"Wait, what is that!"

Glin appeared at my side, swiping the pills from Kaito before Moto did. "They're pain killers, and they will fight off infection. She should take them. The cut wasn't deep, so it doesn't need stitches, but it was exposed to rain, sweat, and mud." Kaito ignored Glin's looks, focusing on his patient instead. "You need to keep it clean and dry for the next couple of days. If you need to bathe, wrap it in plastic first." Kaito took the bottle back from Glin and opened it up, two small white pills in his palm. "And take these. They will make you drowsy, so no driving."

"My cyc . . ."

"We will take care of it."

I was still for a few heartbeats, and they were waiting for my fight or flight to kick in. Instead, I took the pills from Kaito, turned from them all, pushed up my helmet to get my mouth free, and popped the pills into my mouth, a small sound of protest coming from Reglin. Now laying back against the seat, I felt the drugs kick in quickly, making the edges around me look blurry, and my body felt like it was buzzing. Moto was nowhere around at the moment. What little hardcore-ness I had was long gone.

Kaito left for the moment, but I was focused on my dear friends, both looking worse for wear. And we still hadn't achieved what we came here for.

Something was on my head, and it weighed a ton. It made my head flop back, finding my friends' faces as they stood over me. Something was also blocking my view, making it look dark. So, I pushed it up, popping it out of my way and clearing my vision. "Cami."

I snapped it shut again. I liked the difference between light and dark a lot. It made me giggle, so I did it again, hoping to get answers to my important questions.

Pop. "Cami!" Snap.

"Um . . . yes?"

Pop. "What's this?" Snap.

"What's..what?"

Pop. "This thing," I knocked my fist against the thing surrounding my skull, "on my head. There's something on my head!!!" Snap.

"It's a helmet, dear. Just a helmet."

Pop. "Oh….. I should take it off…."

"NO!!!!" Cami and Reglin both screamed and ran to me. Reglin slapped the visor shut and held the helmet on my head while Camillia pried my hands away from the edges.

"We need to get her out of here, now."

I looked around quickly, finding Yuuto's attention on the three of us–watching. My friends glared at me when I gave him a silly little wave while Yuuto ignored it. Guess hot, ganged-up guys didn't wave. Reglin wasted no more time, bending down before my blurry self and whispering. "Jo, how about a piggyback ride? Like when we were kids? Doesn't that sound fun?"

It did sound fun. The most fun thing I had heard of in a long time! The helmet bobbed up and down like crazy as I agreed. Nothing sounded better now, and Reglin swiveled on his toes, giving me his back. I didn't hesitate to grab on, and Cami helped Reglin pull me from the auto unscathed.

With a heavy thud, my head dropped to Reglin's back. I couldn't help myself, black edging around my vision. My helmet whacked the back of Reglin's head and earned a loud groan from both my light-haired friends.

Cami stood next to us as Reglin mounted his cyc, following us like a puppy. He shifted me slightly to ready us for the journey. Reglin took off his belt and wrapped it around my waist, tying me to him as he must have feared I would fall asleep along the way and fall off, which was very likely. I could barely open my eyes, and my arms felt like lead.

"How are you going to get home?" Glin asked in a moment of responsibility.

Cami's face said she hadn't thought about it, so now she was floundering without an answer. "I'll take her home." Behind her was a sheepish Kaito, his eyes darting from Cami to the floor and back again. "If you will let me, that is?"

"Will you be okay?"

Reglin whispered again, giving Cami a chance for brutal honesty with her answer. Although I wasn't sure what he could do about the situation, what with me already strapped to him and eight credits to the breeze. Cami answered with a nod and a smile, trying to be reassuring.

Going slow, I watched the two of them disappear into the night. But I remembered none of the ride home.

Chapter Thirteen

"Heroes aren't heroes because they worship the light, but because they know the darkness all too well to stand down and live with it."
— ***Ninya Tippett, <u>The Mischievous Mrs. Maxfield</u>***

It had been two weeks, and no one had said a word about me getting my cyc back. I had no clue where it was, but I assumed it was within the Cruor and wherever they kept their cycs. Or -to my fear and horror- they trashed it.

Glin said nothing. Not about my cyc or that night. I wondered how long that would last, but I didn't have much time to worry about it or my cyc with finals approaching. After my last final, there was another race. I would figure it out then.

The only final I was apprehensive about was New World History. Professor Smith was a hard ass and took joy in failing people. I would have to stay up all night to prepare.

I didn't trust my mind with sleep.

I tried to make all the words stick from my notes before me to at least manage a passing grade.

In 2918, a sickness hit the Southern Uyhokvine area. It then spread like wildfire through the Crison continent. The economy took the most significant hit, collapsing in on itself and causing all to suffer regardless of wealth. By 2920, the virus was contained, and the world's governments blamed its strength on the low-income/tier. Neither high nor low tier were satisfied with this response as it did nothing about the situation. Great unrest followed.

It was this that led to the War of Class. In 2922, the world was at war as civil wars broke out. Those that were starving fought those with golden spoons. While Gildes had access to the best weapons (all now illegal), most Mutes had only knives, sticks, and rocks to fight with. Even with the clear advantage, the War of Class lasted for close to ten years.

The war ended in 2931, and the result was a world split into two classes, Gilde and Mute, spread across ten tiers. Except Alloys, who belonged to no tier, and my tier,

Untouchables, who were above all the tiers.

Today, the population still dwindles, and many theorize that our society, as a whole, has had a setback in growth. Not just in people but in science, technology, biology, and chemistry. The environment is the only one to benefit from the drop in population as the Earth now holds less than half the number of people it once did. According to theorists, the air and water are cleaner than two centuries ago.

Stopping, I took a deep breath. I knew all of this already, but the dates and numbers were hard to swallow. The collapse of the economy created so much hatred and animosity. With all the blame placed on Mutes, it was no wonder why they were the brunt of every law.

Uncle once told me about his great grandfather, who was active in the war. Great grandfather lost many friends. It was to the point that no one got to know each other in the Mutes' communities since they would get killed off so easily. Even for those not involved, a bomb could go off in their building or street, and they would all be gone.

But even with so many Mutes eradicated, they still outnumbered the Gildes. Numbers didn't matter when it came to money and power. The more the Gilded have under their boots, the better, and they want to keep it that way.

However, this didn't mean that there weren't people who disagreed with the way things were. Or ignored the differences. It's how Alloys came into existence . . . and why more laws were enacted.

2940, the National Board of Senators called for Mutes to be stripped of their titles and removed from the board. This was more of a deterrent as few Mutes held a title at this point. 3941, law 45AA passed and stated that Any Mute can be removed from or denied a position at a Gildes request. So many Mutes stuck to roles inside their community or jobs with low contact with Gildes. 2943, Mutes segregation in schools. 2950, Utirius Omega is the first Career Placement to allow Mutes and Gildes in the same school. It has the highest application rate to this day but also the highest rejection.

I already knew how lucky I was to get into Utirius. But how lucky was Nori? And Kaito? And Yuuto? No, I knew better. It wasn't luck at all. Not for a Mute. They had to work their butts off, more than Cami and I ever had to just to get in, never mind staying and graduating. Law 45AA, aka the

Mute termination law, was still in effect today. It was why I suspected Roxana and Clyd worked around Gildes. Those two had the best posture out of the entire gang. And they wore clothing with the highest thread count. The jobs within the Gilded territory paid better, but they had a higher risk of termination without cause.

A Gilde could walk into any place with a Mute working, saying, "I don't want them here," and the manager or owner would fire them. That was law 45AA.

It kept so many Mutes at the poverty line with no means to improve except illegal methods. Leaning heavily on my arm, I gave up studying for a moment because my mind was too filled with other thoughts.

Uncle Haru, Rene, and Yuuto.

It was possible to survive as a Mute without resorting to the underground. Uncle had succeeded for years now, taking care of his family. They had setbacks, just as any Mute family did. But theirs was worse as a Plunge family. Anytime someone found out who Aunt Caroline was married to, she got fired from her position even if she worked in a Mute area or for a Mute boss. There was still a lot of anger towards

Gildes and fear.

Rene was bullied constantly and came home once with a black eye. She had called me that day, crying so hard I could barely understand her. The worst part for me was I couldn't do a thing about it. My home wasn't that far away, two hours by Electotrain, but my parents wouldn't let me leave. All I could do was comfort her through the glowing Holo. After that, Rene started dying her hair and got different friends I knew nothing about. But I had a feeling they were why Rene went missing.

And now my thoughts went to Yuuto.

How much did the Cruor know about Rene? Did they even know her name? Reglin was deep in with them, but no way they would tag the two of them as related. Rene looked like Uncle Haru and Glin like Aunt Caroline. No one ever thought the two of them were related. Some had confused me for Glin's sister while ignoring Rene when we were younger, and we all played together. So if the Cruor or any of the other gangs did know something, they'd never suspect Glin. At least I had that as some kind of reassurance.

But I struggled to believe the Cruor had anything to

do with Rene. Already a tight-knit group, would they even let Rene join? She wasn't a joiner. Rene wouldn't push for acceptance like Glin—and I. Rene would just walk up to whoever wanted her and blend in. Dying her hair bright colors made her fit in more with the Mutes, something Rene had decided long ago that she wanted to be. No one would know she was a Plunge because Rene was good at assimilation. I couldn't shake the feeling that it was something the creepy group in all black that liked to stare at me would do. Take Rene in without fuss.

That's not something the Cruor would pay attention to either.

At least if we got in, Glin and me, then the Cruor would protect us while we asked around. Maybe. So far, they had saved me from overzealous racers, but I had rescued them from overzealous drivers.

"I wonder how Nori is doing?" I said with a sigh to the wall.

With the racing seasons coming to an end, there were fewer and fewer to go to, so I would have to wait to find out. Nori was strong, and she had her brother to back her up.

Surely, she was fine, right? It wouldn't be like when I nearly lost it to those two racers. I couldn't talk to Glin or Cami because they would have forced me to stay home and miss the next race. No one else knew about it or knew I was Moto, so who could I have talked to? At least Nori had plenty of friends and family she could lean on.

Moto had no one.

That would be sad if I didn't have plenty of friends. And I included most of the Cruor in that category. All but Yuuto and Kaito. Those two didn't like me, which would be what kept me out of the Cruor in the end. I should probably try to play nice and just show them respect. At least that would get Kaito on my side. Yuuto was another story, and I didn't know what to think about him.

Taking care of himself and his sister from a young age -as Mutes- was unheard of. Uncle had told us he would never have survived if it wasn't for a support system, that his entire family would have starved without his mother and father working like dogs every day. Yuuto didn't work, so how had he kept himself and Nori alive all these years?

Something told me racing wasn't the only illegal

activity Yuuto took part in, and I couldn't even find fault in him for it.

He survived, as did his sister. And now they both went to a prestigious school–thriving. It was unheard of. Yuuto was the exception to everything I had ever learned about Mutes and the expectations set upon them.

And I respected the hell out of that.

And then there was the ancient language Yuuto knew. Only Gildes learned any other language besides English and Latin. It wasn't that the different languages were forgotten. They served no purpose other than being pretty. Uncle knew some—his family passed it down for generations. But he only knew one, and it was the same one Yuuto knew. Maybe Yuuto had the same background? He looked like Uncle a lot, same black hair and almond eyes. But his irises were like none I'd ever seen before.

I knew four languages due to being in Gilde primaries and fundamental. Mutes didn't learn anything that wasn't necessary for their survival. Around Reconstruction, any language other than English and Latin was deemed flowery and 'extra' centuries ago—which was right after the end of the War of Class in 2931, another date I needed to remember.

Yuuto's posture was decent, too, so when you add that with his knowledge of a nearly dead language, you had to wonder what he was. With him studying biomechanics, good posture would be a requirement since he would be working with Gildes.

Knowledge and posture that exceeded his tier . . . was Yuuto a Plunge?

Part of me really hoped he was because he would be more likely to help with Rene if he was. It wasn't a guarantee, but maybe Glin and I could appeal to his solidarity? A strange part of me respected Yuuto a bit more, thinking he was an Alloy. It was one thing to get far in life as a Mute or assimilate and another thing entirely as a Plunge. It would mean that someone in his family was a Gilde and loved a Mute so much that they gave up their status.

A Gilde could always become a Mute, but a Mute could never be a Gilde.

And a Plunge was at the bottom of the barrel, the lowest of the low. Because who would ever want to give up status and wealth for another person? Gildes didn't get it. My parents didn't. Aunt Caroline did, and every Mute I've ever met understood.

Love is more potent than any amount of credits or status.

That said, the feelings I had towards Yuuto couldn't be allowed. I respected him. That's what I kept telling myself, but the more I thought about him? He was slowly consuming my brain. Thoughts that should be on Rene and my exams. Even focusing on my notes and reading about Mutes and their struggles while Gildes flourished, I thought about Yuuto's strength. He clearly hated me, but that didn't make him any less amazing.

I respected him . . . that's all I was allowed to feel. Anything more would be pointless and painful. And I had exams to pass, or I'd never see Orcestra again.

Chapter Fourteen

"We are all ordinary. We are all boring. We are all spectacular. We are all shy. We are all bold. We are all heroes. We are all helpless. It just depends on the day."— **Brad Meltzer**

Camillia had one more exam, and Mia had two, but we were determined to celebrate today. The end of exams and the beginning of winter break were more than enough reasons for some fun. With me being the first to finish, I had the longest wait. But with my favorite book just waiting to be re-read and a shady Ginkgo tree, I was all set. I loved the feel of paper against my fingertips, even though *physical books* were antiquated and mostly turned to dust. Anyone who gave me a second glance would probably be confused. They wouldn't know what a paperback book was like anymore. My back against the bark and the sun twinkling through the leaves above me, I could care less about *others*.

I just hoped I could stay awake.

My all-nighter had been worth it. I still felt good about the New World History exam I just finished. Even if most of the so-called 'history' was depressing, I managed to vomit it all out from brain to page, never to be thought of again. Until I took New World History 102 next semester, so there was that to look forward to. More than anything, I needed to bring a good report card home to my parents if I wanted to stay another semester.

It was a bright sunny day, but it was still chilly as time barreled right into winter. The autumn colors were still on the Ginkgo trees' leaves, a golden yellow joining the sun around me. Everyone passing down the avenue was happy with the chatter of their winter break plans, and I allowed myself to eavesdrop for a few moments before digging into my book.

The Princess had just been dropped into a mystical otherworld when a shadow fell over me, and my heart began to beat a strange rhythm. I had been careless, lacked sleep, and forgot about keeping my wits about me as time passed.

"Long time no see . . ." Yuuto's deep cords washed

over me.

I sincerely didn't want to look up, but Yuuto didn't leave me any choice. Looming over me the way he was, if I didn't look, who knew what he would do. "What are you doing here?"

Luck was on my side. He was standing with the sun right behind him, so I only saw his silhouette, keeping his shining orbs from digging in. "I'm looking for you."

"Me?" It was hard, separating my two lives. To Yuuto, I was just Josaline, a silly girl who had been avoiding him for a month now. But to me, he was in both worlds. He knew me as Moto and Josaline, and I had seen all his sides. Josaline was supposed to be angry with him, but Moto wasn't which left me confused in how to feel. He couldn't know I was Moto. It would only complicate things more than they already were. "I'm sorry, but it's hard for me to imagine Yuuto Himura coming all the way to the Humanities campus."

"You don't need to imagine since I am standing right here."

I rubbed my eyes, "Hmm . . . well, I didn't get any sleep last night. Maybe I dozed off while I was waiting."

"Is that your way of admitting that you dream about me?"

I couldn't see his face, but I knew he was smirking. "Sure, when I have a nightmare!"

"Nightmare or not, you must be thinking about me a lot for me to show up in your sleep."

Yuuto had no clue just how right he was, and I hid my face as best I could to keep it that way. I'd kill for my blacked-out helmet right now, my face just like my paperback—readable. Struggling to my feet, I hoped to either come off as intimidating or get a chance to flee. "You wish I thought about you that much!"

Yuuto took a step forward, taking him out of the light and into the shade. Now I could see him clearly, and I found it hard to breathe. "Maybe I do?"

I swallowed the thickness in my throat down to coat my lungs, "I have far more important things to think about than you. Like classes and exams and winter break . . ."

"What are you doing for winter break?"

I huffed, needing to expel some air with Yuuto's continued closeness. "Like I would tell you. Besides, I don't

239

know yet. That's why I am waiting for my friends. So, we can discuss it."

My back hit the tree, subconsciously backing myself up as Yuuto moved closer. I shrunk as much as I could when he bowed over me, placing one hand on the tree just behind my head with nowhere to go. "My friends and I are getting together for some fun over the break. If you have some free time, then you should come."

Yuuto had always felt like an overwhelming presence whenever he was near, but I was sure he'd never gotten this close to me. Or Moto, keeping his distance and using his influence to sway and move me around. I was always under Yuuto's control one way or another, so there was no need to push me like this. It was such a strange difference that it made me wonder what had changed? Here he was, inches from a Gilde on a thickly populated campus.

Yuuto was risking a lot right now, and I didn't know why.

As close as he was to me, I was sure any moment now, Yuuto would hear my heart as it pounded in my chest. It had me tugging on my long sleeve, pulling it firmly down to my wrist. The cut I got at the last race was almost healed, but it had left a pink mark on my skin that had yet to go away. Even with it completely covered, my fear spiked with his inquisitive eyes that looked my face over. No matter how much I truly wanted to, spending time with Yuuto would not be good for me.

"I'm not free. And even if I were, I wouldn't spend it with you or your friends so you can make fun of me."

Yuuto was still studying my face as if reading every secret I ever had off my skin. The smirk he had worn was long gone. "Are you sure?"

"She's sure."

Wrapped up in the moment, I was confused at first. Yuuto was shoved back, and Reglin was standing at my side. Yuuto looked just as confused. "Inu? What are you doing here?"

I had to be Josaline now and act like someone who didn't know what was between the two of them. "Inu? How disrespectful! His name is Reglin!"

Any worry that my knowledge would give me away washed right out the window. Yuuto focused on Glin, glaring at him as he stood between us, so if I gave anything away, Yuuto had missed it. "What were you doing to her, Yuuto?"

"That's none of your business, Reglin."

"The hell it isn't!"

I jumped in between them, both of them looking close to blows. "Glin's my cousin, Yuuto. I live with him, so he has the right to ask!!"

The only reason I could explain Yuuto's anger was that Reglin looked like a Gilde, and Yuuto was worried about trouble his way. Although, threatening a Gilde wouldn't help him unless Yuuto planned on scaring Glin into silence? Or reasserting his leadership status in the Cruor?

Yuuto took a step back finally, still looking us over carefully. "Your cousin, huh?"

"Yeah, that's right. And as Jo's cousin, I'm telling you to stay away."

I groaned loudly. Glin still saw me as the little Gilde shaking in my shoes when confronted. "Glin, it's fine. I can take care of myself!"

Reglin turned his glare onto me, "Were you waiting for him?"

"What?! No! I'm waiting for Camillia and Mia!!"

"Present!!"

Turning away from the mayhem, I felt relief seeing both Camillia and Mia making their way to our meeting spot. Maybe they would be able to help me with this mess.

"Mr. Himura? What are you doing here?"

"I could ask you the same thing, Bunnag." Yuuto looked genuinely surprised at the sight of Mia, as she was him.

"Is it so hard to believe that a Biomed major would associate with Humanities majors?"

Camillia looked fierce, her arms crossed over her chest, grimace on her face, and tapping a toe in irritation. But Yuuto was unaffected, shoving his hands in his pockets and making his escape. "Yes, it is. Not sure why I am even here. See you around."

"Not likely!!" I screamed at his back.

Yuuto continued, unflinching or turning like I no longer existed, which was how things should be, how they needed to be. I needed to stay away from Yuuto as much as possible until I could tell him the truth. It was far too confusing trying to be two different people. I refused to believe the ache in my chest was from anything else other than guilt.

"Reglin, what are you doing here?" I asked once Yuuto was a tiny spot in the distance.

Glin still frowned heavily at me, "I am here to take you home. So you didn't have to drag your tired ass on the Magtram!"

Guilt ripped at my stomach. "Oh. Sorry. That was very nice of you."

"Did you two mention getting Josaline's cyc back from Yuuto? There is another race coming up soon." Camillia asked.

Cami was on the right track while I was still reeling over the most recent events. Instead of wondering what Yuuto was doing here, I should have hinted for clues to my cyc's location. I didn't miss the way Reglin paled at the mention of my secret life. "No, we didn't. But Reglin knows where it is, don't you?"

"I do . . . but I'm not going to tell you."

"What?! Why not!!"

"No cyc, no racing."

It was just like before, Reglin refusing to tell me where the race was all so he could keep me 'safe'. I just found it annoying and insulting. Now he was hiding my lightcyc from me, a cyc that was a gift from him! That was somewhere in the hands of the Cruor!

"Fine! Don't help me! And as you can see, I don't need a ride, so you can leave!!"

He grimaced but left, stomping away and fussing to himself as he did. Once he was long gone, I turned to Camillia. "You still have Glin on Aimless, right?"

Cami smiled and looped her arm through mine, reaching back for Mia. "Sure do. And I'll discuss it with you after you come with me. You guys have to see this place."

Chapter Fifteen

"You don't look so much like a great hero,' Jarrah said. 'I'm pretty sure I'm not,' Mack said wearily. 'My throat is hoarse from screaming in terror. I don't think heroes have that problem."
— Michael Grant, _The Call_

The place was small but cute, reminding me of the photos I'd seen of famous coffee shops back before the Reconstruction. White tile on the floor glittered. I watched it and the back of my friends' heels as they made their way to a booth. The worn leather was soft and warmed quickly from my body heat. Dim lighting above was offset by the bright orange light from the setting sun outside. I would need to leave for home soon, but I had time for some cake, coffee, and a distraction. The place smelled of sugary sweet deliciousness, and I was already drooling.

Mia and Cami sat across from me. I studied the menu, quickly picking a slice of chocolate, raspberry cake, and dark

246

chocolate mocha. When a presence appeared, ready to take our order, I was suddenly at a loss for words.

"What can I get for you guys . . . oh, hi Camillia. And Josaline?! What are you doing here?"

Roxana looked curiously at Cami and then at the rest of us, stopping on me the longest in her scrutiny. "Just . . . hanging with some friends."

When Roxana's eyes danced around the table, I knew she was probably trying to figure out which of us, me or Mia, was Moto. "This your first time here?"

We nodded silently, and I thought it best to focus on my surroundings more. If Roxana worked here, it wouldn't be strange for more Cruor to be lurking. At least Clyd since they were married. The café (as predicted) was in a Gilde neighborhood and filled with them. I didn't see another Mute around. That made me like the place a little less.

Roxana took our orders, and I drooped in to whisper once she was gone. "Did you know she worked here??"

Cami shrugged, "Kaito might have mentioned it."

"Why would you bring us here?!"

Mia was silent, watching Roxana's return while Cami

and I had a whisper fight. "So we could get some information! I thought you wanted into their gang? What better way than to go through a chill and non-terrifying member! Plus, she might know where your cyc is."

I didn't need anyone to tell me where it was. I had Glin's GPS tell me when the time came. But it would be better if I had an idea beforehand to prepare myself for whatever I may have to do to get it back.

When she returned, Roxana placed all our orders before us in a hasty performance, not touching more than an inch of the plates' edge and only touching the bottom of our cups. Something that was Regulations for Mutes working in Gildes' neighborhoods. But then, to my shock, she sat down right next to me.

Silence fell for a second, none of us knowing what to do. But then Cami broke out of it quickly. "Roxana, this is Mia Buung."

They gave one another bright smiles and bowed slightly, more like a nod. "So, what are you guys up to?"

Maybe it was due to Cami's association with Cruor, like Kaito? Or my shortage of fear when I went to Yuuto's place that night, but Roxana instantly didn't worry about us. I didn't know about Mia, but Cami and I were Gildes, and Roxana had no problems openly associating with us even at her place of work. Cami was wrong about Roxana. The woman was fearless and that was intimidating in its own way.

"We are discussing plans for this break!" Cami spilled a little too energetically.

They were all so excited about their free time, which made me a little jealous. "I'm heading home for the break."

Silent, Cami and Mia looked over at me. Roxana read the room or something, remaining silent as well. "The whole break?"

"No, but for Peace Day."

Mia shook her head in clear judgment, "You celebrate?"

Peace Day was only something Gildes celebrated since it was the end of a war they had won. I hated it, but my parents forced me every year. "Not really. Just dinner with my family and a few… family friends." Family friends but not friends of mine, I thought to myself.

"My parents force me to celebrate it with them,"

Cami added with disgust, "but they live in Orcestra, so I'll still be around."

"I'll be spending time with my family too. The Cruor." This time, Mia and I were silent, unsure how much we were supposed to know. "I'm sure Cami told you guys about them? I'm one of them."

"Oh, you are?" Mia asked, doing her best to sound surprised or confused.

Roxana nodded, "Yep. They're the best. You guys should come hang out!"

"That reminds me," Cami started, her eyes dancing to me for a second, "You couldn't possibly tell us where Moto's cyc is, could you?"

Roxana looked a little uncomfortable all of a sudden with the question. "I'm not really sure . . ."

Whether she meant she wasn't sure where it was, or Roxana wasn't sure she could or should tell us, I didn't know. And we would never find out. Before any of us could respond otherwise, another stood beside Roxana, leering suspiciously over us. "Oh! Clyd! I'm sorry, I lost track of time! You remember Josaline, right? And Camillia, of course. And the new one is Mia."

We smiled back at him, catching him completely off guard. "Um… Hi. Nice to see . . . meet you all."

"Camillia was just telling me how Moto was wondering about her cyc? Are you guys planning on giving it back to her anytime soon?"

A frown creased Clyd's face that he zeroed in on Roxana and Cami. "That's between Moto and the Cruor."

"But . . . aren't you a Cruor? And Roxana as well?"

Mia was playing it too close with her concerned question. She was too eager to find out about my cyc, and Clyd now targeted her with his scrutiny. "Yes, but none of you are Moto, are you?"

The table grew silent, and Roxana rose, taking his arm in her hands. "Well, it was nice chatting with you ladies. I'd better get this one home. I think someone's a bit cranky today."

Remaining quiet until the couple left, hot air expelled from me just as I slouched in my seat. "That was too close for comfort."

"Clyd's stare is far from intimidating," Mia added,

drawing her arms over her chest in irritation.

I giggled at her a little; she was so cute. "It's alright. I knew they wouldn't tell me anything about my cyc."

"So now what?" Cami asked, taking a sip of her drink.

It reminded me of mine, getting woefully cold while I tried to play the part. "Now? We stick to the plan. Follow Glin's GPS to my cyc."

"That means waiting until the night of the race, doesn't it? You'll risk running into a Cruor like that."

Worry was clear in Mia's tone, but it wasn't as if I had any other choice. "And if I do, then I'll claim foul. They stole my cyc, and they strike me as the type to take such accusations very personally."

"And what if they don't?"

Cami's eyes dug into me, but I just shrugged them off. "Then it won't be the first time I had to fight for something that was mine."

The look on Camillia's face was one of confusion and concern. It wasn't the first time I fought for something, but the results would need to be vastly different. I would have to win this time.

It was the first time I had taken a Rental, and the lack of a driver was eerie for me. I knew the auto was attached to the tracks and programmed to follow the GPS coordinates I put in, but watching as the auto drove itself was strange. The race was in a few hours, and (according to Reglin's 'find friends') Glin was still at a place over in South Bunkyo. I found an oversized garage with nothing much to speak of around it following his beckon. There were rundown buildings all around the garage, the same as the garage itself, rusting at the edges of the sheet metal it was made of. As to be expected in the area I was in. And a garage owned by Mutes. If they did own it, there were no signs of life currently to tell me for sure. But Reglin was here, or at least, his Holo was. Maybe Yuuto had locked him or his device up as punishment for standing up to him the other day? Reglin and I were not on speaking terms at the moment, so I couldn't ask him if he had gotten any flak for how he talked to his . . . 'master' in my defense.

We also revealed my connection to Glin as Josaline to Yuuto, but it seemingly didn't affect the situation.

The Rental dropped me to a spot close by as instructed, and I now stood in an alley–waiting. I was glad Camillia had decided not to come with this time. I didn't want to imagine what this sneaking would look like with her tagging along. Cami already stood out in this area as a Gilded. Plus, it would make this a lot easier without her involvement.

Josaline was sure Moto was about to get on the Cruor's bad side.

A door on the front opened, slowly pulling upward, releasing the hum of com-motors as it did. They soon flooded out. Cycs first, then autos came out and raced away. The old building struggled to close the garage door, but that was my advantage as I ran in before it fully shut.

There she was, my beautiful cyc. It felt like an eternity since I had seen her, and tears formed slightly at the sight. At least the Cruor had taken good care of her. By the looks of it, they had given her a good shining. They probably made Reglin do it.

They also replaced the pads and regenerator on my brakes (I had meant to get to), which is another lucky break.

Not so fortunate was my missing riding jacket. Nori must still have it. Meaning I was stuck wearing long sleeves with a thick sweater on top. The only things black I owned were a few pants and that riding jacket since my windbreaker was destroyed. I was pretty sure I would get laughed out of the place in my dark pink sweater. The baggy material was thick and covered my butt and thighs. It was also the darkest and warmest clothes I had. It was the best I could do to look like I 'belonged', and my black jeans helped a little, looking more like tights as they fit me like a second skin.

Laugh all they want. I was there to race, not look good. For *anyone*!

With the race in Iswa near the central hub station, I had a long ride ahead of me. Being back on my cyc -alone- was freeing, so I didn't mind even as the crisp autumn night bit at my exposed skin and threaded its way through my clothes. My feet were warm this time (at least). Borrowing a pair of Auntie's shoes, I wiggled my toes against the plush inside of the black, faux fur-lined boots I wore. I had some lined with real fur back home, but I hated them.

As I neared the station, my focus was on preparing

myself for what I faced when I got there. It was hard to imagine anything bad with Reglin giving me the cold shoulder and the Cruor not expecting me to show (at least not on my cyc). The best I could do was ignore them and just try and make some money tonight. It wasn't something I enjoyed, but if I made enough, maybe I could get Yuuto to take it and let me buy my way in? That scenario was even less likely tonight. The Cruor had done nothing more than given me the run around this entire time, and now I had broken into their place.

It also got me clout within the community if I kept winning races. And attention. Both of those would help me get information no matter who I asked.

I was arriving a bit late. A race was just taking off. Jimmy caught sight of me and flagged me down. "Running late tonight?"

I shrugged, "Had a few last-minute errands to run."

"People are already asking for you. I wasn't sure you would return what with all that happened."

"Here I am. Ready to go."

"That'a girl. I got you a spot right up here to wait in."

My return had earned me some distance, getting closer to the line. Jimmy placed me on the opposite side from the Cruor and far enough down to go unnoticed by them. The crowd parted to make room for me but then swarmed back in with questions and dry conversation before I got to race.

I snuck a peek over at their crew without turning my head (letting my helmet hide me again) after the first calls of 'Moto' made it over the crowd. I watched as -one by one- the Cruor found me on the other side, Yuuto turning away from the race entirely to brood. Reglin turned bright red while Kaito laughed. LAUGHED! Roxana had to take Clyd away for some reason, and Nori just moved closer to the front, sporting my racing jacket and looking like a total fangirl. I couldn't catch sight of Buri but what took my breath away was Camillia. I had no clue how she got there, but she gave me the thumbs up and called out my name. My racing name anyway.

Three races I won got me close to four–k, and I managed to avoid all contact with the Cruor the entire time. I thought things would go South right at the start, even as I set myself on the far side of the start line. I still got noticed in large part by those who cheered my name.

The last of my races finished, and the transfer credits chiming away in my pocket, I was ready just to call it a night. There was no way Yuuto would talk to me rationally–he was obviously pissed. As was Reglin, and I was tired of it all anyway. Maybe I could get some information from others around. What with winning every race with ease tonight? But I still didn't have enough to back me just yet. I would need to keep winning into the next racing season. Winter break started the next day. I would rather relax than deal with this drama for a while, but I would be dealing with family drama instead.

A few others made their escape. Most of the races were over, and now it was getting close to dawn. It was the latest I had ever stayed out, and I felt it in my entire body.

I was going the respectable speed (and my new brake pads), so I didn't struggle to stop when some guy jumped out in front of me. Even though I didn't want to, a shiver ran up my spine at the sight of him. It was the creepy guy, his long hair loose and hanging around his shoulders. The stringy strands made his face look slimmer as they framed his face with his slumped shoulders in a defiantly Mute stance. He wasn't that bad looking of a guy. I was sure there were plenty of interested girls, and that wasn't based solely on the cruel looks some of the girls behind him shot me either.

They had nothing to worry about. I was everything BUT interested in this guy. I wanted to speed away into the night, but I also had to make connections if I wanted answers. That included creeps like the one before me -like it or not- and I was sure he had answers for me even without any proof.

"I have been waiting for a chance to introduce myself...."

I didn't like the sleazy way he spoke to me, so I let it be known. "Can it wait a bit longer? I just want to get home."

He chuckled darkly, and something told me it was the only way he knew how. "I fear if I wait, I won't get another chance. Someone will sweep you up."

I sat up, releasing the accelerator but keeping the com-motor running. My way of telling him to make it quick. "I am not for 'sweeping'. I'm just here to race."

A lie, but I needed to get a feel of this guy before

letting go of any valid information. "I figured that out when you turned down the twenty-k. You rightfully won those credits. There would have been no shame in keeping it."

"I would have felt shame regardless. If this is about that money, you should know I can't be bought."

He chuckled again, making my blood run cold. "Hear me out anyway. You might like what I have to offer."

Was he all about the money? Someone who was Mute would have a reason to race for credits. Far more than a Gilde like me had cause to. It would explain a lot and make things a lot easier. I could buy information from him. But then again, Glin could have done the same thing if he had won enough races.

My cyc bounced as I was pushed up by another body that forced itself on the back of my seat. "She's busy."

Yuuto's voice and scent washed over me as he pushed my hand off the brake and hit the accelerator hard. Taking me and the cyc up to high speed quickly, I had no choice but to go along with it. If I moved even to swat his hands, I could throw us off balance and tumbling into the street. I held onto the seat between my legs and seethed–caged in by his arms around me. It was good that I was angry. I didn't want to think what my mind and body would be doing otherwise.

The buildings slowly shrunk in the distance, Yuuto taking us off-road and onto what looked like a pedestrian road. When we stopped, it was completely silent, surrounded by trees and a lake. Not even the birds intruded on us. He had taken us to the National Park near the city's edge.

Yuuto put the stand out hard and nearly ripped my keys out of the starter before hopping off the cyc. He said once he could tell what look I was giving him through my shades. I hoped he could tell how I fumed at him now. "What the HELL do you think you are doing?!!!"

He kept his helmet on, pacing back and forth from me. "What the HELL are YOU doing? Breaking into my garage, stealing, and then rubbing it in my face?!"

"I took back what was mine! And I wasn't in your face about anything. I was making a name for myself!!" In my anger, I leaped off my lightcyc and pushed my finger into his chest, not pulling back even as my finger bent painfully against its hardness. "Now give me back my keys, you jerk!"

Yuuto pushed my finger off him with the back of one

hand and held up the keys just out of my reach with the other. "What? These keys?"

I reached out for them, and Yuuto held them higher, dodging my attempt and holding them up as high as possible. Jumping a few more times, I realized how stupid I was when he started to laugh at me. "ARRRGGGG!!! What is wrong with you?!!"

"What is wrong with you? Practically serving yourself up on a silver platter for *that* guy!"

"What guy? That creepy guy? He jumped out in front of me. What was I supposed to do, run him over?"

"Yes! If that guy ever comes around you again…."

"I can make my own decisions about people. I'm a big girl." I spat back.

Yuuto shook his helmet at me, "You're far too trusting of people."

He had a point. My past told me this, and I had re-learned that about myself with all the close calls I recently experienced. "Then tell me, why should I stay away from that guy? At least give me that!"

A swift tug and Yuuto had his helmet off, tossing it, so

it rolled up to the back wheel of my cyc. "He is a bad guy. A thug. He does hard crimes and craves power."

"I'm going to need more than that."

Releasing a sigh, Yuuto looked up to the sky, dawn lighting it up to a pale grey. His 'Adam's Apple' danced in front of my eyes as he spoke. "You need more than that? Really?"

". . . I just don't see what that has to do with me," I pushed, wanting to know more. Not for myself but about Yuuto, even if it wasn't fair.

"What difference does it...." Yuuto sighed heavily again, dropping his head down to look at me. "Fine. His name is Sora. He is a leader in the Kurio-chi," when I tilted my head in confusion, he chuckled darkly, "that gang around him, a real gang that swallows people whole and spits out their bones.... and he's my cousin." Yuuto ignored my obvious shock that was clear even with my helmet on. "When I was a kid, I lost my parents and had to take care of Nori by myself. When my cousin offered to help us out, I thought it was a blessing. But it turned out that cousin Sora wanted me to be a *runner* for him. When I got too old to pedal drugs, he had me do odd jobs to make him money and fast. One of those things happened to be racing anything with wheels. Sometimes away from Regulators. I don't know what would have happened to me if Kaito hadn't gotten me out, but after what happened to Nori…."

He trailed off for a second, and I wanted to hear more but knew better than to ask. It had something to do with Nori's Biomed leg. The look on Yuuto's face…he blamed himself.

"He takes advantage of people, Moto. Especially those that I show even the smallest amount of interest in."

Yuuto was staring at me while I let his words settle in my brain. "So . . . what you're saying is . . . he wants to use me . . . to get to you?"

"Most likely."

My heart raced in my throat. I had to remind myself that Yuuto was only interested in the racer and not *me*. "Then . . . wouldn't you hopping on my cyc and kidnapping me make it worse??!!"

He cringed, my voice going to another octave at the end of my rant. "I didn't want you getting tricked into working for him."

My hand hit plastic, wanting to slap my forehead but forgetting my current wardrobe. "You think I'm a complete idiot, don't you?"

"Your actions speak loudly," he said with a serious expression on his.

At least Yuuto's words had my heart dropping into my belly instead. It was better that I felt nothing but hurt when it came to him. If only I could stop needing to remind myself that I was there for Rene instead of Yuuto. "Ug. Just give me my keys so I can go home already."

I held out my hand, and Yuuto hesitated. "Promise me you will stay away from Sora and all Kurio–chi."

"I just want to go to bed." I whimpered.

"Then promise."

"Fine! I promise to stay away from them. Now give me my keys!" In my hands again, I wasted no time getting on my cyc and starting the com-motor. The weight shifted again, this time Yuuto wrapping his arms around my waist and making me jump. "What are you doing??!!"

"I need a ride. You weren't just going to leave me out

here, were you?"

"Yeah, kinda!"

"At least take me back to my cyc." He whined.

Never had I wished for my riding jacket more as we sped back towards Iswa station. The heat of Yuuto's hands on my hips and his chest on my back bled through my thick sweater like it was nothing. He either felt my heart pounding and was messing with me or wanted to make sure Sora wasn't lurking somewhere for me because he took his sweet time getting off when we pulled up next to his cyc. I had a feeling it was the former. He had only shown mild amusement while teasing me the four months I had known him.

I didn't wait for him to move away from me and get on his cyc. Unable to stand his nearness any longer, I took off as soon as he was clear. This winter break would be a welcomed reprieve from one Yuuto Himura.

Chapter Sixteen

"That is why enemies can be great motivators. They serve as fuel for your fire."
— **Simon Zingerman, <u>We All Need Heroes: Stories of the Brave and Foolish</u>**

Staying out all night and sneaking in at dawn equated to me sleeping for twenty-four hours straight. I never really made up the time I lost from studying for exams. When I woke, I had missed seven calls from Camillia and three calls from Mia.

"Where have you been? Why are you ghosting me??"

"Sorry, I was asleep."

Camillia sighed loudly into the Holo, shaking her head at me. "If it were anyone else, I would think that was a lie. What are you up to tomorrow?"

"Well, I think I have slept enough to last me the whole break, so . . . nothing!"

"Good."

267

All Cami gave me was to dress warmly. With the freezing temperatures outside, it wasn't a hard sell. Leaving the West sixteenth street station and a three-minute walk later, I arrived at the address Camillia gave me, and my breath caught. Then it released quickly, a long white puff coming from my mouth.

Before me was the Goricart, along with Mia and Camillia, who stood just outside the doors before me.

The building was short and made up of a blonde colored tin. It was rusted in several places but we were near Mute territory. Frankly, if it wasn't for the holograph sign glowing dimly over the front door, I wouldn't have believed I was at the right place. It was still strange, considering what this place was. They should have the credits to fix up the place but maybe the oldest surviving company in the world didn't care how one of their buildings looked. It was also the only one that allowed Mutes in, so it probably got the least amount of business compared to the rest. I had always planned to come to this one with Rene but we never made it here. This was my first time ever so I was busy freaking out. I didn't pay attention to anything other than those three details.

Camillia, Mia, and Goricart.

"Ohmygodohmygodohmygoooooodddddd!!!!" I bounced over to my two dear friends, narrowly missing a large missing chunk of sidewalk, and wrapped my arms around their necks and swung them all around in a circle before facing the doors to bounce some more. "My cousin and I have always wanted to come here. How did you guys know? EEK!! It doesn't even matter, thank you, thank you, thank you!!!"

Mia got her hands up and pressed them to her ears. "Josaline, please. Decibels."

"We will all be deaf at this rate. Camillia, can you please control your friend?"

"Flamingo, people are staring."

Ice filled my veins, and I turned around. In all my excitement, I missed Yuuto and Kaito, who stood with Camillia and Mia, now behind us from my excited freak-out. "What are they doing here?!"

Mia flushed, looking very embarrassed. "They invited us."

Yuuto was grinning from ear to ear while I scowled

back. Camillia grabbed my arm, spinning and pulling me away to whisper harshly. "If you had answered your Holo . . ."

"I told you I was sleeping . . ." I whispered harshly back.

Cami continued to whisper. " . . . you would know that Kaito and I are friends now . . ."

I couldn't stop yelling, "WHAT?!" in my genuine confusion and shock.

Camillia hushed me before continuing. "Yes, so could you please wipe that look off your face? He invited me to come today and told me I could invite my other friends. You are here to support me, okay?"

My friend was pleading with me (begging, really). A Mute and Gilde on opposite sides of the tier spectrum had decided to become friends? They would need all the support they could get. "Of course, I will support you in whatever you want, Camillia."

Flipping her switch, Camillia released me and spun back around, a big smile on her face. "Well, guys, should we go in?"

I took my time, doing my best to contain my excitement as now I knew it would get used against me. Kaito went back to ushering us in. "Everyone else is already inside."

"Everyone?" Mia squeaked.

Before Yuuto could answer her, opening his mouth to explain, I laced my arm through Mia's and began pulling her away. "You know those Cruor, Mia, attached at birth. They're all inside already waiting desperately for all their limbs to return."

Yuuto chuckled behind us but said nothing. We met with the main character of the graphic novel Goricart was based on, War-shi. Normally the character was in an all red suit of armor but Kaito only wore the small hat that went with it. Eiyu-Teki was there as well, a priest or monk that wore a long dark blue vest and matching pointed hat. Kingukonga was a weird orange monkey and the costume looked like roadkill. It was so old. A large Banana and Princess D rounded out the group that we now faced upon entering the dressing room. Rows and rows of costumes were all around us, the Cruor pulling outfits over their clothing. It all smelled like dust and mildew which made it all more surreal. I was shocked to see a 'gang' playing dress-up even as they pulled it over their street clothes.

With frigid temperatures outside and the extra wind we would be creating for ourselves, it wasn't strange that they would put on the additional layers. It was just the costumes on people who were supposed to be hardcore that was confusing. It was more evidence to the contrary. I lacked any belief that the Cruor was anything more than a close-knit group of friends.

Friends that would go to war and die to protect one another but still not a gang of cutthroats.

Mia left me, heading for the rack filled with the small purple dragon, Ryu, costumes, while Camillia was already pulling a pale pink and tight fitted Princess Pinku dress over her head. Nori passed by me in a red, ballroom gown of Princess D. It matched the red tips of her long black hair. She somehow made the puffy royalty look fierce, but paused just long enough to glare at me.

"What did you do to her?"

Still standing behind me, Yuuto had yet to move

towards any costumes. I shrugged at his question, "Guess Himuras don't like me. All the ones I've met so far have it out for me…."

"I don't have it 'out for you'," he said, holding his hands up to do quotes with his fingers.

"Could have fooled me."

I left him, my eyes landing on a Frogette costume. The raspberry beret fit perfectly over my melon head and allowed my braided tails to hang free. I pulled on the matching fuchsia dress, leaving my white sweater dress and thick, light gray tights underneath. I hoped I wouldn't be too cold when I checked my purse and coat into a locker.

Camillia stood, chatting with; Jeb, Eiyu-Teki; Buri, the Banana; Kaito; and Roxana in a dark green and majestic Rose Queen dress. Clyd stood beside Roxana in just street clothes either undecided or uninterested.

All famous cartoon characters from my childhood seemed to perfectly fit each Cruor member, especially Buri in a Banana. Mia was just zipping up her Ryu costume when Yuuto walked past them and out the door. I couldn't stop myself from following after him and finding him crouched to look closely at a kart.

"What are you doing?"

Yuuto's head popped up from the steering wheel as if caught. "I'm checking out the ride."

I stood next to him, looking down at the ancient vehicle. Nervousness had me shaking instead of the cold, suddenly self-conscious now that we were alone. "Did you know that Gōruden is one of the oldest surviving industries globally?"

"Yeah." He said with a smirk, standing and watching me out of the corner of his eye, "Pretty sure everyone knows that. And I'm pretty sure these rust buckets are the same ones they used when they opened this joint."

Ignoring the apparent jab, I looked him over. "Where's your costume?"

Yuuto huffed, looking me over with a smirk. "I don't do cosplay."

"Well, that's no fun." My disappointment (that I couldn't control) was evident in my voice, leaving him behind to go back inside.

"Fine." Yuuto released a rueful sigh and followed me

to the door, holding out a hand, asking me to lead. "Then you pick something out for me."

I grabbed the hand he extended out to me without thought, pulling Yuuto back inside to the costumes. We roamed the racks as I tried to find something that suited him. I wasn't sure how much time had passed when I realized; I was still holding Yuuto's hand. He was holding my hand in return, so I didn't know if I should pull away. I didn't want to. I needed to. Once noticed, it was like an itch just out of reach. It tickled at my brain. My palm was getting hot, and my heart skipped around wildly, so I gently pulled my hand from his, feigning a need for two hands which wasn't entirely untrue.

Grabbing the black and gray felt of the large bat wings attached to a Hammer costume, I held it up for his consideration. "Isn't Hammer the bad guy?"

"Yep. And I think 'bad guy' fits you perfectly."

He rolled his honey eyes and took it from me to return it to the rack. "Next." I picked up a Ni-Banme costume and held it up. "The second in command?"

"The younger brother! And Kaito is War–shi, so it's a

275

perfect fit!"

He looked over the yellow 'armor' made of thin cotton. "I'm not wearing some weird one-piece PJs."

I put it back harshly to grab just a hat. "Then wear the hat like your buddy!"

"I don't have to follow Kaito, you know." I didn't know if he meant the hat or, in other ways, Cami and Kaito looking . . . comfortable with one another, even from different tiers. Yuuto took the hat from me and tossed it up on the shelf. "Who are you anyway?"

"Frogette," I said, flicking a braid behind me, and it hit my back heavily.

"Then I should be Frog."

Yuuto was already picking up the white and light blue hat, pulling it on his head. The beret bubbled up around his ears, and he faced me with a grin. I tried and failed to contain my laugh, sputtering for a second before bending over with it. When I rallied enough to speak, tears were in my eyes, but Yuuto was still busy chuckling.

"It doesn't suit you," I managed through large gasps of air.

"At least it's warm."

I reached up and pulled it down around his ears and the back of his neck as far down as it would go until the beret bubbled only a modest amount above his head. Making it look more like a brightly colored beanie instead. "That's better."

Bright gold crashed into me. I had gotten my face inches from Yuuto's in my poor judgment while adjusting the hat. Both of us were rooted, millimeters from each other, and my arms around his shoulders. His eyes were searching mine, and I wondered how many of my secrets Yuuto could dig out if given the time. I started to shake from going up on my toes, and now they began to ache, which was my saving grace. Effectively breaking the moment, I lowered myself and stepped away.

An awkward silence stretched between us, my eyes to the floor as I begged my feet to move to get away. Yuuto cleared his throat, breaking the stint. "This fits you." Picking up my braid, he tossed it to my back for me, and I pulled my eyes up just in time to see Yuuto pull back his arm.

My brain was frozen in time, struggling to get it and

my mouth to work together again. I took a deep breath and forced my brain and lips to connect. "Too bad there's not a Grave-runner costume here."

"Why?"

"It would suit you the best. Good, bad, you never really know with Grave-runner. He just does whatever he wants."

His arms crossed over his chest, the dark gray sweater he wore was tight everywhere, and I had to focus on his face. "Figures a Humanities major would reference such an old comic. I thought Grave-runner was a superhero?"

"Grave-runner doesn't have any superpowers, just skills he acquired over the years. Which he protects the people with however he can. Making him the bad guy sometimes."

Yuuto smirked down at me. "Skills he acquired, huh? I guess he and I are similar in some ways. Except I'm better off financially than that guy."

I huffed, "I've seen your place. You are far from rich."

"Hey, my place is comfortable. And Utirius is expensive, especially when you times it times two. And then there's the medical bills…"

"Medical bills?" Yuuto was a stone. He had let that slip and now the air was uncomfortable so I saved him by changing the subject. "Are you bragging now?"

HIs lip twitched, begging to smile while Yuuto forbade it. "It's not bragging when someone is looking down on you."

Yuuto was grinning, but I wanted him to be mad. I didn't like the warm fluttering my heart was doing at the moment. It kept happening when I so much as thought about Yuuto. "It's just respect", I told myself repeatedly, but that was starting to get tired.

Stepping around Yuuto, I wanted to get away and enjoy the fun. But he stopped me, grabbing my arm as I passed, and forced me to be nearer than before. "Where are you going?"

"Out. To the karts?"

"You are just going to walk away in the middle of a conversation?"

I tried to get out of his hold without looking like it was bothering me. "The 'conversation' was over. And you have your costume, so what is left?"

"It didn't feel over to me. More like you ended it. If you have something to say, then say it."

Yuuto's face was blank, and I couldn't tell what he was feeling. Like a mask over his face. "Fine, I have something to say. Let me go."

Pondering over it for a moment, he released me after one too many heartbeats to be expected. My freedom was gained. I did all I could to get away from Yuuto and look natural. The last thing I wanted was to indicate that I felt anything towards that man.

Escaping to the outside, the karts before me, I caught sight of a scared-looking Mia. I was about to comfort the dark beauty when Buri beat me to it.

"You alright?"

Buri never looked more ridiculous in his banana costume, but it seemed to make Mia relax a little. "I'm fine . . . I just . . . I've never driven anything like this before. It has no magnets!"

He shrugged, the yellow cloth wiggling on Buri's entire body, and I giggled as I passed him looking for my kart. "Me either. But that's half the fun, isn't it?"

"If you say so."

Buri wrapped an arm around Mia's shoulders and warmly smiled as he squeezed her. "I'll keep an eye on you. Don't worry. You'll be safe if you stick with me."

Mia managed a nod, the strange banana man leaving her to hop into the kart right behind his new friend. It was cute. I liked them together for some reason. Maybe because Mia was so quiet and calm while Buri was wild, the two would complement each other well.

There were a few empty carts before me, some claimed by the staff/tour guides driving with us. I watched as the others quickly walked past me to claim their vehicle. Yuuto strode out of the costume shop, hands in his pockets and unperturbed. The only one ever bothered by our encounters was me. Nothing bothered Yuuto.

All the months I had known Yuuto, I had always seen two sides to him. Cool and calm or polite and warm. Sometimes, those two were at the same time. No matter what happened, Yuuto was always collected and professional. He handled any crisis without breaking a sweat, and the only time he showed any stress was when it came to his sister. But as he got closer and passed me, I had to admit. I was at a loss for the face he wore now. It was one I had never seen on him before.

He looked . . . exasperated.

Yuuto knew I was Gilde even if he had no clue how far up the chain I was. With his aspirations in Biomed, there was no way he would allow himself to get tangled up with me. I had nothing to worry about when it came to feelings being mutual. All the more reason not to allow me to feel anything towards him. Yuuto must be worried about associating with so many new Gilde, Cami's class more evident than mine.

Out of nowhere, music blasted in front of me. Mia turned as much as possible to find the Banana, dancing like a fool in his seat. Buri had grabbed a kart with an AUX plug and had his Holo playing tunes. Banana Man must have prepared for it. How many people had AUX cords handy? Peeking behind me, I saw a few other Cruor dancing in their seats. Roxana and Nori as well as Cami. But the rest were stoic like this wasn't a game.

It wasn't long after we were all pulling out, lining up on the street. The instructors gave the rules out, reminding us not to go any faster than sixty MPH and not bump one another. The karts were real, and this was "not a game". A shame since it would be entertaining to knock one another around.

Following the set track, the one we had to keep ourselves on as nothing was holding the little kart to it, we set out towards Loport and Ocresa station. The kart's freedom, magnet–free, reminded me of being on my cyc, and I loved it.

There was light traffic, being the middle of the afternoon, but no matter how slight, it still made Mia nervous, her hands shaking on the wheel.

Mia looked confused when she had to stop herself at the red light. But that was normal. Mia had no experience driving off the rails like the rest of us. Save for Cami, but she was currently at the back of the group.

Then, it occurred to me that I should be acting like Mia, unused to the lack of magnets.

Banana Man Buri continued to blast music but eyed

me carefully for a moment before 'letting it go' and going back to his silliness. The music wasn't loud enough for me to hear when moving, but it was loud and clear as soon as we stopped.

With my cover not blown, I relaxed, getting out my Holo to make some memories. I wished I had my digiCam, but I didn't know we'd be coming here, so I only had the camera on my Holophone. Pulling up next to Mia, I noticed Mia was still freaking out. My Holo was up in my hand, blocking Mia's face from my view until I lowered it enough to make eye contact. "Mia, say 'hi'! You're on digiFilm!!"

She looked meek with her small wave at my Holo's camera. The whole experience left Mia winded and shaking. I switched hands, placing the Holo away from us and extending my now free hand out to her. She took it without hesitation and held it tight.

"It's okay, Mia. It's all perfectly safe. I won't let anything happen to you."

Banana Man appeared on the other side of me, coming to a brutal halt. "Yeah, I won't let anything happen to such a beautiful girl."

The light changed, and the gentle Mia stalled. Buri was laying it on thick, and she wasn't used to that sort of attention. It was something obvious before, but now it was screaming at me.

Mia was a wallflower.

I didn't know why. Mia was gorgeous and super bright.

Somehow, I had ended up in a mock race with Buri the Banana Man. It had me closer to the music, enjoying his choice of tunes. If it weren't for the tiny kart that maxed out at seventy and the ridiculous costume he wore, it would be just like that night we raced together. I didn't worry, though, the differences in the situations made up for the similarities, so my identity was safe.

We came to another light, and autos were beside us now. A few people stuck their heads out their windows around Buri and me. I saw no one did it around the others— too many Mutes in the group. A few kids were in the auto next to me, excitedly waving like we were celebrities. Getting to my feet, I gave them both a high five before the light changed again.

It was a long trip, getting dark, and apparently, we were only halfway through it. We had a break at the historical landmark, 'Freedom Tower'. I hadn't seen it since my first summer in Ocresa, but it looked the same. Rene and I ran around the base for an hour that day, passing out in the back of the auto on the way home.

Rene would have loved all of this.

Shaking the memories and tears from my head, I called out to everyone and forced them to gather together. They groaned, but I didn't care, getting them to do a group shot in front of the tower.

"We aren't tourists," Nori whined but curled into Jeb.

A glance his way, and I saw Yuuto was glaring at the couple. Wonder how much longer that would go on before he stepped in and squashed it? Was Yuuto even okay with Alloyed relationships?

The chill wrapped around my heart had me diverting my thoughts to the task at hand, grabbing a random stranger and convincing him to take the shot. Glancing again, I saw Yuuto roll his eyes, disapproving of my trusting nature as both Moto and Josaline. But it wasn't something I could turn off.

Now, I faced the next challenge of the night. A large boat before the group, they all began to board. It looked like we were going for a ride on the dark waters where no one would hear us scream.

Chapter Seventeen

"Men have to have heroes, but no man can ever be as big as the need, and so a legend grows around a grain of truth, like a pearl."
— **Peter S. Beagle, _The Last Unicorn_**

Kaito had talked the others into taking the long tour all so he could take Camillia on the boat ride. The whole plan would have been better if it wasn't the middle of winter. But the sparkling skyline on the water was lovely. The large boat's water propulsion was the only sound, sucking in water through the front and pushing it out the back, like the com-motor on a cyc or auto. However, switching air for water is much louder.

Rainbow bridge was next, at the halfway mark. I stuck to the boat's helm, freezing but getting some beautiful shots of the night skyline and the lights dancing on the black water.

"Are you going to spend the whole time recording this or actually live it?"

I didn't so much as glance, keeping my attention on my Holo. "Both."

Leaning against the rail next to me, Yuuto caught the shiver that ran through me. "Cold?"

"No." My answer was too quick, and I couldn't look at him. This was not good. My heart was dancing around in my chest like crazy, and I hated it.

"You said you and your cousin always wanted to do this?" I stared back at him. Because I didn't understand his question or what he wanted me to say. "I'm just struggling to see Reglin into something like karts."

My gaze flicked to the water so fast. I almost flung my eyeballs into the dark water. "I didn't mean Glin. I meant my other cousin, Reglin's sister."

"He never mentioned having one to me?"

If Glin hadn't brought up Rene, I didn't dare to. I trusted Reglin's decision to keep quiet about her for now. "Why would he? He's just your dog."

Yuuto was silent, and I hated the part of me that cared

if I offended him. "You got me there, I guess." Now I hated how much more I liked him, owning up to his flaws. "I saw you racing with Buri."

Oh no, had Yuuto been watching? Did he know? My mind was a wash with these thoughts while Yuuto waited for an answer I didn't have. "So?"

"So, how about you and I race?"

I almost dropped my Holo into the water, pulling it into my chest after quickly regaining myself. "What?"

"You, me, a race. You want?"

Not good. Not good. "I . . . uh . . . I don't race."

"You mean you don't race with me. Are you that afraid of losing?"

"NO! Who says I will lose??"

Crap, my competitive nature was coming out. Along with my cheeks burning, I knew I looked like a mess. Probably scary, but Yuuto just chuckled. "I do. Buri was just playing with you. Going easy. I won't be that nice."

"Why would I want to race you anyway? What's in it for me?"

Yuuto thought about it for a moment, and I considered

jumping over the rail. But Yuuto would probably just jump in after me. "You pick."

"And if you win?"

"How about we just race for now and decide after we have a winner?"

I tried to fight the smirk from forming on my face but failed. "We can't go faster than sixty, and we can't bump."

"Are you afraid I will cheat?"

If there was one thing I was sure about when it came to Yuuto, he didn't cut corners. Not with racing or school. The smile I had been fighting broke free with that, and I answered honestly. "No, I know you won't. You wouldn't want me to use it against you."

"Ha! She knows me so well. Rainbow bridge is next. We will have more than enough space."

It was a bad idea, and I knew it. But I couldn't help myself. "Alright, you have a deal. From one end of the Rainbow bridge to the other. Winner's choice."

I held out a hand for him, and he took it, squeezing it a little more than needed. But I didn't react past returning the favor. Neither of us released our hold for several moments, like a challenge. The one who let go first was the loser. We stared each other down while refusing to lose.

His thumb started moving, stroking the skin on the back of my hand, and my smile faded away. Even with the stupid hat on his head, I felt drawn to Yuuto in a manner I didn't like. He was Cruor -a gang member- an underground thug that I was supposed to get information from. I was in this to find my cousin and keep the other cousin from disappearing. That's all. No more, no less. But the longer Yuuto held my eyes and hand captive, his thumb stroking my skin and his glowing orbs burning into my memory for good, the thought that he was nothing more than a contact slipped from my mind.

"We're docking soon!!!"

We both jumped, pulling away simultaneously with Buri's call. I fled after that, hiding just out of sight but not earshot.

"Sorry! Didn't mean to intrude!" Buri's apology lacked all sincerity.

"That's all you ever do!"

There was a slap and a grunt. I assumed Yuuto

punched Buri. Hopefully, just in the arm and not the jaw. I didn't have time to figure it out. I was too busy learning how to breathe again.

The boat docked with a loud thump of the lock on the ship, sounding the end of the ride, and everyone returned to dry land. Save for me, as I was busy pacing on the other side of the boat.

"Jo!" Cami called out.

I didn't stop or lookup. I just went back and forth. Mia tried, "Josaline, what's wrong?"

Stepping in my path, Cami grabbed my shoulders and stopped my pace. "Jo, talk to us."

"I agreed to a race with Yuuto," I said quickly with one breath as though it would make it better.

"Wait . . . here? Or as Moto? I'm confused . . . " Mia asked.

So was I. I sat on the rail, eyes dancing in thought. "We're racing on the Rainbow Bridge. But it's fine, right? I've never raced him before, so there is nothing to compare."

"Then why are you freaking out?" Cami asked.

"Yuuto is good, isn't he? He wouldn't have done so

well if he wasn't?" Mia still sounded worried.

"Are you afraid that he will figure it out if you beat him?"

I shook my head at Cami's question. "No, I don't think so."

Mia sat down next to me, patting my knee with warm affection. "Then what are you afraid of, Josaline?"

"I'm afraid . . . I'll like it."

My double life was trying to bleed together, and by the looks on Mia's and Camillia's faces, they saw it too. I was in trouble.

"Well, I knew you were brave, but I didn't think you were crazy!"

We were no longer a threesome. Roxana and Nori found us and came in behind. "Brother will wipe the floor with you, you know?"

Cami did an odd laugh, attempting to stop it, and it came out as a snort. "Nice jacket."

Nori glared at the blonde for a second. The leather riding jacket Moto loaned Nori -a month ago- was over her red Princess D dress. "She didn't ask for it back, so why let it go to waste in my closet?"

Cami glanced over at me with a smirk that she tried to hide. Roxana sat on the other side of me, wrapping an arm around me.

"Just let him win, okay?" Cami was thinking about my secret while I was thinking about my rep.

The thought of letting Yuuto win hadn't crossed my mind, but it would certainly keep my identity secret.

Nori huffed loudly, "Like she could beat him if she tried."

I gave Nori a warm smile, not bothered by her words. Hard to feel insulted when the one running her mouth wore your jacket like a trophy. "I will give it my all regardless."

"What did you bet? What do you each get if you win?" Roxana asked me.

Glancing at Mia and Camillia, it was clear they were worried. "We left that to be decided when there's a winner."

"Isn't that a little dangerous?" Mia warned.

I shrugged, "Too late now."

Mia, Camillia, and Roxana gently pulled me from the boat while Nori followed closely. As if I'd run away or something? My experience was mostly with two wheels, but I did have a little with four. Everyone was getting back into their karts after Yuuto announced our race. Save for Nori, who stood by Yuuto's kart with him, the two discussing something. Then he ruffled her hair and pulled on the jacket she wore. The distance between them and me still didn't hide what I knew to be sibling affection. Yuuto was picking on Nori in a manner that all brothers did. Probably about wearing Moto's jacket, and the whole scene made me homesick for the first time.

Just a few more hours, and I will be back in the country for the holiday. Today had been a good distraction. I was nervous about being back home with my parents. But I had a sound report card to give them, so I was likely to return to Ocresa and my friends.

Pulling up next to Yuuto, the others went ahead. Clyd would be the referee of sorts. The only other person with us was one of the tour guides. Their job was to stop any cheating, even though there would be none.

Yuuto had taken off his Frog hat, so now he looked normal. I took mine off as well but still had the dress to make me different. The thing I truly liked about the costumes was that they covered all who wore them with the same material. There was no distinction between Gilde and Mute in these outfits.

Revving his engine, Yuuto got my attention, and he shouted at me over the noise the little corn oil motors made while roaring. "First one to the end of the bridge, winner takes all."

I managed to hold off my shiver until he looked away again. The last thing I wanted him to see was how "winner takes all" affected me when it came from his lips. Buri was a good ten feet away from us, and he counted us down with his fingers up in the air. When he reached zero, Buri waved his arms as big as possible, and we both pressed a foot down on the accelerator.

Buri was back in his kart (and on his way) when we hit where he once stood. The Rainbow Bridge was fully lit, nighttime ticking away, and living up to its name even centuries after its conception. The branches of the Rainbow bridge that once went to other parts of the city were torn out long ago. It no longer touched the Mute neighborhoods. It was more for show, and we were the only ones on it.

Rainbow lights up the towers and the city lights behind it. It was one of the few remaining markers of the Ocresa from history class. Like a twinkling fairyland, it was very much like being in another world–because I was.

It was easy to forget what I was doing, using my knees to steer and throwing my hands up into the air as I called out to the night. Yuuto stayed at my side the entire time and shook his head when I retook the wheel to look over at him. I lacked the care, my face hurting from smiling so much.

After that, he took the lead, and I got serious, coming around behind him and back at his side. We passed Mia and Buri, going slow together. Buri called out to us, and I turned to watch the two of them shrink behind me.

I moved a few inches in front of Yuuto, the two of us still side by side as my front bumper pushed ahead of his. We were so close that Yuuto's laugh made it to my ears over all other noise. I forced myself not to look over at him. The end of the bridge was coming, and I had yet to take the lead fully.

Swinging to the right, I put some distance between

our karts and then hit the accelerator to take the lead. It lasted as long as it did for Yuuto, him pulling up to my side again. I looked over with the end in sight and found Yuuto grinning with determination in his eyes, bright golden orbs glowing in the night. I had never seen him race before. Although this hardly counted. Still, my heart was racing faster and harder than my little kart engine was at the moment.

His front bumper pushed ahead, but he caught my stare, and his smile dropped. I wasn't even sure how it all ended. The two of us stared at each other instead of watching the road. We had to brake hard, coming to our senses right before it was too late, and we rammed full speed into a barrier. We slowed, and the others pulled up around us.

"Nice work, Jo!"

Jeb clapped a hand on my shoulder, fully waking me out of my daze. "Huh?"

The tour guides pushed us to move along. We still had a lot of ground to cover to get back to the start. Buri was busy giving Yuuto a hard time. "You had her, man. What happened?"

"Wait . . . did I win?"

"Don't you know?" Mia asked.

Roxana had one hand on her steering wheel and the other in Clyd's hand. "It was pretty close. It would be hard to tell."

Nori came to a quick and loud stop next to me. "You tied."

She looked the least pleased out of all of them, disappointed in her brother most likely. Yuuto shrugged back at me. "Tiebreaker?"

A smile split my face even though I tried to frown. "We can't. The tour guides are already uneasy as it is!"

"Tomorrow then?"

My frown came easily this time, shaking my head at him. "I'm going home tomorrow."

Roxana squeaked out a whimper. "What? You are? What about Peace Day??"

Roxana looked so sad. I almost canceled my trip right then and there. I hadn't expected a Mute to get excited for Peace Day, but I guess it was still a holiday regardless of its History. But I had no choice, I had to go home, or they would come after me. Or rather, send someone after me. "That's why I'm going home. To spend Peace Day with my family."

"You'll be back for A Day, won't you?"

Now Buri sounded sad. "I don't know . . . "

"Of course, she will!" Camillia was behind me, Kaito by her side. "We're all going to spend the Anniversary together. Right Josaline?"

They weren't giving me a choice, save for Yuuto, who had remained silent the entire time. All of them wanted me around except him. "If that's what you guys want...."

"It's decided then! Let's all dress up, go to street festivals, and eat breakfast together!!" Nori was suddenly very excited. I had never pictured her as the sentimental or traditional type.

Chapter Eighteen

"I think—the hero observes that nothing is so frightening as a labyrinth with no center."
— **Jorge Luis Borges, <u>Selected Non–Fictions</u>**

Standing side by side, I let Glin knock. He hesitated, his hand hovering over the wood. "Are you sure you want to do this?"

"Why wouldn't I?"

I wondered if he would give me the same excuse. I didn't need to be involved, and he would handle things and take care of himself. And that I should have stayed home during the Anniversary Day. Regardless, I had lasted as long as I could stand at home. No way I would stay another night there. I would lose my mind.

Glin took a different route entirely, though, tugging gently on my sleeve. "Mom's robes look great on you."

I quickly ran my hands down the slick silk—white

with a spray of pink and purple flowers in varying shades, perfectly matching my pink curls. The design spanned across the bottom of my long sleeves and faded away as it went up to my shoulders. Even though it was Aunt Caroline's, it felt made for me.

Reglin knocked, and we waited, leaning over to tug on the white undergarment (that was extra layers for the cold), so it showed just enough. Clyd opened the door, looking us over with interest before stepping aside with a strange smirk. The dark green of his robes made his chocolate skin look smooth and his white tats pop. If I ever felt comfortable enough with him, I would ask Clyd what his tattoos meant. And where he got them in white.

Clyd's robes matched his wife's. Roxana was wearing red rose printed robes with dark green accents that were very pretty and made her hair look like twisted honey.

"Do we have to wear these things??"

Buri pulled at the baby blue-collar of his jacket -that made him look pale and golden- with his waistline out of whack. Jeb was even worse, his white undergarment showing too much under his robes. The pair looked sloppy in their

303

traditionals.

"Yes, we have to wear them, and you have to wear them precisely!!" Nori fussed back, pulling both of them in, and began straightening them up. The beads of her hairpin clattered together with her every move. It all reminded me of the historical dramas my great Aunt made Rene and me watch. "You would think -doing this every year- you two would be able to dress yourselves by now!"

Buri fixed, and she moved on to Jeb. "You look beautiful." I heard him say and kept quiet to listen on. The pair matched in a manner that could be considered coincidence. Noir's black robe had a few blood-red roses on the sleeves. It fitted with the Cruor dress code so no one would question why Jeb wore black and red checked robes. It looked like Jeb had trimmed his beard and Nori had curled her hair. A beautiful couple to say the least.

Nori tried to hide her blush, pulling Jeb's robes completely apart to put them back together. "And you look dead. You have yours crossed wrong. That's how you dress a corpse in the ceremonial robes!"

"Good thing I have you to, set me straight?" Jeb

countered with a smirk that set off Nori's blush again.

Pulling my attention from the show before me, I continued to take in the room of people, finding Camillia and Kaito before the others took notice. Clyd and Roxana both wore a look of amusement I couldn't figure out. So I went to Camillia's side. Her bright sunflower robes matched her personality perfectly, as did Kaito's pure black one.

"You look so pretty, Cami."

She slightly twisted like she was a model and grinned, her pin-straight, platinum-blonde hair flew out as she spun. "Thanks. Kaito got it for me. Anniversary Day present."

Of course, the fabric was beautiful but thin. Cami would want to blend in at a Mute's A Day. The Anniversary of the Reconstruction. An event that was almost as devastating as Peace Day for Mutes. All my robes remained back in my closet at my parent's house. If I wore one of them here, I would get called out instantly as a Pryce or another family at our level. I was lucky Auntie's fit me, and I didn't dare ask to borrow one of Rene's. It would kill me to wear it without Rene right beside me in one.

I took my time entering the living room. The last time

I was there, it had been . . . hurtful, and I was trying hard not to think about that. No one looked like they didn't want me here, but I could have said the same thing last time. I had been so blind then that I was broadsided by the Cruor's words and my feelings from them.

Mia popped out from behind us, entering just after Glin and me, looking cute in her bright teal and white polka dot robes. It made her green eyes pop. Her black, pin-curled hair bounced with her movements, held back behind her ears with jeweled clips. She was a gentle match to Buri with his light blue robes. It was a coincidence that Buri jumped on as soon as he had the opportunity. That was when Kaito noticed me and who I had with me. I watched for a moment as confusion bloomed on his face and then as it changed to irritation.

"Josaline, you look stunning!" Mia cooed softly.

Turning from the 'show' that was Kaito, I blushed deeply and bowed my head in embarrassment. "Thank you, Mia. You look beautiful yourself."

"Doesn't she? I've been trying to tell her, but she doesn't believe me."

306

Mia gave Buri a small and playful push while ducking her head in bashfulness with me. The adorable display caused me to miss the darkening looks on a few faces, but I caught onto them soon enough. Glin was grabbing onto me tightly, ready to fight or run. Either one would have been hard with us in robes, Glin's gray and white striped ones were the most modest in the room. And the oldest since they were handed down from his grandfather.

There was no chance we'd make it but I seriously doubted we were in any kind of danger with the Cruor. Especially tonight. The worst that could happen would be getting kicked out onto our butts.

"Inu? What are you doing here?" Nori gasped.

I tried to set my face to the appropriate amount of displeasure from the name since Josaline wasn't supposed to be used to it. Motor was. But I was distracted.

As if on cue, Yuuto entered the living room. His robes were perfectly wrapped, his white undergarment sticking out just enough under his black robe. He was pulling on a light gray jacket as he walked but froze mid-stride, Yuuto's eyes stuck on me.

"Isn't he part of the Cruor?!" Camillia had the appropriate amount of offense in her tone, where mine should be.

But I struggled with my lives again, staring right at Yuuto, unable to look away. "I brought him."

Everyone stopped with my admission and glanced back at Yuuto. I expected the same simmering glower to be on Yuuto's face that was on Nori's and Kaito's, finding it very odd that he wore a small smile while everyone else was shocked. It was a surprise but a pleasant one. He looked nice when he smiled. Very nice.

The others were silent, and I broke out of my trance, finishing what I had started. "And please, his name is Reglin. If any of you call him Inu again, I will smack you."

Glin put a hand on my shoulder, signaling that I had done enough. But I was determined to get Glin to a higher, safer status within the Cruor and get information on Rene.

"Who the hell do you . . . "

Grabbing her shoulder, Yuuto silenced Nori's fuming quickly, still smiling as he looked back at us. "Reglin, it is then."

Nori shoved Yuuto's hold off of her and glared up at him. "Are you just going to give in to everything a Gilde says? She has no respect . . . "

"It would be disrespectful of us, Nori, not to do as she asks. After all, he is her family."

The room was so silent. We could hear the jaws that dropped. Buri picked his back up to laugh loudly in the silence. Glin stood in front of me, blocking me from them in a protective stance. It instantly had me worried. Not for his safety. I was sure the Cruor would never hurt us. No, I was worried they would notice the similarities in how Glin protected me and how he protected Moto.

"Call me whatever you want. As long as you are nice to Jo, I don't care what you do to me."

I gave him a shove, effectively moving him from in front of me and to my side. "The point is, you have all been cruel, and we all have things we don't know about one another. Right?"

A low murmur broke out among the group, no one able to disagree with my words. I was winning. Since it was me, I wasn't outing Glin's Plunge background. The two of us appeared as Gildes, even if on the low end.

Yuuto left Nori's side, holding his hand out to my cousin. "Reglin, please join us for A-Day."

The tension was thick as Reglin hesitated. It deflated when he took Yuuto's hand and shook it with enthusiasm.

"Welcome to the Cruor, Reglin!!" Roxana shouted out, and no one refuted her.

Chapter Nineteen

*"No, what he didn't like about heroes was that they were
usually suicidally gloomy when sober
and homicidally insane when drunk."*
— **Terry Pratchett, <u>The Color of Magic</u>**

It was just the girls, walking together in a small clump

with all the boys behind us. We strolled, and Nori was inside,

away from the crowd we pushed through. No one said

anything about it, and I kept my eyes from her as she walked.

Not once had I seen any proof of her Biomed leg other than

the night her jeans ripped to show metal beneath. That was

Moto, though, not me. So there was nothing I could say on

the subject if no one else did.

Glancing behind me from time to time, I repeatedly

checked on Reglin in his new spot. He walked -quiet- off to

the side while the others clowned around as usual. Kaito was

stoic, watching the new blood with interest that had me

concerned. If anyone figured the two of us out, it would be Kaito.

No matter how many times I told myself not to look, I still flicked my eyes toward Yuuto. And each time I did, my eyes met his citrine ones as he watched me. It made my breath catch in my throat each time. I had been dumb enough to look five times now, but I wasn't counting.

The air was a happy one, primarily, as the women of the Cruor chatted around me.

"Mia, are you gonna join the Cruor now?" Roxana asked.

Mia looked confused and stuck, "I . . . I mean . . . why would . . . "

Camillia came to her rescue. "I don't think you guys want Mia or me. We're useless."

"So is Inu, but he's still one of us now."

I rolled my eyes at Nori's blatant dig and giggled at Roxana. "Since when is the Cruor so eager to add new members?"

"Since forever! I want some girls to hang with!" Roxana wined.

"Hey, what about me!" Nori cried.

Shrugging, Roxana pushed a little ahead of the group as if she knew her words would start a fuss. "You're not actually a Cruor, Nori."

"What?!" All of us, save for Mia and Roxana, yelled.

Now at the front of our little clique, Roxana walked backward to speak to all of us. "Well, she's not. She's just Yuuto's little sister. If you asked him, he would tell you, 'no way in hell is my little sister a part of a gang!'"

Nori looked shocked and offended but said nothing. Because it was true, and even I knew it. How he coddled Nori after our one race? When Nori was in pain? Yuuto was ready to have Moto's ticket removed and even dislocate my arm to make things even. It was hard to imagine Yuuto ever hurting me, but it was Nori. He would do anything for his family. His past, where Yuuto's cousin used him, is proof of that. All the terrible things Yuuto did, the things that still haunted him today, he did for Nori. So, it wasn't a shock that he wouldn't want her to be a part of the Cruor, even if they were harmless.

Lost to my thoughts, I lost the others in the crowd.

Now the festival was right before me. Between me and it, about fifty people were also there to play. It was a mix of Mutes and Gildes, so I blended in fine. But it was primarily Mutes.

Everyone spilled and congregated at the old building that the small street festival surrounded. Once a beautiful ancient structure, it was now covered with art and illustrations of different beliefs. I found it stunning, the mixture of different cultures that once existed? Given this day was to celebrate the end of such ideas, it felt strange to be here now to honor them. At the same time, it was comforting to see that these things were still breathing.

The traditions that survived even after all the years of trying to rub them out of history were impressive. It showed the steadfast resilience of humanity. A practice I was unknowledgeable in. I watched others out of the corner of my eye as I pressed my hands together before my chest and closed my eyes. Everyone was doing something different. A few got on the ground to kneel and prostrate themselves. I took the easier route since I had no clue what I was doing.

I whispered my wishes, begging whoever was

listening to grant my heart's deepest wish. "Bring Rene home safe."

It was a cold night, but I didn't feel the frozen air like I would otherwise with my layers and the many warm bodies around me. The chill that ran up my back caused my fear to spike. Still bent in prayer, I didn't move, slowly righting myself with the others but not turning around even with my brain screaming at me. My skin tightened on my bones in anticipation, my throat restricting along with it and becoming sore.

A few next to me glanced behind and frowned before moving away quickly. Whatever it was, it wasn't just me. Determined to face my fear, I took a deep breath and counted to three before turning around.

Stepping out to turn, the circle of Cruor around me stopped me. The fear and anticipation melted away like sugar in a flame, but my curiosity was still at a peak. They were trying to lead me elsewhere, away from whatever had the hair on the back of my neck standing on end—and trying hard to keep me from looking over to my right. So, of course, I did. And I found Yuuto in deep with the creeper–Sora. Black eyes met mine, and I quickly hid them from the man. My warning bells knew Sora was bad news even when I was unaware of his closeness. I wasn't supposed to know who that guy was, but I was pretty sure it was normal to find him creepy.

"Who is that talking with Yuuto?"

Jeb didn't even look, he was busy trying to pull me away. "No one."

I wanted someone to tell Josaline. It would make things much easier for me and my double lives. "Doesn't look like no one. It looks very much like someone to Yuuto."

"Josaline, you know who not to talk to. You know that that guy is bad news with just one look. So, let's let it go, alright?" Jed said, his voice tight with irritation that he aimed elsewhere.

Reglin had one hand in mine and the other on my elbow, aiding in leading me away. Everyone wanted me to stay away from Sora. "Alright, I'll let it go."

I didn't need to push. I already knew Sora. Yuuto had told Moto everything I needed to know about the guy. Seeing him so far away from the racetrack was unsettling, though. What the hell was he doing here? Were more of the Kurio–

chi around lurking? He had been so close to me. Why? No way he knew who I was. That I was Moto. So, what was he doing so close to me? Was it a coincidence? That was a hard one to swallow on my best day. Had Sora seen me with the Cruor? Was that all it was? Was I a connection that Sora was desperate to sever?

Yuuto had severed his ties to his cousin, but Sora was still gunning for him. I didn't know why, but it was clear Sora wasn't done with Yuuto.

My heart ached at the thought, turning to glance again and finding Yuuto alone this time. He looked so lonely, his back to me and his head slightly down. Flexing his shoulders, I could see the tension they held even under his layers. Allowing myself to be led, I watched Yuuto as he slowly shrunk in the distance. The further away he got, the stronger the pain in my chest became. Only when Yuuto's head popped up and he began to turn did I look elsewhere, ignoring the looks Reglin gave me.

"Are they treating you well now, Reglin?"

Jeb released me to my cousin, going back to Nori's side to help her in the crowd and let us talk. "You no longer need to worry."

"So, they are making you one of them? You'll be able to get information on Rene now?"

"I said you no longer need to worry."

Lie. Reglin was lying to me again. I could hear it in his voice and see it in his face. He was no better than before I showed up to help. Reglin was a Cruor now, so that had to do something for him and our cause?

Reglin a Cruor. It was almost comical. The ability to get him out of 'dog' status had been within Josaline and not Moto. But Moto would be the one who would stay by his side, racing and gaining favor and information. That was something Josaline could never do. And maybe something Reglin could never do either, looking like a typical Gilde. There was no telling if anyone in or outside the Cruor would talk to him about Rene—especially if they found out he and Rene were Plunges.

Always on the outside, no matter what.

Chapter Twenty

"Heroes are those who can somehow resist the power of the situation and act out of noble motives, or behave in ways that do not demean others when they easily can." — **Philip Zimbardo**

The majority of the group gathered at the bottom of the festival's street, the events and food before us. It took a few moments for everyone to get back together—such a large group in an even larger crowd.

Camillia took my arm, and she reached back for Mia's, calling the others to follow. "Let's go check out the booths!!!"

I was skipping -nearly dragging Mia- while Camillia managed to keep up. It was a holiday. The last thing I wanted my friends to do was dwell on wicked people and thoughts.

The booths stretched down the path as far as the eye could see. Large white lights on strings lit the way, swinging in the breeze above us on either side. It kept you on the right street or path, lighting up the otherwise black night.

Smells wafted in the air, a mix of food cooking and the aromatic bodies of the visitors. All the booths had lines in front of them, but none looked too bad. It was a grand show, like walking through a market back in pre-collapse times. I hopped in the line for old-fashioned sugared and fried bread without a word while the other girls moved on to nearby booths. Now I was alone yet surrounded by people.

Looking around, I saw no one I recognized. Since moving to Ocresa, this was nothing new to me, but Sora lurking around had me shivering. The heat of the stand before me did little to soothe me.

A lite weight dropped on my shoulders, warmth flooding down my arms and back as it did. The musky smell of pine overtook all other scents, the jacket I now somehow donned covering me from the cold and foreign odors. "If you're cold, you should wear a coat."

Even with Yuuto's kindness, he still managed to be condescending. "I didn't want to cover up my robes. Besides . . . I was fine until a moment ago."

His arms crossed, Yuuto looked either annoyed or bored. I wasn't sure. "I suppose it's a shame to cover such pretty fabric up."

My cheeks burned, and I made sure to busy myself with pulling my locks free from Yuuto's jacket instead of looking anywhere in which he could see my flush. "It's my Aunt's."

"Nice of her to let you borrow it. Even if it's too nice for this event, you're drawing too much attention."

Yuuto looked around as if there was still a threat, and I wasn't sure if he was complimenting me or simply stating some fact. With no feeling in his tone, the coat he placed on me had a new meaning. It wasn't because it was cold or Yuuto was nice. He was covering me up.

Sora may have left, but Yuuto was still on edge, standing beside me in line but keeping himself busy with his eyes on the crowd. So, I pushed my arms through the sleeves of his dark grey jacket and didn't say another word.

One person before me, an elder Mute, struggled with her sleeve. The strings of her drawstring-style robes slipped from her wrinkled fingers as she tried to get her wrist bare to pay. It was an older style designed to cover and keep warm. That way, a Mute wouldn't need a coat they couldn't afford. This woman's robes showed her white undergarment a little at her collar but she had clearly taken very good care of it over the years. Her dark deep brown eyes were shining with tears of embarrassment.

Ignoring everything else, the danger, stress, and hiding my location from my family, I stepped to the woman's side with my arm stretched out and bare to take my credits. "Here."

After a moment, the man took it, and the woman protested but gave in quickly. While they made the woman's order, I helped the elder tie her sleeve back to her wrist. My fingers brushed her dark olive skin. It was soft and warm and she smelled of roses. "Thank you."

With a kind smile from the woman, I returned it with mine. "Happy A-Day."

The woman's last act was to pick up my hands and kiss their backs before leaving for the crowd. Either my borrowed robes and forced slump hid my social standing or the woman knew I wouldn't mind since I helped her with her sleeve. If Regulations had seen us, they could have given us a hard time.

I was about to leave the booth, having spent my treat money already, when a small tray appeared before me. "I can't pay."

I flushed with chagrin at the man holding the tray up for me to grab. "Paid for!"

The guy was in a rush, shoving it into my hands and moving on. Forgetting myself, I looked around for Yuuto to find him a few steps away, waiting. "Did you pay for this?"

Arms crossed and leaning against a booth, he was going for nonchalant but still clearly searching the crowd. "You were so busy with that grandma. The line was about to swallow you whole."

"There is nothing wrong with helping one's elders . . . "

"Didn't say that."

"Your tone did."

Straightening, Yuuto dropped his arms and glared down at me. "Your ability to put words in my mouth is absolutely astounding. My tone has nothing to do with you."

"If you told me what was bothering you, maybe I would believe you."

"Your cake is getting cold," Yuuto answered, turning and saying nothing else as an answer.

With a small distance between us, we walked the rest of the booths. I had finished my treat by the time we reached the end and circled back. I regretted not bringing some transfer credits with all the fantastic food booths. Wallowing in my anguish, I saw it.

"Yuuto!"

Yuuto jumped, but I slapped my hand to his arm and pulled him along hard, not stopping until we stood before the booth. The open design allowed us to find an empty spot on one of the four long sides. Lit below, the white block surrounding the booth glowed as it formed a barrier between the gamesman and those who played. The table came up to my ribs, and the pieces were already splayed out, ready to go.

"Mind Puzzle?"

Mind puzzle was an old Mute game where you matched pieces together, blindfolded, as quickly as possible. Gildes had something similar, only it wasn't a game, and you did it with a holo. Uncle had taught it to me long ago, and it was free. They just asked for donations to the community. I hoped to chill the guy out. Yuuto was too high-strung currently, and no one deserved to feel like that, especially on holiday. I dug in my purse for something but was coming up empty. I had already spent traceable and couldn't do more so my wrist implant wasn't an option. I could have sworn I put credits in my purse from racing but I was coming up empty when Yuuto reached over me to drop in some credits. That out of the way, I looked up at him expectantly.

"Tiebreaker."

"What? You're not serious?"

I nodded, smiling at his continued confusion. "Winner will be determined by speed and accuracy."

"What, because I'm a Mute, I know how to play?"

I realized my blunder a little too late. Yuuto was frowning with his offense. "I know how to play. I can teach you?"

His glare lasted another second before he snickered at me, "I'm just messing with you. I know how to play. But there's only one here."

There were other puzzles around, but only one that was free. The one before us was the shape of an apple, so it would be complex with all its rounded edges. "We will go one at a time, then."

Yuuto eyed me carefully, hesitating. But then he sighed loudly, relenting and pulling out his Holo. "Ladies first."

Picking up the blindfold, I held it out to him, and he looked confused again. "If you put it on me, you can't say I cheated!"

Rolling his eyes (glowing with his amusement), Yuuto failed to hide the slight smile on his lips. He covered my sight before I could see if it grew any more than that. Yuuto was standing before me and wrapping his arms around my neck to tie the strings. His hands went to my shoulders when he finished, steadying me.

"Can you see?"

"Nope."

"Are you sure?"

I grew still and silent, his breath on my cheeks as he spoke. It caused my knees to wobble, and I grabbed onto his wrist in hopes of steadying myself. ". . . Y . . . Yes . . . "

Yuuto chuckled, his breath washing over the side of my face. His skin brushed against mine, his mouth at my ear. "You are far too trusting, Jōji."

Everything spun as he turned me, his newly declared nickname for me washing over while he gently pushed me to the table. I had no clue what it meant, but it sounded like the same language as Inu and Mōtāgāru. A language I, and everyone else in the world, knew very little. Maybe it was just a shortened version of Josaline?

His fingers caused my skin to tingle as Yuuto guided my hands to the puzzle pieces. Not once had I considered Yuuto a threat, not one that would physically hurt me. But now, he was dangerously close to having my heart. That was scarier than any bodily harm Yuuto could do since I was pretty sure -once in his hands- he would crush it.

He led my hands to the plastic apple pieces next to the small gravity field that held it in place and hopefully started the timer on his Holo. "Go."

My fingers ran along the edges, discovering the pieces with my touch. Holding each one for a few moments and then placing them together. The dim hum of the magnets that held the lifelike apple puzzle up and together was my only clue to my accuracy. I could feel Yuuto's eyes on me, burning me as my skin continued to warm up.

With my last piece in place, I found the edge of the blindfold, pulling it up and revealing bright gold eyes that were curious on mine. "How did I do?"

Yuuto shook his head instead of speaking, so I grabbed his wrist to look at his Holo. Still in his hand, I pulled myself around so that my back was to him, escaping his glowing gaze. But that had me wrapped in his arm and close to his chest. He made a tiny sound when I took his Holo from him, stepping away.

"What are you doing?"

I snapped a picture of my 'apple' before grinning back at him. "We can't judge these, we're both biased. The others will have to do it."

Yet to let go of Yuuto's Holo, I pulled the blindfold off completely and held it out to him. Now it was his turn. "Aren't you going to put it on me? So, I don't cheat?"

Hesitating, I carefully and slowly set down his Holo

and moved closer. But I wasn't fast enough for Yuuto as he gently grabbed an elbow and pulled me near. The little gasp that slipped from my parted lips was more than enough to have my cheeks in flames again. He bent down to me, and I wrapped my arms around his neck, my fingers grazing his scalp as I tied the blindfold tight. His hair was so soft. I had to stop myself from running my fingers through it more than I already had.

That would be awkward.

Once finished, my hands went to his shoulder and slipped to his chest when he stood. I should have backed away, but I needed help with my balance—feeling feverish. "What face am I making right now?"

He shook his head at me, "That won't work."

"Why not?"

"Because I don't need to see your face to know what you are doing with it right now."

Now I really needed help to steady myself, feeling like the ground would swallow me up any second now. Yuuto had said the same thing to Moto weeks ago, which had me wondering if he told it to many or just me. "Fine." The thought of Yuuto telling others how he could see their face just as he had told me made my chest ache.

So I took it out on him by flicking his nose hard. "Ouch! What the hell was that for?!"

"Didn't see that coming, did ya?"

I giggled while Yuuto rubbed the soreness out from my attack. Hands that I pulled away soon after and placed on the small plastic pieces. "Okaaaay, go!"

Watching Yuuto's work was memorizing, his fingers gently caressing each piece and placing them correctly. It only made my heart race more, and my blood felt so hot.

Finished, he pulled off the blindfold, and I busied myself with the timer and took a photo. "How did I do?"

"We tied."

"Again?!" Yuuto yelled with a smirk.

All I could offer was a shrug, holding onto his Holo for another second before he swiped it from me. "Hey, what are you doing?"

"We need to find a judge, right? Let's go!"

Yuuto pulled me by my elbow back into the fray, his arm grazing mine as we walked. I took a step away to stop it, but Yuuto just moved over and cleared the small space again. "How do you plan on making this a fair process?"

Yuuto pulled out his Holo again, looking between the two photos. "Easy. We ask someone to pick the best one without any more details than that." It sounded reasonable, but I didn't particularly appreciate how he was eyeing our pictures. "Although I know you already lost."

"Excuse me?"

He held the two pictures before my face, "Look at yours. You call that an apple?"

I reached for the Holo, but he swept it up out of my reach. "Aren't you supposed to be Biomed? Then you should know when something is perfectly shaped when you see it."

"You've been hanging around me for months. So should you."

Yuuto was referring to himself, posturing as the most attractive man alive. The dumb part of my brain agreed, but luckily, it didn't control my mouth. "Wow. You're so full of yourself, aren't you?"

"Just being honest," he said with a smirk, "your shape looks weird."

Now Yuuto was talking about our photos again. I tried again to swipe his Holo, but Yuuto pulled it away. So, I pulled out mine instead. "Mine looks just as good as yours, thank you. Sounds to me like you're nervous?"

He shifted closer, placing his fingers on my elbow again to guide me around a clump of people. "What do I have to be nervous about?"

Yuuto diverted into me as he said it, putting his mouth dangerously close to my ear. I had to swallow nervous sludge down my throat before I could speak again. "Nervous of my perfect shape!"

Yuuto stopped and looked down at me. "Well, you got me there, Flamingo."

I no longer knew which one we talked about, the apple or me, especially with the change in pet names again. The crowd went around us, splitting like a river around a rock, and I had to force my head down. Yuuto had the amazing ability to make me feel like he only saw me. His eyes focused on me hard as I stood before him. He did it to Josaline and Moto, so it must be something he did with everyone. I did all I could to shake the cold feeling that thought put in my heart and held up my Holo. Instead, the camera flipped towards me.

"What are you doing?"

I felt it was obvious, "Taking a Digi-pic!"

Yuuto's fingers brushed mine as he took my Holo from me, and I practically dropped it into his hand from his touch. I thought he would steal it, so I couldn't take the shot with him. Color me surprised when Yuuto lifted it, his height and long limb getting a much better angle than short, little me ever could, and took the shot. And then a couple more.

Handed back, I looked at the photos. The first one had me staring up at Yuuto in shocked confusion while he smiled. I got my act together for the next one and the last one . . . Yuuto was smiling at me and not the camera.

I felt someone touching me, and instead of flinching like usual, I slowly pulled my attention back to Yuuto, knowing it was him. He took advantage of my distracted mind to play with a curl that had come loose, pulling and wrapping it around his finger only to release it and watch it bounce. I watched him intently, and when he caught on, Yuuto pulled back quickly as though he didn't realize what he was doing.

As if needing a distraction, he had his Holo out again, "Maybe I should delete this so you don't embarrass yourself?"

I scoffed, "Coward."

"Excuse me?"

"Mines better, and you know it. You're afraid of losing!"

The look on Yuuto's face had me wondering if I had struck another nerve. But he covered it with a smirk and held the Holo out of my reach again. "I'm only trying to protect you, Josaline."

I jumped, my fingers grazing the Holo, and a shocked look grew on Yuuto's face as I landed right before him. "I don't need you to protect me. I can take care of myself."

Our conversation had turned again, and I was no longer talking about our bet. Jumping again, Yuuto twisted it out of my reach, no longer taking any chances. Now, it wasn't a Holo. It was proof. Getting that communicator proved I could take care of myself. When I reached up for it again, Yuuto grabbed my outstretched hand and spun me around like a top.

A little dizzy, he grabbed my elbow and held me both still and close, "Whether you can handle yourself or not, I'm not going to stop trying to keep you safe."

My brain settled (as did my sight), leaving me stuck again in his sticky, honey eyes. This time my throat was stuck with it too. Although whispered, Yuuto's words were ringing in my brain at high volume. It was just because Sora was so close. Yuuto's protectiveness and words had nothing to do with me and how he felt. Not about me anyway. He didn't want anyone hurt because of him. It would be a terrible burden, and I understood that. And yet, my heart still drummed against my ribs, completely missing the true meaning of the moment.

I blamed the large and beautiful smile he wore as he spoke to me. It was different than the one he flashed on a typical day, and I tried not to notice how I only saw it when he talked to me. Of course, I only saw it then because I didn't see him any other time to know! Except when I was Moto, but who would smile in that situation? But this smile reached his eyes and made them sparkle, flecks dancing that I couldn't stop watching.

"Josaline?"

Saved by my name, I broke from the sugary chrysalis of Yuuto's stare to Mia. Buri was right beside her, and they both looked bewildered. They were standing before us, looking very comfortable with each other. Given how I was playing around with Yuuto, I wouldn't be surprised if they thought the same of us.

I quickly recovered from Yuuto's hold, running up and wrapping my arms around Mia. "Finally, someone I know!!!"

"And who am I? A stranger?" Buri cried, fully offended.

Looking up at him, I could feel the heat of my flush still on my cheeks. "It's good to see you too, Buri."

"Happy to see you two."

Yuuto was back to his warm and polite smile. The one I loved and had me spellbound, he tucked away again.

Buri nudged closer to Yuuto, "What eh . . . what were you two up to?"

Yuuto raised an eyebrow at him and his tone, but Buri had meant it to be suggestive. "Just enjoying the festival."

"Oh yeah? How much?"

Buri was dangerously close to a punch, and he knew it. Yuuto frowned heavily at him now. I desperately wanted to change the subject, returning to Yuuto's side and taking his Holo. "You two can be our judges!"

"Judges? What are we judging?" Mia pulled out of Buri's embrace, neither of them noticed she was still in it.

"Our tiebreaker."

Buri looked around hastily. "There's a racing booth here?!"

Yuuto's irritation grew the longer Buri was near, smacking the back of Buri's head hard. "No, you idiot. We played Mind-Puzzle."

Buri held his injury and winced as he spoke. "You played what now?"

"Never mind," Yuuto mumbled under his breath.

Mia was already leaning into me to look at the Holo. "What do you need from us?"

"We timed ourselves but got the same. So the determining factor is accuracy. Who did a better job putting the apple together?"

Taking the Holo, Mia returned to Buri, looking at the pictures together. It was obvious which one was the winning apple, as they instantly agreed. Returning the Holo, Buri left it on the one they picked.

"This one is the winner."

Yuuto and I collided together, both scrambling to look at the winner. Doing a jig, I had to take deep breaths as my heart did as it pleased, a combination of Yuuto pressing into my side and seeing his apple as the winner.

"Told you mine was better."

I was pouting, but I didn't care. I was going to use my win to ask about Rene.

"What did you win?" Mia asked with a hint of fear in her tone.

Mia was the only one being rational, and it had me waking up, realizing the danger I was in now. But the way Yuuto looked at me . . . it had my face on fire. "That's right. I get to pick my prize, don't I?"

Yuuto dipped in close. Mia covered her eyes as it looked like Yuuto might take his prize right then and there. But he stopped inches from my face. I was frozen, unable to blink while his eyes roamed and his breath wafted over me. "I want you . . . "

"That's a bit much, don't you think, Yuuto? She's a bit young and innocent for such illegal talk." Yuuto turned his face from mine to growl at Buri. But Buri just chuckled, reaching over to pull Mia's hands from her eyes. "Yuuto would never be that crazy, Mia."

"I want you . . . to make me a treat."

". . . make you a treat??"

"Yep . . . for Coupling day. It's a big deal here in the city if you didn't know, country girl."

"WHAT?!"

"And no store-bought crap either. I want well-done, homemade goods from you."

I felt like I was hyperventilating, the air I sucked in doing nothing for my lungs. Mia was at my side to save me. "Calm down, Josaline. It's not that bad. We can all make sweets together."

That calmed me, taking in a breath that finally gave me oxygen. "That sounds like fun. Thank you, Mia."

The two men were clowning around. Buri gave Yuuto

a hard time about something, but talking softly enough, it didn't make it over the crowd. "Buri, how long have you known Mr. Himura?"

Mia's formal address threw Buri for a second, just as it had me the first time. "I dunno." He glanced at Yuuto, who offered a shrug. "Seven years?"

"What about you, Mia?" I asked, not hiding my curiosity.

I already knew vaguely, but I wanted to know more, and I didn't care that Yuuto was staring at me in confusion as I asked. Mia blushed prettily, either from the attention or Buri, who now had his arm wrapped around her shoulders. "A little longer. Yuuto and I were in the same class in Primaries."

"You're the same age as Yuuto and Kaito? So you're older than me?!" Buri asked, shocked.

"I am. Is that a problem?"

Mia was already trying to pull away from him, but Buri firmly pulled her back to him. "No! Not at all. It's just . . . you're so cute. I thought you were the same age as Jo and Cami."

"So . . . you don't mind that I'm your senior?"

I had only known Mia briefly but never had I seen her flustered before. I thought it was adorable, and so did Buri, it seemed. "No. I think it's hot."

Mia's head popped up, her entire face turning bright red over her beautiful, dark skin. Buri swooped down and planted a kiss on her cheek. Neither said a word, returning their attention to Yuuto and me. Out of the corner of my eye, I caught the trim look of shock on Yuuto's face, but he cleared it away quickly for the couple before us.

"Hey, guys!!"

Roxana and Clyd made their way through the crowd, starting to thin, given the late hour. Roxana released Clyd and bumped mine and then Mia's hip with hers. "Did you guys get a kiss for good luck?"

There was nothing hushed about Roxana's question. Buri answered with a quick "Nope" to hide his disappointment, while Yuuto was stoic next to me.

I was flustered, and it was obvious. "Don't be ridiculous! We didn't kiss!"

I always sucked at hiding my emotions when I needed

to save my ego. But only couples kissed on A-Day, and it was supposed to be good luck for their future relationship. Yuuto and I barely had a relationship at all.

"That's too bad." Clyd joked.

Yuuto shoved Clyd, not okay with his teasing in the least. Probably because Yuuto didn't want to be associated with me like that—romantically. It was illegal anyway as my parents would never give us their approval. This evening, he was near me because Sora was so near a few hours ago. But I hadn't seen Sora or any other familiar faces all night.

"Has anyone seen Reglin or Camillia?" I asked.

"Nope." That was the general answer.

"How about Nori?" Yuuto had slipped on his -overprotective- protective detail. Thanks to me.

"Haven't seen her either," Clyd answered, looking around with the realization.

Stretching his arms up, Buri yawned and re-wrapped himself around Mia. "Let's find them and go get food. I'm starving."

Someone bumped into Buri, the crowd swelling again. Then someone bumped me, nearly knocking me to the ground. Yuuto wrapped a protective arm around me after that. We had been heading towards the exit, as did the crowd, too many moving faster than us. Then there was a scream from behind.

"That was Nori!"

Yuuto tossed me to Clyd and all of us took off behind him as he cleared a path with his shoving. Everyone was suddenly in a rush to get out of there. We were the only ones going against the current like salmon. I didn't like it because something was very wrong. But since Nori was at the center of it, I pushed through my fear and the crowd, determined to help.

Only a few others remained, forming a circle we had to break through. Nori, Jeb, Camillia, and a bleeding Kaito were in the middle.

We entered the circle, Kaito on the ground holding his hand as blood seeped from it, and my stomach tried to turn upon sight. Yuuto and Mia didn't hesitate, grabbing hold and examining the wound. "It's not bad."

"Not bad, Kaito? There's a hole in your hand!"

Camillia was white, kneeling behind Kaito and

holding his shoulders. Nori awkwardly paced, her Biomed leg unmistakable with her walk, while Jeb tried to calm her down.

"What happened?!" A frustrated Buri yelled.

Jeb, the lone sane one at the moment, was the only one to pay Buri any attention. "Kaito got stabbed."

"We can see that!" Clyd growled.

Everyone was together again except Glin. I did the only thing I could think of and pulled out my Holo without any other thought.

"Are you calling a Regulator??".

Roxana's eyes were wild, a combination of terror and rage. "No, should I?"

No way Kaito getting stabbed was a coincidence or freak accident, not with Sora creeping around just hours ago. There had to be more Kurio–chi around as well. It would be silly to think someone like Sora would come alone. A Regulator wouldn't even respond to this, thick in the Mute territory. Not to mention the attack was made on a Mute. It would only put us in more danger if Regulators deemed the situation worthy because they would only come to mess us up. It would cost me more than credits to get anything out of Regulations other than the Cruor in trouble.

"Who are you calling then?" Nori broke out of her pace to throw her rage at me.

But I didn't even flinch. "Reglin."

They all grew silent, the only sound coming from the two Biomed majors. "Someone tell me what happened. Now!" Yuuto demanded.

"He saved me." Camillia was shaking badly now, barely holding on to Kaito. "It was crowded, and I got separated. Some guy grabbed me and tried to take me. But Kaito stopped him. Then he pulled a knife. Kaito took the cut for me. His hand stopped it from going through my ribs."

"Where's the bastard?!" Nori was in full fight mode now, but one look from Yuuto had her stopping all action.

Camillia was looking all around, searching, "He ran off."

"Why did you scream, Nori?" Mia was cool and calm, which was not surprising.

"I couldn't think of a better way to get you all here."

The conversation went on behind me as Glin finally

answered. "Jo? Where are you?"

"Where are you?"

"I got . . . caught up. I'm coming to you. Where are you?"

I gave him quick directions, then put my Holo away. Going to Camillia's side, I instantly held her.

"Where's Reglin?" Camillia stuttered.

"He's coming. He got caught in the crowd rushing out."

Clyd huffed loudly, "That guy has been MIA almost all night . . . "

"And I'm sure he spent the entire time looking for me!"

I was glaring at Clyd, which oddly made him silent. Jeb and Yuuto helped Kaito off the ground while Mia pushed the injured hand above his head. "First aid stand is at the other end."

Even when Reglin found us and took Camillia, Mia, and me away, the group remained silent.

Chapter Twenty-One

"Heroes are those who can somehow resist the power of the situation and act out of noble motives, or behave in ways that do not demean others when they easily can."
— **Philip Zimbardo**

Maybe it was guilt, Camillia asking for it, or Yuuto insisting, but Nori had given Camillia Moto's riding jacket back. The timing couldn't have been more perfect, having found the card Jimmy had given me all those months ago in a pair of my jeans. The words 'Detailing' and 'Metal Work' printed under his name came to my notice for the first time. Jimmy's place was out there. On the city's edge, a dirt path led to his garage doors. But it was still full of people and projects.

I was glad the Rental didn't have a driver (as eerie as it still was to me), so I didn't have to answer any questions or get strange looks, sitting in the back seat with my helmet and jacket. Jimmy rushed over as soon as he saw me. "Moto! Wait till you see what I've done for you!!"

It had been a month since A-Day, and things were tense. But the loss of my lightcyc had only made me more so, waiting for Jimmy to finish it. One of his men rolled my cyc out, and I skipped over to it, feeling the weight begin to lift off my shoulders a little bit the closer I got to it. Jimmy had painted it black, the spoiler and metal plates gleaming in the sunlight. But the black was just the beginning, rolling it further into the light and showing me the glitter. It was like a hot pink shrapnel-filled bomb went off next to the drying black paint. In the dark, it was one cyc, and in the light, a completely different–just like me.

"It's beautiful!!!"

Jimmy chuckled at me as I continued to bounce in awe. "I thought you'd like it."

"What do I owe you?"

He shook his head at me, "It's on me."

"What??!"

"You have won me a lot of money, Sweetcheeks. Consider this thanks."

"Wow . . . that's so nice! Thank you!"

Jimmy leaned in slightly, whispering with a smile on his face. "Not all of us are so scary."

I jumped on him, hugging Jimmy, and he chuckled some more but then cleared his throat as he gently pushed me away. "Watch it now. you're going to ruin my street cred." I giggled, but he turned back to his 'employees' to yell. "There's nothing for you here! Get back to it, you shits!!"

One last quick wave, and I took off. The frigid February air bit at me through my jeans, but it didn't slow me in the least. Fluffy clouds carpeted the sky, looking and feeling like snow. It would still be several weeks till spring, and the next race, but my cyc was ready–as was I.

New determination had bloomed in me from A-Day. The dark events had shadowed the rest of the night, but one thing was clear: the Kurio-chi were not to be messed with. I didn't know why they'd zeroed in on the Cruor (maybe they were always on their radar), but it felt personal—like Moto was the cause somehow. It felt very cocky of me to think that, but I wasn't helping either way. I needed to find Rene before things got too messy to fix.

Zipping through the streets of Ocresa, I considered it practice, making my way around the slower-moving auto attached to the rails. A few turned their heads to watch me pass as I was not secretive about my illegal activity, whipping around without magnets. It was the least of my worries, and I needed the release of speed more.

I was hindering about going home yet (unsure I was ready) and decided to turn the other way. The open road was calling me at the moment. Any thoughts about returning to my stifling room were too much for me. Planning on going around the block instead of straight home, I tucked in and flew around the corner.

I loved this feeling, the freedom it brought, and the adrenaline that coursed through my veins. Something like this really shouldn't be illegal. That may be why it was. Because it felt too good to be allowed? Soon, nothing but the road opened up before me, speeding away from all the slower traffic.

But then, I wasn't alone.

Humming beside me, we both came to a stop at the light. Even with my new paint job, I was just as recognizable as the man beside me, Yuuto, flipping up his visor to speak. "Nice paint."

There was an edge to his tone, but since he had no reason to be upset with Moto (or Josaline, for that matter), I just chalked it up to the same pressing tension I'd felt from Anniversary Day. The last and only time we had raced was on those little karts. Now was my chance to do it again -for real- and it already had my heart racing.

Instead of replying verbally, I returned to the road ahead and revved my com-motor. It took a few seconds longer than I expected, but Yuuto accepted the challenge. His com-motor returned my call and revved next to me. Sinking back in, I watched the light and hit the accelerator as soon as it turned green.

Yuuto stuck beside me, only splitting apart to go around an auto, cyc, or a materials transport in the way. He took the lead and an exit for the highway. I watched as he slanted in deep to take the U-turn access. He barely slowed, and neither did I.

We popped out. The raised road was sparsely populated and free for us to play on. Opening up even more, I powered past Yuuto. Reglin told me that I knew Yuuto was a talented racer, but so was I. There was no telling who would win this race.

The buzz of his com-motor came in close, and, for once, I wished he could see the smile on my face. As it were, I couldn't see his expression either, but I felt it was the grin he wore when he was picking on me. Mischievous to his core.

Still in the lead (if only by a little), I took an exit, leading us off the highway. The traffic was dense, leading us towards a park at dusk. Not even a single pedestrian was around when we turned into the greenway entrance, splitting the auto-stoppers and slipping through.

Given the temperature, the park, our personal playground, was empty. Playing, we both took turns dipping low to the side and at one point, Yuuto cut a couple of donuts, making me almost fall over with laughter.

Leaving the park, we sat together at a light. Yuuto flipped his visor up again. "I think we forgot to race."

I nodded in agreement, laughing as I did. Once we hit the park, the thought of winning left my mind. The look

Yuuto gave me had me worrying he could see through my helmet. I turned away, even if it was pointless. He couldn't see through. My helmet wholly blacked out. Yuuto just looked like that at everyone.

Like he could see right through them.

The light was set to change any second. I wondered if we would continue our race when more com-motors hummed around me. My throat swelled with worry as men in all black formed a semi-circle behind us. This group immediately wanted Yuuto and me to know there was no escape from what they had planned. Their dark colors were a giveaway, but I could only guess they were with Kurio–chi and that they had their magnets turned off, too. Was one of them him, one of them Sora? They all had dark helmets, not as dark as mine but still hard to see through.

Looking back at Yuuto, he slapped his visor shut, letting me know they were not friends of his either. As if I didn't already know that. Maybe he thought Moto was confused about his relationship with any Kurio-chi? Neither Josaline nor Moto was. I deeply understood the danger they all posed, especially to Yuuto.

The green light glowed across the intersection, and all the com-motors roared as air filled their systems, and we took off. The road was damp and slick, getting worse now that the sun had set. It caused one of the guys to spin out when he tried to take off. Three remained at our sides, trying to close in on us.

One got too close to Yuuto, so Yuuto kicked the guy's thigh hard, sending the Kurio-chi member in a spiral he quickly recovered from. The one on my tail came up beside me and tried to grab my handlebar. Having been through that before, I hit the brakes hard to put him far ahead and myself out of reach.

Yuuto followed, hitting his brakes, and we both took a hard turn back onto the highway. I thought we lost them, but they showed up at the next turn-on. Now ahead of us, they zig-zagged before Yuuto and me. Trying to intimidate or something, they looked like idiots as Yuuto and I slowed some more and took the next exit.

Now I was lost; I had no clue where we were, so I followed Yuuto diligently. Things started to look familiar just before Yuuto pulled into the garage from which I stole my cyc months ago.

We cut our com-motors and parked our cycs inside the garage, but Yuuto left the door wide open. "What are you doing?!!" I hissed as he removed his helmet and stood by the door. "Shouldn't we hide?"

"Why? They know where this place is."

"Then why did we come here???" I roared at him.

He roared back, "If you have someplace better, then go! I won't keep you here."

There was no way I was leaving him alone to deal with four guys. Maybe more if they rallied and got some help before coming over. I also ran the risk of being followed if I left in time for them to see me go. The last thing I needed was for this group to know who I was and where I lived.

"Guess the joy ride is over."

Yuuto opened his mouth to say something more but stopped, the sound of approaching lightcycs silencing him. They parked on the street and sidewalk in front of the door, blocking any comings and goings. Like we were going to run.

Now, there were five of them. Way too many for

Yuuto to handle. I stuck my hands in my pockets, my fingers wrapped around my Holo. The most I could do was call Cami, who could call Kaito, but that was better than nothing. Yuuto might be pissed, but I would take his anger over his bones being broken any day.

Yuuto squared up, ready to fight, and I squeezed my Holo so tight it popped. One of them led the way, holding up his hands in surrender. "We just wanted to talk."

"I've got nothing to say!"

Yuuto didn't drop his stance, and the guy took off his helmet. The fact that he was a Mute wasn't shocking; his bright green hair was glowing in the dark. "Not with you, with Moto."

I stepped around, but Yuuto grabbed my arm, keeping me from getting closer. "What do you want?"

"Sora wants a word with you."

"So . . . you just happen upon me in the streets and decide to try and kill me?"

"Just a test, Sweetcheeks."

I cringed, my stomach doing a flip-flop at the 'pet' name. The same one Jimmy called me. "How did you find me?"

I had a pretty good idea, but I hoped I was wrong. One of the guys at the back pulled his helmet off. It was the same guy that had wheeled my lightcyc out to me at Jimmy's. "You! You followed me?!!!"

"Jimmy told us he was working on your lightcyc. It was pure luck you came for it during my shift."

Yuuto held me back again as I fought to get to the guy, my anger washing away my fear. "You jerk!! I trusted you! You and Jimmy!!"

"Jimmy was too busy bragging to notice anything! He's an idiot!"

Pulled back against his chest, Yuuto held me still. "Chill, Moto." This time, I wished I wasn't wearing my jacket, desperately wanting the comfort of Yuuto's warmth. "She isn't going anywhere with you and has nothing to say to Sora."

"And here I thought Moto was a strong and independent woman. But she still needs a man to speak for her."

Biting my tongue, I didn't take the bait, and Yuuto

gave me a small pat on the shoulder for it. "The Cruor won't be intimidated by a bunch of punk-ass losers like you or your boss."

The two without helmets grimaced, and I was sure the others were doing it under theirs. The group leader pointed at me and sneered. "She's not Cruor, though. Moto's a free agent and up for grabs."

"I am not up for anything…."

Yuuto squeezed me, shutting me up again. "Moto is Cruor and therefore off-limits."

The one that had followed me laughed, looking dangerously at me. "No one is off-limits, Cruor or otherwise."

That's when Yuuto shoved me back, putting me behind him. "I have been polite up until now, but if you don't leave now, you will have to limp away. You are on my property, so kindly get the hell out of here."

Yuuto stepped back, pushing me back with him, and shut the garage door without warning. He didn't move again until it was completely closed, glaring at the men as they stood still on the other side. The sound of their com-motors as they left echoed inside the otherwise silent tin room. Growing quiet, Yuuto turned. I nearly tripped over myself as he took two quick steps it took to clear the space between us with his long legs.

I tried to back away, but he caught me, his hand grabbing and stopping me as his fingers dug under my helmet. Pulling me back to him, I waited for him to rip it off of me (the street racing rules no longer protected me with Yuuto this pissed), but instead, he just held me still.

"Would you please, for the love of credits, STOP BEING SO RECKLESS!!!"

"Reckless??!! How the hell was I reckless?!!"

"You are too *freaking* trusting!!!!"

His breath fogged up my visor on one side, while my breath did the same to the other. He still held tight to my helmet, his fingers touching my chin. "I trust you, " he said.

He loosened one finger, running it across my cheek and back. I waited for him to pull it off to reveal me to him, making no attempts to stop him. "What if I hadn't been there? Huh? What if you'd been alone?"

"I wasn't...."

"Out of luck! Always out of luck that will run out at some point."

"So . . . are you saying you won't always be around? Because all my so-called luck seems to revolve around you."

The breath Yuuto released took the tension out of his body, his head coming to rest on the top of my helmet. His eyes closed. I watched him through the visor as he suddenly squeezed them tight. "You really shouldn't trust me either."

"Hence the helmet."

"That's currently mine to take."

"And I'm not stopping you."

Yuuto stood back up, gently pushing me away and releasing my helmet. I didn't go far. At some point, I grabbed hold of his coat's lapels and held them tight. He grabbed my hands and held them in place when I tried to release him.

"I guess a welcome to the Cruor is in order."

"I'm not a part of the Cruor."

"If I'm honest, you have been -in a sense- since you showed up the second time. You know my sister idolizes you?"

"She doesn't know me…and neither do you."

"And whose fault is that?"

My grip on his coat loosened, but he still held me captive. "I heard you had a run-in with Sora on A-Day."

He squeezed my hands out of response to the memory. "He messed around."

"Messed around? Camillia almost got sliced open!"

"But Kaito protected her. Sora is sadistic, but he knows better than to hurt any of my crew- not if he wants to get what he wants."

"What does Sora want, Yuuto?"

His hold loosened and disappeared. "You should get going. They are long gone by now. But you probably shouldn't go home."

"Didn't you just say they won't mess with your crew? I thought I was Cruor?"

He chuckled softly, backing away slowly. "Who said it was them you had to worry about? Maybe I'm the one that's going to follow you?"

I shook my head, and his smile faded. "You won't do that. I trust you."

"I'll believe that when you take off that helmet for

me." Yuuto turned his back to me and opened the garage door. Once open, he still didn't face me. I only saw his face again in my rearview mirror as I pulled away. But his face remained in my mind the whole way home, replaying all the different looks he gave me tonight and the words he said.

Was I a Cruor now? Really? It had been out of pity, really, to protect me. I didn't take it seriously, but I would have to wait and see if it was valid with the far-away racing season. Yuuto would probably forget by then. I wouldn't; Yuuto's tone and touch were gentle enough to make me shiver from the memory alone.

I circled for an hour before deciding it was safe to go home. All the tension I had gotten out from my ride was back again, thanks to the run-in. Sora was gunning for Moto and me, and I had no idea why. I could use that to gain information, but I needed to be wise and careful about it.

The last thing I wanted was to be trapped inside the Kurio-chi like a slave to their demands.

Glin was waiting for me at the top of the stairs. I glanced up at him once before going around him, completely ignoring him. "Where were you?"

"I went for a ride."

Glin didn't look too happy with my answer at nearly eleven o'clock on a school night. "At this hour?"

I had planned on being home much earlier, but Yuuto and the Kurio-chi kept me out much later. "Moto goes out later than this all the time."

"Moto is Josaline and my Cousin."

I stopped at my door and dug a toe into the carpet. "I ran into Yuuto, so we had a little race."

"What?"

"Then some of Sora's guys followed me, and I had to give them the slip."

That wasn't the whole story, and (with my struggle) I was sure it was obvious. But Glin knew it was pointless to push it. "Are you alright?"

I shrugged to try and go for indifference, playing with the handle of my door. "I'm fine. The Kurio-chi didn't keep up. We're safe."

"Are we? That Sora guy has taken an interest in you all because of Yuuto."

"It's fine, Glin. I'm just going to continue to ignore the

guy."

"What does he want from you anyway?" I shrugged again since I didn't know the answer, but I still felt guilty. "You should stay away from him. Sora and Yuuto. Especially Yuuto."

My head popped up at that. "Why do you keep pushing me away? I want to help you, and this is how I do it!"

"I never asked for your help, even though you've gotten sidetracked from everything. We're supposed to be getting information on Rene! This is getting us nowhere. All I've done is try to say nothing while Yuuto tries to put the moves on both Moto and Josaline!"

"He is not putting the moves on either of me!"

"Oh, come on, Jo. I know you are not that oblivious."

I bit my lip, debating whether to believe it. "Yuuto might towards Moto, but not Josaline. There is nothing between them. Why would there be?"

"Oh, I don't know. Because you're beautiful, smart, happy, and talented."

"Pretty sure only you see me that way, Glin. But

thanks!"

"Not to mention your family is controversial."

I stopped him, holding my hand up and glaring back at him. "No one knows about my family. Only Cami and she would never say a word. If they knew . . . it would only make it harder for me to get any information."

I left Glin in the hall to his silent contemplation while I had mine. I never stopped thinking about Rene, but I'd be lying if I said it was all I thought about when close to Yuuto. At some point, getting close to Yuuto had become something more than just information, which made my stomach twist with guilt. It was all on me, though. Glin has done as he promised, working on getting close for information, and I will continue doing the same.

Getting and staying on Yuuto's good side was essential to finding Rene.

Which meant doing things I was extremely uncomfortable with and doing them well–including making sweets for him. I would have been so screwed this Coupling Day if I hadn't met Roxana. But, if I didn't know Roxana, it would stand to reason that I wouldn't have to make Yuuto chocolate. Chicken . . . egg . . .

Couplings Day was meant for friends and lovers to declare their connection. It was like a thank you for being in my life. I had previously bought treats for friends (as per tradition), but I'd never made anything for someone before. You typically do that for your significant other or partner. And since the only ones I've had were the ones my parents picked out for me, I'd never wanted to make them anything.

When out of the twenty I made, only four came out good enough to give, I felt pretty good about myself. I decided to split the rejects and give them out to my other friends. That way, it would feel less like I was giving Yuuto truffles that meant more than friendship. Two truffles for each of them. Roxana even helped me box them up; they looked professional. Mia was right beside me when we finished up our gifts, handing over hers with a flourish that made us both giggle. Having found every one of the Cruor and Camillia, I only had Kaito's and Yuuto's left to give.

And I was dreading those two the most.

Camillia was with me, a small cake in her hands for Kaito. It was the second time Camillia had crossed the campus and given a gift. However, I wished Camillia had given me some kind of warning as my first.

There were swarms of them, girls everywhere from all over Utirius Omega. A few found their lovers and moved on, but most of them circled two individuals in particular. "Camillia.... why didn't you tell me...."

Camillia's mouth was almost to the ground, so she had to pick it back up first to answer. "It.... it wasn't.... LIKE THIS before!!!"

"But.... there were other girls around?"

"Yeah, a few. About ten."

"You mean five girls each?"

"No, I mean ten each."

"Oh god. I'm getting out of here."

I turned, planning on running as far and as fast as possible, but Camillia grabbed hold of my scarf before I could. "No, Josaline, no. We worked hard to make these sweets and to look super cute. We are way cuter than any of those girls!!"

Looking down at my light pink panda tunic and black tights, I wondered just who Camillia was talking about.

367

Especially with my bright pink hair in wild curls today. "Cami…"

"Don't you dare; you look adorable!"

Camillia did. Her bright red jumper and black boots had her looking like a model. In contrast, I looked like her manager.

"Cami!"

We both turned, Kaito breaking free of his crowd and Yuuto following close behind. Girls were holding out gifts, but they had accepted none, it seemed. Their hands were empty, and the girls all whimpered and moaned as they stepped away. Yuuto and Kaito didn't accept any of those girls as lovers or friends. The two might as well have been famous, a few girls trailing behind them until they caught sight of Camillia and me. Then they stopped and glared.

I was still staring at the mob, trying to find a way to make it back to campus alive with some of the looks I got while Kaito took his cake from Camillia. The sheer number of girls crying as he gave her a quick peck was overwhelming.

Quickly, I handed over the chocolate I intended for

Kaito. The group's cries caused me to cringe: "Thank you, Josaline. I hope you didn't just bring me chocolate?"

Kaito glanced behind him. Yuuto was waiting a few steps away. Forcing me to leave Camillia's comfort, I stepped up to him and thrust out his gift: "Here."

He carefully plucked it from my fingers, the single action causing twice as many girls to burst into tears behind him. "This isn't bought chocolate, is it?"

I forced the lump down into my belly and out of my throat. "No."

The group let out a few wails. "Good. Kaito's better be 'friendship'." I managed a nod, and he smiled. Thanks."

"You're welcome." Feeling very much like a robot, I turned to run.

Just as Camillia had before, Yuuto caught my scarf, the damn thing tangled around my neck and my curls, making it impossible to leave it behind. "Jooooji." He yanked me back and wrapped an arm around my waist to hold me still. "Don't you want to see me open these?"

Some of the cries started to sound more like growls. The group of girls was turning into a pack of wolves. "I want to keep all my hair, thank you."

Yuuto was chuckling, but I found none of it funny. "They are all bark, don't worry."

"If you have all these girls here to make and give you Coupling sweets, then why did you have me do it too?!"

"I thought I was doing you a favor. This way, you have *someone* to give treats to."

I ripped out of Yuuto's hold, turning and getting up on my toes to put a finger in his face. "I don't *need* anyone to make chocolates for!"

"What else would you do? Make them all for yourself?"

"If I wanted some chocolate, then yes!"

"That's just sad."

I growled, anger ripping out from my soul at the man. "You know what? I take it back." Stepping away, I went over to Camillia and Kaito. "Those, there in your hands, are 'store-bought' chocolates. Since you MADE me make them for you!"

My last act before stomping away from Yuuto and his multitude of fans was to jump up on my toes and kiss Kaito on the cheek. Angry wails came from the other side of the onlookers, but I no longer cared.

Chapter Twenty-Two
"Being a hero, the man had observed, is largely a matter of knowing one's cues."
— Lev Grossman, _The Magician King_

The nerve of that guy. Yuuto did all of that, ALL of it, just to bully me. Get me to make him sweets, bring it to him on campus, and then embarrass me even further in front of all those people. I didn't care that much about other people or what they thought, but the fact that Yuuto thought I did and then tried to embarrass me in front of them? *Unbelievable*!

And what the hell was up with all those women? If they thought Yuuto was so great, they could have him for all I cared. I didn't care that Yuuto's body looked as if chiseled out of stone or the way his eyes glowed when he smiled or how Yuuto was willing to stand up to five for one person or how just a touch from him made my heart fly or how I literally flew when we raced or rode together. Or how Yuuto took care of those he cared about to a fault.

None of it. I cared about none of it. And I would have nothing more to do with Yuuto. We were rivals—racing to compete and nothing more. I wouldn't even call him a friend!

Mia was waiting under our tree, and it only then occurred to me that I not only left Camillia behind, but I had kissed her *hopeful* on the cheek. I had kissemissed in front of *a lot* of people too. Regulations would be here to pick me up any second now. It was against the law to kiss anyone you weren't either engaged or married to. And to do that, you had to be registered with the government which required both parents from both parties approval. It was more than signing a document. Blood, fingerprints, and an ID scan were required. Hard to get and impossible to fake.

"Josaline, how did it go?" Mia's kind smile faded away. "Are you alright? You are really pale?"

"Oh, God . . . Mia . . . I messed up….I messed up bad."

"HEY!!!!"

We both turned, a puffing Camillia coming up fast

373

behind us and I ran off to meet her, dropping to my knees before her and thrusting my clasped hands up over my head. "FORGIVE ME!!!!"

"Jo . . . get up, people are staring," Camillia helped me to my feet, "don't worry about it. I know you weren't serious. Kaito gave them all one look and they put their holos away, so no one called Regulations. So, I'm not mad. Plus, it was worth it to see Yuuto go off. Although, you did almost get my boyfriend knocked out."

"I'm sorry about Kaito, but I'm struggling to see Yuuto do anything over me. Especially to Kaito. Yuuto is such a jerk! Nothing more than a big bully and a jerk! Why did he even have me make him Coupling Day treats anyway? He didn't need them. he had plenty to choose from. God, he is such a...."

"Jerk?" Mia and Camillia finished it for me.

"I just want to get out of here and forget this day ever happened. Can we do that? Is it even possible?"

Camillia grinned from ear to ear, and I started to feel a bit scared. "Oh, we can forget. I have just the thing!"

My fear continued as Mia and I followed Cami -with

no indication of where we were heading other than it would take a Magtram to get there- to someplace that promised to make me forget today's embarrassment. I didn't think it was genuinely possible…until we arrived at our destination. If there was a place that existed for the love-lorn, this place was it. Everywhere else had hearts and clasped hands. This place was devoid of all that. And dark. The atmosphere matched the mood of all those inside, including me, at the moment.

The music that played was low but had a heavy beat that no one danced to. I had heard enough about these types of…places to know what it was. And although alcohol wasn't illegal, it was heavily frowned upon–especially when consuming in public.

I was a bit shocked Cami knew of a place like this. If she were to take us anywhere, I expected it to have dancing. Not that I wasn't glad this place wasn't one of those. this place didn't seem like her style at all.

Pushing Mia and me to the long bar and into seats, Cami sat as well with a huff beside me. I was hidden from the rest of the room with Mia on the other side, but I still tipped back and forth to take in the sights.

A woman (Mute with pretty green, almond-shaped eyes) stepped up to us. Cami didn't give either of us a chance to speak. "Candy Apple shots, three."

"Do you visit places like this often?" Mia asked, leaning around me to look at Cami.

"Not really. But enough to know my way around."

Our 'shots' appeared, and Cami tried to pay. But the woman stopped her and pointed for all of us to look. "The man there, he paid for them."

Cami gave the man a pleasant smile and a wave but quickly pulled her attention back to us. "Alright, Ladies, happy Coupling day!"

She slung her glass back, and we did the same. It was sweet, syrupy, and burned all the way down to my belly. "Ug, what was that?"

"Candy Apple shot! I thought you guys would enjoy it." Cami said with a wave of her hand.

"I prefer something a little stiffer," Mia countered, flagging the woman down again, "U–okka soda, please."

I was stunned, as was Cami. Mia blushed heavily but said nothing more. It looks like I was the only one without any experience. It was why I was confused when Mia's drink appeared with two more Apple shots. "The man over there...."

The woman pointed, and we looked. A different man than before, I was starting to notice a theme. "Um.. thanks?"

The woman nodded with a wink, and I quickly shot back the drink, noting that it burned a little less this time. And that I felt a little different all over as well. Cami giggled, and I joined her even though I found nothing funny.

"Uh oh. I think we're in trouble, girls." Cami said through a sugary grin.

I lost track after that, how many drinks we had, but eventually, Cami pulled us from our seats and pushed Mia and me to the door. The fresh air didn't help like Cami promised it would, stumbling around on the street now for many to see.

Again, we were being led by Cami, following even more blindly than we had before. Given how I felt now, fuzzy and warm instead of humiliated and heartbroken, I would follow Cami anywhere. She made things better no matter what the problem was.

I was sure the area was familiar, that I had been here before. It wasn't home, but we didn't dare go there. "Cami...where are you...taking us now?"

Cami wobbled on her feet before Mia and me. I wasn't wobbling, but that was because I had sweet Mia supporting me. Or I was supporting her. I couldn't tell.

"We're going someplace *sweet*!"

Cami yelled the word 'sweet', making my belly rumble. I hadn't eaten all day, too nervous about my chocolate and then too pissed. "Yuuto sucks!"

"We know, dear," Mia said, patting my shoulder, "you've said the same thing for the last... however long it's been now."

"Well... it's still true now, just like then!"

Cami nearly fell over in a fit of laughter. The wall of the building we walked next to held her now instead of herself. "Ooooh, there it is!!"

Taking off, we followed as best we could after her. But Cami was all over the place. I didn't know how much of that was real or in my head. the whole world was a bit sloppy. When Cami tripped towards the glass door, it wasn't my imagination, falling heavily on it with a loud *thump*. She was lucky she didn't go through, but the glass was strong. Very strong as Mia and I soon fell to it too. We all got a good look inside, and I realized where we were.

"Alright! Great idea!"

Cami cooed from the praise and we all started knocking… and knocking… and knocking. The place was dark, but *I* knew I didn't care. We wanted in. A few minutes past annoying, Roxana appeared. It was dark, and my eyes were fuzzy, but I was pretty sure she had a broom in her hands like a sword. A few steps closer and the tension in Roxana faded away to irritation, which she used to fling open the door and drop us to our faces.

"What the *hell* are you guys doing here?!"

We were a giggling mess on Roxana's floor, an immaculate floor, I noted. Rolling onto my back, I looked up into the dark and scary eyes of the female Cruor. "Oh man, are you gonna snuff us out?"

Thoroughly confused, Roxana began untangling us and helping us to our feet. As much as I waivered on mine, I preferred the floor. "Are you guys…wasted?" Her eyes searched us. Mia nodded her head hard while Cami and I snorted. "I didn't think Gildes drank?"

Roxana scratched the back of her head, still confused. But when Cami jumped on a pole in the room, Roxana started pushing us deeper into the café. My butt hit the booth hard, the cushion jumping up to smack it and sting. Ignoring that because I was *hot*, I focused on stripping my clothes off.

"Josaline! Don't go past your outwear, or I swear I'll call a Regulator!"

Snickering at her, I nodded closer so she could hear me. "What will they do? They don't care! They don't give a shit about anyone but themselves and money!"

I was still laughing while Roxana had grown quiet. Mia sat next to me, her pretty head on my shoulder and her black curls tickling my chin. "They'll do something to me. I'm a Plunge."

My brain might have been spinning, but Mia's admission still made my heart jump wildly.

"You are?" Cami squeaked.

Mia tensed, and I wrapped an arm around her before she could run away like Rene did. "My father is a Gilded, and my mom a Mute. It's why I work so hard, so the Buung family will accept me. But all they call me now is *Assimulated*."

I had heard it all, repeated to me from Rene's lips while she cried. Alloyed, Hybrid, Assorted, Fused, all words for those who mixed ranks. Plunge was the worst since it was a high Gilde and a Mute. At the same time, Assimulated meant you blended in well with others. Mixing high with low was considered even more worthless than a Mute.

Mia sobbed after that, and I pulled her tightly to me. "They don't accept you? Then screw them! You're awesome!"

Roxana touched Mia, a sweet and watery smile on her face. But she sobered quickly. "I need to get food into you guys."

She disappeared, and I grinned at Cami. "Best. Idea. Ever."

Roxana returned with plates, and one was slid in front of me. Chocolate. Oh my god, chocolate! It was better than booze. It was better than Boys. It was better than racing. Okay, it wasn't better than racing, but it was still amazing.

I was on my third slice of chocolate… something while Cami and Mia had finished theirs a little while ago. I'm not sure what Roxana intended, giving us leftovers from the Coupling day celebration. But by the exasperated look on her face, she didn't achieve it.

My fork full, I waved it around at them all. "You guys are the greatest. you know that?" All but Roxana nodded and cheered in agreement. "You're the greatest people on this Earth! You guys and my cousin."

Cami leaned on her palm, smooshing her cheek up with her weight. "Reglin? He's alright. Couldn't get into the Cruor without you, though…."

"No, not him… although he's a favorite… I mean Rene, my other cousin…."

"Other cousin? How much family you got?" Roxana quibbled.

"That I like? Not much. I like my brother and my Uncle Haru and Aunt Caroline and Glin and… Rene," I cried, but it came out as a sigh, "I want to find Rene so bad."

"You lost her?" Mia asked, staring with wide eyes at me.

Shaking my head was terrible… but good, new bubbles forming and making me giggle with my tears. "No, I didn't lose her. she lost herself. Or got lost. And no one wants to look for a lost Plunge girl."

Mia gasped, and I petted her knee. Roxana sat up a little straighter. "Rene is a Plunge?" I nodded, my head bobbling. Fun. "What's her last name, Jo?"

"Ito."

Roxana got to her feet in a rush, but all our attention was not square on her. "I remember her. Haruto was pulled in by Regulations and questioned for hours about her! Is that why you're so *interested* in the Cruor?!"

She was pissed, flames in her eyes. But I didn't get it. what did she have to be so mad about?

"What's it to you?" Cami asked boldly.

"Because she… people are interested in Josaline… Jo, you're important to us. Are we not important to you?!"

Roxana was close to tears. I pushed around Mia to grab her hand in mine. "You're important to me, Roxana." When she calmed and sat back down, the mood shifted back to the bubbly one it had been. "Can I call you Roxy?" When she didn't answer, I moved on. "I'm just racing to get information about Rene, but I care about the Cruor."

Roxana stiffened at that, and I didn't understand again. Did I offend her with my lackluster reason for racing? I was about to ask, but she hopped out the booth again—this time with a smile on her face. "I need to make a call. You guys... don't move."

Easier said than done. my body was vibrating.

"Oh my god... Josaline...." Cami gasped suddenly, her eyes wide like she had just realized something. "We should go dancing."

I looked to Cami, my eyes nearly falling out of their sockets. "That's a great idea!"

Even Mia was on board, proving just how great an idea it was. We had just decided on a place when Roxana returned. Cami leapt on the tall girl. "ROXY! WE'RE GOING DANCING!"

"Uh.. no, no, you're not."

"Aw, please!" I begged.

"Can any of you even dance?"

Taking it as a challenge, we all fell out of the booth

and started showing off our skills. I managed to keep from falling on my face, a real achievement. I leaped onto Roxana, and when she nearly dropped me, I got back to my feet and shimmed around. Cami was shaking her hips, and I copied her. Mia was spinning like a graceful top… I didn't even try to replicate that. After a few leaps around the place, I flopped back to the booth, panting, and everyone joined me. Cami was still wiggling in her seat, causing me to snort.

When our breathing calmed (and Roxana still didn't let us leave), I got bored. Staring at the sugar packets on the table, I started balancing them on my nose. The bell above the café door dinged, signaling that we were no longer alone.

"KAI!!!"

Camillia flopped a little, trying to get out of the booth but struggling to remember how. She got it (eventually) wrapping all available limbs around the man, and he grunted from the additional weight. It took all I had not to release my laughter at Cami from my chest. five packets now on my nose. Mia was watching with rapt attention when they all fell.

We tipped over the tabletop into a heap, giggling like crazy till we couldn't hold ourselves up. Slipping down, Mia

385

threatened to go all the way under the table, and I was close to joining her. Camillia would follow as she fell back to the booth with us.

"Did you give them anything to eat?" Kaito asked, all serious.

"Yes. But it only made the drunks more hyper!"

My heart was racing, and my skin was buzzing. And not all of that was because Yuuto was here–staring at me. It was Roxana. she gave me chocolates, so I jumped on her as much as I could from my spot. "Roxy is the best! She fed us so many sweets! Best partner ever!!!"

"That's sweet Jo but, I'm not your partner," Roxana murmured.

"But you are!! The best . . . best one!"

Mia popped up suddenly. "I gave Ziyad chocolate!!"

"Yeah, we know. Buri won't shut up about it," Yuuto groaned.

"He told you it was homemade?"

The boys all nodded. Buri grinned as he did, and Mia turned magenta. I left Roxana and went to Mia, pulling her into my arms. "It's okay, Mia. Buri likes you! He didn't do it to embarrass you. he was excited! . . . .." Mia nodded, her color going back to normal. My anger flooded me out of nowhere, and I turned it on Yuuto. "Unlike SOME people!"

"I didn't embarrass you . . . on purpose…."

Yuuto's weak answer only infuriated me, and Haruto dared to intervene. "Yuuto, see how drunk she is? It's a pointless conversation."

My fury was out of control, feeling hot all over from it. "You're on HIS SIDE???"

Backing away with his hands up, Haruto hid behind Roxana. "I'm on nobody's side."

Camillia started to giggle, gaining everyone's attention at her manic episode. "Kai's on your side, Jo. I'll *make* him."

"We should get them out of here," Kaito suggested.

They all agreed, but we didn't. "I can't go home, not like this!!!", "Uncle and Auntie are going to kill me. Reglin too," and Camillia, "Daddy is going to lock me up this time."

Buri just laughed, taking a spot next to Mia to comfort and snuggle her. Roxana, on the other hand…."If you don't want to be seen like this, why did you get wasted in THE FIRST PLACE???!!"

"Camillia said it would help me forget. So I drank a little, but . . . then they kept sending us shots.."

"Who sent you shots, Josaline?" Buri asked.

Camillia laid her head on the table in front of me. "Everyone. Every single man in that bar. I got us out in time before it hit them too hard, but it was a close one."

"Why the hell did you drink them all? Don't you know men only send drinks to get you to leave with them?"

Now Yuuto was mad. Good. I wanted him to be just as pissed off and hurt as I was. The jerk deserved it.

Mia tried to soften the situation, "I didn't want to be rude."

Camillia just shrugged while I looked right at Yuuto. "Maybe I wanted to leave with them?"

Yuuto said nothing but everything moved in near-perfect rhythm as he reached into the booth, grabbed me, and hauled me up on his shoulder. Buri was ducking with Mia, missing my near slaps to their heads when I was aiming for Yuuto. I kicked and screamed, but nothing I did to him gained my release. I didn't stop, though, not even when he set me back on my feet outside. My hand flew without care and made contact with his face. There was a tiny spark of satisfaction. But it was quickly chased with the guilt I had to swallow.

Cami was howling with laughter, calming just enough to speak. "Josaline, just get in the auto."

The others were already seated inside. Mia and Buri got in on the other side while Camillia took the front seat. Forcing me to squeeze in between Mia and Yuuto. He held me in place with an arm over my shoulders and I hated how it made my skin tingle to be so close.

So I continued to fight against it.

He finally let go, giving up. Yuuto was too bruised to continue. "I'm going to sit on Mia! She is way nicer than YOU!"

Yuuto said nothing, only proving he didn't want to deal with me in the first place. And I was okay with that– thankful! Because I wanted nothing to do with him!

Once in Mia's lap, she groaned. "Jo, you are heavier than you look."

Guilt washed over me shockingly fast. "Aw, I'm

sorry, Mia."

I gave her a hug to make up, and Buri reclined away from us. "This is really hot."

Buri was howling in pain when we pulled apart for some reason, gripping his knee tight and rocking as best he could in the tight space. It had me and Mia confused, the dark beauty wearing concern and confusion on her lovely face while Yuuto glared at Buri and shook his hand as if hurt.

"What should we do with them? We can't take them home. Their caretakers will think we did this to them." Kaito asked from the driver's seat.

We all started begging them not to take us home again. I didn't want to know what Glin would do with my cyc if I came home wasted. I didn't want to lose another cyc to another overzealous male.

"We could take them to my place. Nori is out for the night at a friend's house." Yuuto offered, and my heart found a new home in my throat.

"Mia can come home with me."

Yuuto shot Buri a look but Mia perked up. "It's okay."

I looked squarely at Mia -searching for signs of fear

or protests- but all she did was blush heavily. Not something I could refute. The couple got out, Mia extracting herself from me. Once out, I crawled over to the side Mia and Buri stood on, leaning out the window at the two of them. "Buri. You better be a gentleman. I mean it. I will hunt you down, mister."

With Cami asleep, it was up to me to be the voice of reason or threatening or whatever. Not sure if I pulled it off, I was still wearing my panda tunic. I was sure I was a mess but hopefully, that made me scarier.

We pulled away with my head still out, and the frigid air whipped at my ears. I slowly sat back and found myself too warm. Yuuto was next to me again. I guess he thought I'd fall out the window. I couldn't move; his concern confounded me as I searched for an explanation and came up short. "What are you doing here?"

"I came and picked you up, remember?"

He did? I don't remember that, but it was nice of him. "Oh, thank you, Yuu!"

I hugged him. Yuuto pushed me back after a short second, and it felt like my heart broke. Then he offered me a small smile, not the one I liked so much but a smile nonetheless. "You're welcome."

His eyes were so bright and slippery. Just like honey candy, and they made my brain feel like it was dipped in it. "I didn't mean to drink so much. I promise."

"I know, Jōji."

I really didn't. Why did I drink so much again? "I was upset."

"It happens."

That's right. I was upset… over…. "I was upset because YOU'RE SUCH A JERK!!!"

I slapped his chest as hard as I could and flung myself to the other side of the auto, as far from him as possible. Yuuto sputtered, surprised by my attack for some reason, and Kaito laughed heartily from the driver's seat.

"Shut up!"

"You did ask for it, *Yuu*."

I ignored them, focusing on the world as it passed by at a decent pace. The scenery began to change, and then a drastic snap to decayed buildings surrounded us. Back in a Mute territory only made me ache, thinking about Rene, my

Uncle, and Yuuto. And they were just the Mutes I knew. Thousands, millions more had suffered like them and worse!

My heart pounded in my chest, and my brain refused to be still. I was bouncing around from moment to moment in my memory. From the last time I saw Rene to Yuuto smiling down at me on A-Day. Then it flashed to Glin with his plan and racing Yuuto the night the Kurio–chi surrounded us. The auto came to a stop, and the last thought in my head was Yuuto mocking me this afternoon.

When the door opened, I flew out of it, passing Kaito and Yuuto (who tried to grab me, but I refused to let Yuuto touch me). I wasn't supposed to be falling in love with Yuuto. I was supposed to be finding Rene! It was a good thing he was a jerk. It reminded me of what I was here for.

Yuuto chased after me, and I swung myself up on a pole. He reached for me, but I dodged, planting a foot into his shoulder to spin him away. While he was busy getting his equilibrium, I shot further down the street, making it around a corner to an alley before he got his eyes on me again.

The alley was empty save for a rusted-over vending machine from a time when people got food and drink from boxes taking paper money and pieces of plastic. Using the wall behind it, I shimmed my way up and sat on the top just as Yuuto's molten eyes found me. Taken aback, he slowly approached me. Where I sat, the only thing he could reach was my feet. I kicked, trying to keep him from getting a hold. But he still caught one of my ankles. Before my sluggish brain could pull it away from his touch, he yanked me down by it.

Yuuto was nice enough to catch me, but then he flung me over his shoulder again. That wasn't nice, not at all!

I kicked and screamed again, but he didn't put me down like before. Until we were inside his place, and even then, it was just to shove me into a room and shut the door. It took my wasted mind a little longer than it should to figure out I was in Yuuto's room. Why did he put me in here? To be extra cruel? Like I wanted to be surrounded by his life and his smell all night. That was just the last thing I needed right now.

I found the small window inside and tugged it open. There wasn't even a fire escape outside it, and it was a long, long way down.

I was trapped.

If I went out the door, Yuuto would definitely stop me. And as tired as I was, I knew I couldn't fight him, not anymore. What would that look like? Me unable to control myself or get out of his grasp? We had already broken some rules with touching but given my state, Regulations would have given Yuuto a pass. It made me shiver. Which also reminded me I had left my coat... somewhere. Oh great, I lost my coat. That was going to be a hard one to explain. Even if I could get out of this place and back out to the street, I'd freeze to death on my way home.

At least the cold might sober me up.

I flopped to the bed, and the action caused a sob to push out. The dam was broken, pulling my knees up to my chest in hopes of controlling my shaking. When that didn't work, I fell back to the small bed. It was the same size as the one I had at Auntie's, but that was the only similarity. Dark blue sheets and comforter. It was everything you would expect of a man's bed. And worse, it all smelled exactly like Yuuto. And not when he was fresh at school. the few times he had been close enough for me to smell there. No, this was his natural scent, warm skin that was clean and lacked any cologne. Cologne still lingered in the air, so I still smelled the earthy pine scent as well. Right now, I had my face deep in his sheets, and it was just like my nose was pressed against his skin.

It haunted me.

It was getting harder and harder for me to think of only Rene when playing Moto or being Josaline. Any time the Cruor were around, I struggled. Because I liked all of them, they were friendly and fun. It was hard to imagine any of them having anything to do with Rene's disappearance.

Why had Regulations dragged them in then? It wasn't like I trusted Regulators, not in this case or any other. But there had to be a reason. Otherwise, it would be too random.

My brain was too messed up to think about this now, especially while lying in Yuuto's bed. It only confused me more.

Like why Yuuto showed up tonight in the first place? Did he just want to see his handiwork firsthand? That didn't seem right. Yuuto would have followed me or something. And he wouldn't have brought me to his home or his bed. No matter how much of a jerk he was, Yuuto was still a nice guy deep down. He wouldn't leave some wasted girl alone to defend herself, even if that wasted girl was me. Moto was the only person Yuuto showed any respect or care for outside the Cruor.

Yuuto liked Moto.

And why wouldn't he? She's cool and in control. Or at least, she pretends to be. Was it normal to be jealous of yourself like this? Because I really wanted to bitch slap Moto. It couldn't be a healthy thing, and I hoped it was all the alcohol making me feel this way–inadequate.

Rolling onto my back, I left a wet spot on Yuuto's pillow from where I had been.

Great.

All of this left me feeling so unsteady with my thoughts, feelings, and plans. I was supposed to think of the Cruor as a means to an end. Feel nothing for them and only use them to get information on Rene. But instead, they were my dearest friends, people I trusted with my life. And Yuuto… he had me struggling to focus on Rene as I should be.

I liked him. I hated to admit it, but I did. I really liked Yuuto. He was dangerously handsome and clever. Talented and smart. I had no doubt he would break through the Mute barrier and become a very prestigious person. The last thing he needed was a silly little girl like me throwing him off his track. Especially a Gilded, that would only make things harder for him.

I scoffed at myself. Like I was doing anything of the sort. If today taught me anything, it was that Yuuto didn't need me or want me in the slightest. He had plenty of fans, and they were all beautiful.

I was just the girl that slapped him.

Cringing, I relived the memory. I had slapped Yuuto in the face. If he didn't hate me before, he did now.

That had me crying again, turning back to the pillow to weep to sleep. A strange sleep that didn't feel restful at all.

Chapter Twenty–Three

"But heroes, at times, had to be fools."
— ***Steve Berry, <u>The Venetian Betrayal</u>***

I was dreaming of Anniversary Day before everything went to pot. The smell of Yuuto from his haori draped over my shoulders. It was everywhere, surrounding me, the scent of pine, and his skin and…. coffee. It was freshly brewed.

Yuuto was putting the blindfold on me only this time I bent down and brushed my lips across his knuckles. I had seen engaged and married couples do this. It was a show of respect and kindness. This was something I had never seen my parents do, but that wasn't surprising.

When he didn't react, I pulled back. "I'm sorry!"

"No, I'm sorry, Josaline," Yuuto suddenly said as if it was pent uptight before, "I didn't mean to upset you so much."

I hopped, my fist coming down on Yuuto's chest again but not very hard. But I didn't pull back, resting my upper body on his. "Why are you always so mean to me?"

"I'm not mean to you." Yuuto sighed, and I danced on his chest, "I show you attention which is more than I do for others."

I had my face pointed at his chest, trying to get the tears to stop. But when I pulled my face back up, I felt wetness. "Yes, you are, Yuu. You are mean to me. Really mean."

Yuuto didn't understand, not even in my head. His words and actions hurt much than anyone else's. His hands were on my back, pulling me closer, and there was fear in his voice and his eyes. "Josaline…"

I had to make him understand. I had to make this Yuuto get why he affected me so much. Or I would die. "Everything you say or do….and it is so much worse because I like you. I really like you even though you just torture me."

"Jo…"

"But don't worry, I get it. I saw all those girls today chasing after you, and I know the last thing you need is another one of those. Or worse, a Gilded wrecking everything you're working towards." A sob interrupted me, and Yuuto's face switched from soft and sad to angry, "I guess that's why you had me come to you today, to show me where I stand...."

"Joji! Just . . . stop talking."

There was more to say. more I wanted to say. But I couldn't. Yuuto's lips brushed against the back of my hand, returning my sentiments of respect. The world faded away, both of us lost in the moment as we floated on a cloud. Laying across it, holding each other tight, we whispered sweet promises in between kisses. Like how I was his, and he was mine. Things that didn't make sense in a world where Gilded and Muted weren't allowed to be together easily. But this was a dream. It was too kind and amazing to be reality.

My hold on him was tight, arms and legs wrapped around him, but he was still ripped from me. The cloud popped, pinks flashed to black, and I was on my cyc, racing through the city with Yuuto next to me. However, this wasn't fun. We were being chased.

One of the men got alongside Yuuto and kicked his cyc hard, sending him wobbling and then flipping—Yuuto completely lost control. I was running, my cyc was gone and my feet pounded endlessly on the pavement. I pushed. Yuuto never seemed to get any closer, but I finally reached him. His helmet was long gone, cracked and crumbled to dust, so I placed his head in my lap.

Yuuto looked unscathed, like nothing had truly happened. But then blood pooled out under us–all from him.

Honey gold eyes, fading to gray, looked into mine. "Why didn't you...tell me?"

Yuuto's hand reached up, grabbing my cheek, and I realized my helmet was gone as well. I was still in my Moto get up. My identity was revealed and revealed too late.

"I'm sorry. I didn't . . . I wanted to, I just . . . Yuu.."

He gave me a small smile and then faded away to nothing. I was alone, kneeling on the street and pool of blood before me. And laughter.

Aching from my scalp to my spine, I was pulled up to my feet by my hair. The shadowy face was inches from mine, and their breath reeked of death. "You're all mine now, Moto. Or should I say, Josaline Pryce? The daughter of the Vice President of Commerce??? The Heiress to the Untouchable's throne! What a pleasant yet unexpected find! I must be the luckiest man alive."

His laugh filled the air again, digging into my skull paralyzing me. It was too much. the blood, the cold, the pain in my brain and heart. I just wanted it all to end.

Sitting up, I regretted it, my head still splitting in two after being released from the dream. I was in a strange room, and a strange bed but my clothes were the same as before. Wrinkled but fully intact save for my shoes. And my hair, sitting on the mangled curls as I took a look around.

It didn't take me long to find a picture of a chubby Nori. She was small and in a little yellow dress covered in mud with both her legs intact. That meant whatever happened to Nori happened later in life.

Nori was cute and happy, a sweet baby. Smiling hurt, too, but I did it just the same, carefully rising and tracing the frame that sat on the small desk in the corner.

"You're awake."

Yuuto's voice was soft, but it still stung. As did the fast twist my head did to find him standing just inside the door. "Am I? I feel like death."

Chuckling softly as well, Yuuto came to my side, looking at the photo I still had my fingers on. Then he ran a tender hand across my cheek, pulling my hair back and off my shoulder. "Yuuto..." He looked confused, like I had called him by someone else's name. "How did I get here?"

"You . . . don't remember?"

Yuuto was frowning -deeply- and for some reason, I felt guilty when I shook my head 'no'. His eyes left my face, stepping away from me. It started small, but the distance snowballed. Yuuto's chuckle was broken at first, but it soon became a full laugh. My head swam, and my heart trembled.

"Yeah . . . that seems about right. What do you remember?"

His face was strange like Yuuto didn't know how he felt. "I'm . . . I'm not sure. Wait.." I inhaled quickly, the rush of the memory stirring me and his eyes widened at me. "Did I hit you?!"

A smile, small and loopy, came with a sigh. "Yeah, a few times."

"I'm so sorry! Ooooh, I got your neck bad, it seems."

Yuuto grabbed the spot, knowing exactly where I was

talking about without looking. But his face was blank, his eyes going wide again in shock. "You seriously don't remember, do you?"

"Huh-uh. Is there something important I forgot?"

He was silent, thinking it over. But then he shrugged, "No . . . nothing important." Yuuto breezed past me, picking up his book bag. "I'm going to class. You should stay and rest. And drink water!"

Patting my head as he spoke, it all felt so awkward. I must have done something horrible to him last night. "Yuuto…"

"I'll talk to you later."

Yuuto gave a short wave and then ducked out fast enough to put out a fire on the other side of town. I couldn't keep up. my brain spinning while on fire all made my stomach want to jump ship. There were voices outside the room, so I moved towards them, finding Cami and Kaito talking quietly and quickly to one another.

"My hair hurts."

They both looked up at me and ended whatever conversation they were having before my appearance.

Cami moaned pitifully, "Tell me about it." Kaito placed coffee and Aspirin before her then went to the living room to sit alone. "Thank you."

"You're welcome."

Kaito sounded gruff and I wondered if he caught the mood Yuuto left in? I plopped to a chair and then lowered my head to the table. My bright strands hurt my eyes, standing out painfully against the white tabletop of the small dining set.

"What happened last night?" Cami asked softly.

I didn't raise my head. the table muffled my voice as it made it through my thick curls. "I don't know."

"What?"

We glanced at Kaito, his outburst both out of character and hurtful to my ears. But he kept his focus on me. "I don't remember anything after . . . walking to Roxana's bakery."

Kaito was blank, staring at me dumbfounded. Then he turned away like it never happened. "Interesting."

"What? Why? Do you know what happened?" Cami pumped.

I pulled my head up from the table and looked over at Cami. "Don't you?"

"More than you, it seems." She mumbled into her coffee.

"Can you fill me in? I need to know so I can fix this."

I was desperate, the way Yuuto looked at me and left? It felt like a large rift between us, which was the last thing I wanted. "Fix what, dear?"

"Yuuto. Things are bizarre, and I don't know why. I think I hurt him. I hit him a lot last night, apparently . . . "

"Don't worry," Kaito interrupted, "Yuuto isn't the type to get upset over things like that."

"Do you know what his problem is?"

Kaito turned, looking back at us from his spot in the living room. "I think it's best you don't know."

"What kind of answer is that?" Cami yelled a little too loud.

He ignored her, returning to the paper in his hands. I moaned and changed the subject, grabbing up my hair and pulling it around to braid it. "I should just cut all this off. But I'm afraid *the hair* would cry."

"Cutting it would make wearing a helmet easier."

Cami and I both froze and then slowly turned to Kaito, who still held his paper as if he had said nothing at all. "What did you say?"

"To be honest, that was what kept me from figuring it out for so long. How *do* you get all that hair up into your helmet?"

My glare shifted quickly to Cami. "Did you tell him??!!"

She grabbed her head again from my squeals. "God. No Josaline and please, decibels."

"I figured it out on my own, thank you. It wasn't too hard. Once I knew about your tie to Reglin, it was simple."

"Who . . . who else knows? Is that why Yuuto is upset???"

"As far as I know, I'm the only one. But I wouldn't put it past Yuuto to have it figured out soon. He's very clever."

I still held my hair in my hands, frozen mid-braid. "Jo! Your neck!!!" Cami cried, and I cringed.

"You just complained about my decibels…."

Her fingers pressed to my neck, and it hurt a little. "You gonna explain this to me, young lady?!"

I pulled away from her touch and pressed my fingers to it instead. "I don't...it's sore. What is it?"

"A bruise," Kaito yelled quickly.

His eyes shifted from Cami to me and back. The blonde shook her head and huffed. "Fine. It's a bruise. But what is she going to tell her family when they see it?!"

"The truth. It's a bruise."

Kaito was causal about it, while Camillia acted as though she might fall over from a stroke. "You guys are weird," I muttered loudly.

"Either way, you should both hurry and go home. I called your families and informed them you ate some bad food. They will want to see you both in one piece as soon as possible."

Bad food. It wasn't a lie, technically. But (when I got home) the way Glin was watching me, I was pretty sure he didn't believe the story. "Josaline, what did you do last night?"

I was currently clutching my head as it laid on the

kitchen table. "I caused the death of many things."

"Like what?"

"Like brain cells."

"Are you going to explain your neck?"

I popped my head up, hand going to the spot and covering it. "Yeah, I have no clue. I must have fallen and hit my neck somehow. I don't know how a person does that, but I guess if anyone could, it would be me."

"You're....you're telling me that . . . *that* is a bruise??"

I pressed a finger to it, shrinking slightly. It still hurt. "What else could it be? It looks a little weird, though, right? Maybe I should go to a Doctor? Maybe I have weird blood that causes weird marks."

"Jo, you have fallen a lot over the years. Did your bruises ever look like that before?!"

I took a moment and honestly thought it over. "Well . . . no, I don't think so...."

Suddenly, he jumped up so fast his chair fell backward. "Are there any elsewhere?"

"Any what where?? Keep your voice down, please!"

He pulled me from my seat and shoved me towards the stairs. "Go. Go now and take a bath and make sure there aren't any . . . *bruises* anywhere else!!!"

"Okay, okay! I was going to take a bath anyway...."

Glin was almost as weird as Cami about the mark. No, weirder cause Cami didn't make me strip and check for more. I wouldn't be surprised if there were more. I'm a bit clumsy even when sober.

Oddly enough, my knees were a little banged up. Like I hit them both on something with equal amounts of force. That would explain my tights, small rips in the knees that made them ruined. Roxana arrived before we left Yuuto's with my coat and stories of us dancing all around the café after eating a truckload of chocolate, which explained why my ankle was a little sore. I must have twisted it trying to dance.

With all that, the only dark spot was on my neck. I propped myself on the mirror, inspecting it closely. After Camillia got over her trepidation about it, she thought it was hilarious for some reason. But I guess such a strange spot for a bruise was somewhat funny. It was shaped like an oval and primarily red with purple around the edges. All my marks had been purple, no red at all. It was almost like the shape of a mouth, the ends angled to look almond-shaped.

It looked almost exactly like the one on Yuuto's neck.

That wasn't normal, right? Two people having similar bruises in the same spot?

My brain was two sizes too big for my skull and it didn't appreciate *thinking* at the moment. It wasn't important anyway. I had far more critical things to consider. Like how to get on Yuuto's good side again. Not that I was ever on it before.

Maybe it was better this way? Even if it made me want to cry, I needed to distance myself from Yuuto and his hypnotizing eyes. Focus on Rene and getting information. Races wouldn't start back up for a few more months. Which meant I would be waiting until spring for another chance. It was going to be one long winter, that was for sure.

Chapter Twenty–Four

"To be heroic does not have to mean possessing the ability to stand against the evils of the world, either well or successfully, but just that one is willing to stand."
— **Mike Alsford, <u>Heroes and Villains</u>**

Focusing on my schoolwork did nothing to the slow tick of time. Waiting for the races to start again slowly turned into waiting to see the Cruor again. That wasn't true. I saw Kaito and Buri often since they were dating my best friends. And we saw Roxana when we visited her café and Haruto when her picked her up. I saw Jeb from time to time, and Nori didn't like Josaline at all. So really, I was only waiting to see Yuuto.

Whatever I did to Yuuto, he wasn't going to talk about it or forgive me. He had been avoiding me since that night. Not that it was hard. But before, he used to just show up, and now nothing. It told me that whatever I had done was terrible.

My biggest worry was that I had revealed myself. That was the only thing I could imagine that would have Yuuto so upset. finding out the girl he had been chasing was me. Moto was lame Josaline, an honest, plain Jane. Someone he could barely stand to be around for longer than a few minutes.

Finally, there were only a few days left until the next race. I was trying my best not to think about it, which was impossible given my current company.

"Kaito, can you teach me to drive off the rails?"

Kaito choked on the tea he was sipping, the three of us hiding in a booth at Roxana's work, which was hard with my bright hair, and Kaito the only Mute as a customer. The soft cushioned bench squeaked with age as he jerked to look at Cami. I glanced up from my research paper to laugh at his exasperated expression before it disappeared.

"Why would you want me to?"

Cami shrugged, "so I can race, of course."

It was a strange conversation in such a spot. the soft lighting and smooth jazz playing softly above were hardly the setting of illegal activities. But what did I know?

"Your parents gave you a limitless spending account.

What do you need to race for?"

"Maybe I want to look cool like Moto?"

Kaito chuckled, "That has very little to do with racing."

I took that as a compliment whether he meant it or not, beaming back at my report on Gilde relations in 2993, mainly focusing on laws *against* Mutes.

"Have you heard from Yuuto?"

That was to me, but I wished it wasn't. Cami could have easily asked Kaito. He knew the answer too. "Nope. And I'm fine, thank you."

"Wish I could say the same for Yuuto," Kaito muttered.

"What's that supposed to mean?" Kaito just shook his head while I bristled. "If he's so upset, then he should face me like a grown-up. It's the least he could do." No one disagreed, but that seemed more out of survivalism than actual understanding. I wanted to change the subject right now. "Kaito, have you met Cami's parent's yet?"

He shifted a little uneasily next to the blonde. "Not yet."

The frown Cami wore with her downward turned eyes told me not to push it. I only asked to see how serious they were. If they wanted to be together (more than just friendly hanging out), Kaito would have to meet Cami's parents soon. It had already been longer than polite, verging on criminal. I didn't know if Cami's parents would approve. If they were anything like my parents, it would be a cold day in hell before they signed off on the Alloyed couple's registration, which meant either breaking up or breaking the law. But my family helped write those laws. Cami's parents were far more liberal. Another reason I should just leave Yuuto alone. Even if he were interested, we would never get my parents' 'okay'. I seriously doubted he considered me worth the risk to his life and future.

These thoughts and conversations had turned the air bitter, as talk about Mute laws always did. But with us, Cami and I, just going over Amendment 901A, the marriage and relationship law, it was impossible to ignore at the moment.

Kaito did better than we did but being a Mute, he was used to it as he slung an arm around Cami's shoulders and rested it on the back of their booth. "I'll meet them soon. It'll be alright."

And I got my answer. They were *very* serious about one another. Not that I was surprised, Kaito was a completely different person from the guy I first met, and that all had to do with Cami.

I had the large, bright purple mug held to my lips for a sip of chocolaty goodness when a body fell next to me, nearly spilling it all over my sweater. "What's happening?!"

Buri's bright red and black checkered flannel stood out far more than the subdued crimson hoodie Kaito wore. But the two were in their red and black as usual, reminding me that they were still in the club and I was not.

Mia sat next to Buri, squishing me against the window. "Just homework."

Mia pulled out her work with my sarcastic tone and didn't miss a beat, getting deep into it without a word. Buri frowned. "Damnit, she'll be at it all night now."

"As she should be. As should we all." Kaito offered, stoically even with his arm around Cami, who rolled her eyes. "You most of all, Buri."

"And what about you? I don't believe it all just comes

to you. You have to work just as hard as the rest of us!" Buri fussed.

Kaito drifted in a bit with a smirk. "Some of us just know how to manage our time better."

Kaito must have struck a nerve with Buri irritated and Kaito amused. But the blond man soon turned it all around, a smile back on his face. "Everyone ready for this weekend? I know I am. Ready to win some credits! You coming to the race, Jo?"

Glancing at Kaito, he spared me a look but said nothing. As much as I wanted to avoid the topic, I didn't have any choice. "Why would I come? I'm not even allowed, am I?"

Mia's hand flinched with her pencil, listening in. The only one not in the know was Buri, and it felt weird playing the part just for him. "You're allowed if we bring you! I've been trying to convince Mia to come with, but she has 'too much work.'"

"Thanks but no thanks. I have too much to do as well. Maybe next time?"

Buri sighed loudly, dropping his head back to hit the

top of the booth. "Man, I thought for sure you'd take me up on it. Yuuto's gonna be a pain this weekend without you around."

Kaito huffed in agreement while I huffed at the ridiculousness of it all. "If Yuuto wanted to make things right, he would come to me himself. Not send his buddies to do it for him."

"Yeah, not gonna happen."

"Then that's his fault."

I didn't take Yuuto as a coward, so the truth was, he didn't care enough to fix it. Which meant I would no longer feel guilty about whatever it was I did to him. Or think about him as anything as just another obstacle between Rene and me. That's what I told myself for the rest of the day and long after we all left the café, even after we split and went home. And after the remaining hours before the first race of the season.

It was barely spring and still cold, so I wrapped up as tight as I could. Thick, black tights tucked into Auntie's boots (that I was borrowing again) and a little sweater under my riding jacket, I was dressed to go.

My cyc under me, I took off from my home and into the night, unsure what it would bring me for the first time in a while. The slight shake in my hands had nothing to do with my cyc floating beneath me. I had written Yuuto off, so why was I so nervous about seeing him tonight?!

With my new paint job and turning a new leaf in my life, I had plenty of reasons to be excited, including getting out on the city streets and opening up my com-motor for the first time in weeks. A few cherry trees glowed in the holographic's lights. In full bloom, their pink color matched my hidden locks inside my helmet. They were nearly hidden as well -rare and expensive- blush-colored trees dotted City Centre streets, marking the extravagant places off like beacons in the night. If you looked real close, you could see a few hanging off a roof or balcony of the high-rise apartment complexes, showing who was genuinely wealthy.

The streets soon turned dark and dirty as I entered the Mute neighborhood. No pretty trees here.

It wasn't long until I arrived at the race site after that. Nearly all had turned off their com-motors, but it was far from silent—everyone enthusiastic about their return. The sounds all echoed, the raised highway above them. My cyc gleamed in the electolamps—the bright pink glittering and winking like the stars. I was greeted with cheers of happy energy and many happy faces aimed at me.

Jimmy got to me first, making sure everyone knew he was responsible for my new look. Then he bowed in to apologize for what his man did, explaining that he was more than fired, but I didn't want to guess what that meant. The last thing Jimmy did before leaving me was to guide me to my new spot. It was right on the line, the meaning not lost to me, and directly across from the Cruor. The road between them and me I never felt a more obvious metaphor in my life.

Buri showed up a little late, probably due to Mia somehow given the good mood he was in, smiling and laughing as he joined the others, hopping off his cyc right away. Camillia was chatting away with Nori and Roxana (another new addition to the Cruor), proving it was just me on the outs. Reglin sat a short distance from the others on his cyc, looking around the crowd as if to search for someone, and he wasn't looking for me. That had hairs on the back of my neck standing and worry spreading through my lungs for some reason. Kaito was with Haruto, making last-minute adjustments to Buri's cyc. Yuuto reclined against one of the thick round columns, the cement pressing back into him, a frown on his lovely face. Their shades of red all varied, but even Cami wore a berry red leather jacket on top of her black top.

My cyc as my seat, I tried to take in more of my surroundings, but I was drawn back to the Cruor, feeling eyes on me. I knew who before I even turned, but I still couldn't stop myself. Yuuto was looking at me dead on. My blacked-out helmet didn't keep him from knowing he had my full attention, pushing off the column to frown deeper at me.

He pointed at me and then to the ground in front of him. I didn't move, confused and slightly scared at what he wanted. But when he continued to stare, it was clear. I shook my head, telling him 'no'. Standing up straight, he did it again, the two of us having a silent conversation in our heads.

"You, come here."

" . . . .No."

"You are Cruor. you belong here with us."

"I'm not Cruor."

"Yes, you are. Now come here, or I will drag you...."

I released a heavy sigh so he could see it across the street. *"....Fine!"*

Slowly, I rolled over to 'their side' and came just inside their circle before turning my com-motor off again. Everyone had gotten quiet, even a few who didn't belong to the Cruor. But it broke quickly.

"Alright, with Moto in the gang, we will make so many credits!" I tilted my helmet to the side, and Buri took a step back. "You're not here for the money. I get it."

"You should be. Money can get you a lot of things in this world."

Kaito was smirking at me, looking like he knew more than he said. He had figured out who I was but had he figured out why? I wouldn't put it past him, but unless Glin had said something about Rene, I didn't see how. Nori did a cute little hop over to my side (something her Biomech allowed), a broad smile on her face that reminded me of her brother a lot.

"Glad to see you could make it!"

I was grinning inside my helmet at her. "Where else would I be on a night like this?"

She shrugged, her smile a permanent fixture. "It's not like I know about you and your life outside of this world? Or inside this world?"

"That would bother most people, you know."

Nori played with the frayed hem of her dark red sweater, looking cute in her black tights. She matched me in that respect, wearing my black tights but no red. "Yeah, like my brother." Nori popped up her head at that as if she had said too much. "But I'm not bothered! You have your life, and I have mine!"

The first race took off, a bunch of wannabes showing off as usual. I still sat on my cyc, facing the starting point while Roxana and Nori stood nearby, Camillia busy with Kaito somewhere. Roxana and Nori talked around me, but I was busy focusing on other matters, forcing myself to honestly look at the crowd and try to figure out who might know Rene. The only group that truly stood out was Sora's and his Kurio-chi. As desperate as I was for info on Rene, I wasn't crazy or stupid. If they had information, it would come at a steep price. One I wasn't sure I could afford.

I was busy searching, but I couldn't ignore Yuuto as

he slowly stood beside me. I still tried, watching him out of the corner of my helmet instead of turning my head. "You going to race tonight?"

I dodged, shooting his question right back at him. "Are you?"

"Maybe. If the challenge is interesting enough."

"I'm sure nothing is interesting enough for you."

My anger was simmering just below the surface. Yuuto had been avoiding and ignoring me since Coupling day. I was pissed and hurt, and I wasn't sure I could wrangle it all in to be Moto, who had nothing against Yuuto currently.

Yuuto sat on the guardrail before me, not taking his eyes off me. "Are you mad at me??!"

"No! Why would I be mad? I have absolutely no reason to be!" I was going to get caught at this rate.

"I agree, and yet, here you are, mad."

I needed something, anything, and it couldn't be a lie because I sucked at those. "Maybe it has nothing to do with you. Did you ever think of that?"

That wasn't a lie. I was also pissed at the lack of headway on Rene. He shrugged, "Sure, but you didn't seem to have problems with anyone else. Reason would stand that your problem is with me."

"Oh, you're just so smart. Well, then you should be able to figure it out!!!"

Danger! Danger! I was screwing up, and I couldn't find it in me to stop. My heart was aching no matter how hard I tried to ignore it, angry at Yuuto for his treatment of Josaline and mad at myself for failing at being Moto. Moto didn't care about Men, not stupid ones who lacked the backbone even to face a person! I needed space, and since Yuuto wasn't going to give it to me, I made it myself, getting off my cyc and moving closer to Nori and Roxana. I wish I could say I was surprised when he didn't follow me. As more time passed and Yuuto kept his distance (a distance I both loved and hated), it pricked at my skin until I could take it no more.

"I'm going to race."

Nori and Roxana just stared at me, so Haruto answered. "Okay. Have fun."

I spared Glin a glance before leaving to speak with Jimmy. He was still deep in thought, not talking to anyone and off to the side. Glin hadn't said a word to Cami or me (that I had seen). As a member of the Cruor, his life had been far less hectic, home more often and no longer leaving at random hours for long periods. He was no longer a dog, but he still didn't look satisfied. If anything, he looked worse.

Another thing for me to worry over. Glin was acting close to postal, his flint silently burning away to nothing. Exactly what would happen when the bomb went off was another unanswered question that I couldn't deal with right now. I needed to blow off some steam and get back into character before my cover was completely blown.

Jimmy put me up against some decent competition. It was nice to feel challenged. Even if I still floated over the finish line with several seconds to spare.

I was considering shoving my winnings into Yuuto's face, my inner voice trying to convince me that Moto would *totally* do that and say it was for her 'debt' he claimed I had. But when I returned, the Cruor were all pale, a mixture of panic and fractured outrage.

All of the Cruor but Glin, as he was nowhere in sight. I spun on my heels, turning towards the location that held the full attention of the blood gang, only to catch the fleeting red and black of Glin's tacky Hawaiian shirt as it disappeared into the cloud of black Kurio-chi.

Chapter Twenty–Five

"Our culture has filled our heads but emptied our hearts,
stuffed our wallets but starved our wonder. It has fed our
thirst for facts but not for meaning of mystery. It produces
"nice" people, not heroes."
–Peter Kreeft _Jesus Shock_

I last caught sight of Reglin as he entered Sora's den.

Too much time had passed as I waited for him to come out

again. My mind was racing. What possible reason could he

have to go over there and talk to Sora? Did Yuuto tell him the

whole story about our run-in last month?!

Glancing back, Yuuto was pacing. The others were

standing just out of his way, urging him to calm down and

offering up ideas on how to *fix* this. It was all just talk if all

they did was stand around.

Before anyone could wrap their brains around it, I

swung over the guardrail and launched myself towards the

black swarm. Voices called out to me and after me, but I made it to the group. A few lightcycs swerved around me since I didn't even think to look or wait for the race to be over. I had watched Reglin force his way in, and I prepared to do the same. But once they caught sight of me, they split out of the way and let me pass. It wasn't long before I stood in front of Sora.

Reglin stood off to the side. The two talked until I arrived, and Reglin paled at the sight of me. Did he not expect me to come after him?

"Ah.... Moto, Moto, Moto. It has been too long."

"Not long enough if you ask me."

Sora chuckled, and a chill ran up my spine. "To what do I owe the pleasure."

I pointed at Reglin, and he turned white. "I want him."

Sora put a hand up to his ear and slanted over slightly, the auto he sat on creaking from the strain. "I'm sorry? What was that? I can't quite hear you with that thing on your head." If he expected me to take my helmet off for him, then he was an idiot. When I made no moves to remove it, Sora sat back with a grin on his face. "Alright, I get it. Nothing like a little mystery to get the blood flowing. You like my imagination to running wild, don't you?"

"Give Reglin to me, now."

Sora stood, taking three long strides before standing before me. His face in my helmet, I took a good look at his soulless black eyes and swallowed my terror. "You're in no position to be making demands, little girl."

There was a new reason for me to be thankful for the helmet. It kept Sora from seeing how hard I was trying to contain myself. "Funny, your men seem to think I do."

"They moved because I told them to. I wanted nothing stopping *the* Moto from coming to *me*."

I pinched the back of my hand to keep myself from shivering visibly. "You knew I would come?"

"I had a hunch."

Sora snarled down at me, his eyes dancing around my visor and then back at Reglin. "What do you want for Glin?"

Tilting his head up, he put a finger to his chin as if thinking it over. A sneer formed on his face as he returned it to mine, and without warning, he grabbed my shoulders. My hands were out before me; I held him back as Sora tried to pull me against him. My stomach was rolling with panic and disgust, and I could hear Glin's cries as he tried to get to me.

Someone was holding him back.

Then Sora's hold disappeared. He was suddenly back against his auto in a less-than-comfortable position. "She is Cruor. You can't touch her."

Yuuto was on one side, Kaito on the other, and my heart slowly returned to normal as Sora continued to keep his distance. "I'm starting to rethink that agreement."

"Even without the agreement, you have no choice. You know what will happen if you touch one of my people, and I don't think you want a war, not with everyone on my side." At Yuuto's words, those around us stepped back slightly. Now, release Reglin. You can't touch him either. He is Cruor, too."

Sora shook his head slowly, his smirk returning. "No, no, he isn't Cruor anymore. He defected. Reglin freely gave himself to the Kurio-chi."

With my hands still on my cousin, I screamed back at Sora. "What?! He isn't free. You're holding him hostage!!!"

Yuuto held me back again, shouting over my head. "I want to hear it from him!"

The guy that had Reglin in a lock-up released him, Glin stumbling slightly from the roughness. "One race, I win. he gives me what I want. And I am free to come or go. Moto gets left alone."

My hands hit the sides of my helmet, slapping loudly but not covering my anguish. "Oh God, Glin, no."

"What choice did I have? The Cruor knows nothing, and you just keep putting yourself in more and more danger. You were *never* supposed to be involved in this!"

"You could have talked to me about it!!! I was helping you. I want it as much as you do!!!!!"

"And you were going to stay. Don't lie to me. You wanted to stay whether I was there or not. You are a member of the Cruor for life."

"Glin…"

Yuuto stepped between us, ending anything more between us. "You understand what you are doing?"

Reglin nodded, and Yuuto turned, taking me with him as we barreled out and back to our spot. Yuuto had a hold on

433

my wrist, keeping me from running back when all I wanted was to run from him. Once back in the safety of the Cruor, I ripped free, or he let me go, I wasn't sure. Either way, I was released, so I shoved Yuuto as hard as possible.

He wouldn't face me, and the others mostly had their eyes on the ground. The only ones who would look at me were Camillia, Roxana, and Haruto. And even they had sadness in their eyes. None of them ever cared for Glin, save for Camillia. Not like I had. None of them knew or understood…or cared. And right now, I couldn't stand the sight of them.

No one tried to stop me as I left, hopping on my cyc and driving off into the cold night. But I couldn't go home. Whether Glin was there or not made little difference; the worst had already happened.

The Cruor weren't that bad. I wasn't sure why Glin had defected because now he was in the middle of a real gang. They would not play nice. I had seen the aftermath of what a real mob would do a few times. The memory made me shiver uncontrollably to the point that I had to pull over.

I flung my helmet off -not caring if anyone saw- and

sobbed.

I wasn't sure how long I stayed like that. Or how many hours passed after I finally went home. I didn't answer my Holo for anyone, not even Mia. Forcing myself to go to school was a terrible choice, and as soon as I stepped onto campus, I knew it. I had to get out of there. It reeked of broken promises. The promise to go with Rene and then the promise to get her back? Glin was supposed to be with me: safe. Instead, he was in just as much (if not more) danger as Rene was. With no information on Rene to this day, there was no way to know who was in more trouble, and that only made my stomach twist. At least I had a good excuse. I was far too sick with worry and guilt to do school today. So I made for the exit as fast as I could.

When Mia, Camillia, and Kaito were waiting at our tree, I knew better than to stop for them.

"Josaline?!"

Mia and Camillia were pleading with me. Mia may not know what was going on, but she could tell things were hanging by a thread.

I stopped because Mia and Cami were my friends

long before they knew Moto. It wasn't their fault, not that Glin left or that they knew nothing about Rene. My body hunched in defeat before looking back at them with a sad smile. "Sorry, guys. I'm not up for talking right now."

"Then . . . we don't have to talk!" Camillia sounded desperate. Like I would disappear any second now, and I honestly felt like I would.

"You should at least listen to us."

Kaito was stern, not bending in the slightest at my broken state. But I changed, fixing my damaged parts and standing tall to face him. "There is nothing you can say to me that will fix this."

"Please, Jo."

Everyone was heading to class, the avenue clearing while we remained. Cami, Mia, and Kaito were pleading with the person who used to be their friend. I didn't feel like that person right now. I didn't even want to go to class.

I smiled at them, and it was painful. "I'm sorry. I haven't been sleeping well. I'm going home."

"I'll call you later!"

It sounded like a threat or promise, Camillia telling

me to answer in her own way. I didn't even turn around, waving as I walked away. It bit painfully at my chest. But it didn't change the fact that I couldn't handle them right now. Everything and nothing had changed.

Coming home to an empty house didn't help. Glin hadn't been home since the last race. I wasn't sure what he had told Auntie and Uncle. I hadn't seen much of them either. I never felt more alone, including my days living in the country with my *family*.

For a moment, I considered calling my brother. But what could I tell him? If I mentioned street racing again, he would come after me and drag me away. Or tell our parents, who would do the same and worse.

No, I couldn't talk to him or anyone else in my family. The only one I could talk to was waist-deep in it and not taking my calls. I tried every day since Glin joined the Kurio-chi, and he had yet to pick up.

No harm in trying again, right?

I had Reglin's number glowing before me when my Holo came to life on its own, Cami calling as promised. I was sure if I didn't answer, she would show up on my doorstep.

Her face illuminated. I tried to hide my dark emotions as they plagued me. "Hey," I said shakily, "what's up?"

Cami only sighed at my attempt at normality. "How are you doing?"

"Isn't it obvious?" I answered, choking on a sob.

Shaking her head, I had a feeling a scolding was coming my way. "Jo... you know it's not our fault."

"I know."

"And it's not Yuuto's fault either."

My grimace was involuntary, "I never said it was. But even you have to admit, Yuuto did a crappy job of protecting his people. People he considers his family."

"Glin acted on his own. He was never into being a Cruor. It was obvious even to me. When are you going to be honest with me and tell me what's really going on?!"

Cami was angry, and I guess she had a right to be. After all, she had put herself in danger without really knowing why. Now things had changed so much I wasn't sure I should tell her. Not because I worried she would tell Kaito but because I was afraid she wouldn't. Cami cared very much for Kaito. This would be a secret she had to keep from him. He understood our secret, me as Moto, but this was different, and I didn't know how he would feel about it, knowing or figuring it out like before.

"I…can't. Not now. Maybe never. I'm sorry."

"Seriously? After everything we've been through…."

"It's because of what we've been through that I can't tell you. I won't have you keep secrets from Kaito."

Sadness bloomed on her face. "I…I care about Kaito. A lot. But I care about you a lot, too."

"I know. I won't ask you to choose. Until I'm ready to tell all the Cruor, I can't tell you."

Cami didn't look satisfied, but I didn't give her a choice. I wasn't going to tell her, and I had another call coming in—my Uncle.

"I have to go. I'll talk to you later, I swear."

She didn't believe me and hung up without saying goodbye. There was a ruined friendship. I would have to fix it later. I couldn't give Cami what she wanted now. And I couldn't cry now either, answering before I missed the call.

"Uncle. What's up?"

He looked highly disheveled. So much so that it had

my heart dropping to the floor in concern. "Josaline. It's your cousin…" he took a long pause, and I waited. I waited like death was behind me, waiting with me. "He's in the hospital."

"What?"

My body was reacting in ways I didn't understand nor could I control. My spine shook hard as I fell to my knees. "Calm down, Sweetheart. He's just sick. He has a high fever, but the doctors are taking good care of him. He'll be fine."

"Oh god…" I struggled to breathe because, if anything, I expected him to be dead, "what hospital? I'll come right now…."

"No need. Stay home and rest. You have homework too. We don't want you around all these sick people. Caroline will be by soon to check on you, alright? Got to go!"

It was weird. I was pretty sure my Uncle was lying to me. But I didn't know why. If Reglin was sick, of course, I wanted to see him. It was just a fever, too, so why was he in the hospital? It had to be very high for them to keep him overnight like this. There were only a few Mute-friendly hospitals in the city. I could find them. It would take a few hours.

But I didn't want to disrespect my Uncle's wishes.

Maybe Reglin was angry with me? And didn't want to see me? Or they didn't know what he had or how contagious it was?

Either was very likely

Chapter Twenty–Six

"Where once we aspired to be more like our heroes, today we try to make our heroes more like us."
— *James Rozoff*

Tonight was the night of Reglin's big race, and he was still in the hospital. A hospital that I was not allowed into for some reason. For all I knew, it didn't allow Gilded in, even as visitors. I had been mostly alone in their house for days now, but the solitude had only given me time to think. It wasn't clear before if Reglin would be able to make it to the race, and I had yet to hear just what was wrong with him. My uncle had a different answer each time and claimed it was due to a misdiagnosis. I was starting to think they needed to switch hospitals. Maybe that was how all Mute hospitals were? I hoped he was getting the best care available.

Even if Reglin was still sick, I had decided my next

move long ago. As night fell, and there was still no word on Reglin, it only strengthened my resolve.

I hopped into my dark denim skinny jeans and rolled my skin-tight, long-sleeved, hot pink shirt on top. My riding jacket and helmet lived in the garage on top of my lightcyc. With those on, I hurried to the spot Digi–noted to me days ago.

The nights were still cool. I zipped my jacket up tight, the cherry blossoms glowing in the dark again as I zoomed through City Centre. Crossing Rainbow Bridge brought back some warm and fuzzy memories. Ones that were not enough to change my anger at a particular dark-haired gang leader. Nearly every member of the Cruor had spoken to me about Glin, giving me sympathy and support.

All except Yuuto.

Even if he was still angry about Coupling Day, this trumped that. He cared so little for my family and me. He couldn't even come to me and give me some reassurance or own up to his mistakes. It made my chest feel hollow because the man I liked and respected fell far from my expectations.

Yuuto was right, after all. I was far too trusting.

Crossing another smaller bridge, I found myself at a shipping yard of the Higrelo Terminal Park. The skeleton of a Ferris wheel loomed in the distance, long dead and abandoned, a rusted reminder of a different life. Where we were, there were little external lights, and the stars showed themselves overhead. It was far different than the previous race locations, making my bones quake with anticipation and fear.

The crowd was particularly rowdy tonight, and it had me more on edge. It was either the location, the upcoming race between Cruor and Kurio-chi, or both. I wondered how it would go, learning that Reglin was a no-show?

Sora and a few of his underlings were at the line, talking with Jimmy, who looked a little uncomfortable but still doing fine. I wondered if they had smoothed over the whole 'following and threatening his customers' thing? Or if Sora just bullied Jimmy into letting it go.

It didn't look like the Cruor were here yet, which was a bit unsettling. However, it didn't matter. I didn't need or want their help with this. They would only get in the way tonight.

And Yuuto...our rivalry/friendship was officially *over*. I should never have considered him as such from the beginning.

The men at the line gave me all their attention as I parked my cyc in the empty Cruor spot and strolled up to them. "Reglin won't be able to make it tonight."

"Oh?"

"He's sick."

Jimmy was torn, looking back and forth as if worried something was about to happen. But he added nothing to the conversation.

Sora sneered, "Well . . . that won't do. I guess that means he forfeits."

I had been expecting this. "You mean you won't be honoring your agreement with Glin?"

"I am honoring it. I set up a race for Reglin and everything. And now I get to look the fool because he has a cold. The race will go on, and if Reglin isn't here to race, he comes in last by default. Making him mine."

"I'm going to race for him."

Sora's brow twerked upwards, "Oh?" I nodded, and

Jimmy looked pale. "Does that mean you will take his place in all aspects?"

"You mean . . . if I lose…."

"You're mine."

Although I hadn't expected this, I couldn't say I was all that surprised. "Fine, I will race in Glin's…."

"I'm racing for Reglin.."

I could feel my blood drain from my face, turning my head slowly to see Yuuto walking up without a care in the world as if it were just another day. He stood next to me, and I looked behind to find the others, but they weren't there. "Where is everyone?"

Yuuto glanced my way, trying to keep his eyes on Sora. "Just you and me tonight, Moto."

"So, you're going to take Reglin's place then?" Sora asked.

The grimace on Yuuto's face deepened. "I don't have a choice, do I? Since you and your *boys* beat the crap out of him."

"What?!" I screeched.

The air felt thin like nothing I breathed in did

anything. I looked at Sora, waiting for him to confirm it, already knowing it was true down in my bones. "What can I say? The little *Alloyed* wouldn't give me what I wanted." I jumped, thoroughly planning on getting a few slaps, hits, and scratches in before Sora's men pulled me off. My anger burned away any fear I ever had of Sora. But Yuuto caught me, holding me back with my feet off the ground. "Woooo, God damn, that's hot. I don't even need to see your face. I'm already in love."

I was still struggling, pushing Yuuto's arms around my waist. "Stop it."

If I didn't have my helmet on, he would have been whispering right in my ear. But Yuuto had to say it loud to get it through all the plastic. It sent Sora into a fit of laughter when I listened, calming in Yuuto's hold and getting released soon after. I knew how it looked, but I didn't have much choice. If I wanted my freedom, I had to cool it.

"I'm still going to race." I ignored the stern glare Yuuto was shooting me.

"I'll tell you what, Hellcat. You win, I'll let you get one shot in."

"Just one?"

Yuuto grabbed my arm, expecting me to jump again. Sora smirked. "Yeah, you have one shot at doing whatever you want. You can hit me or kiss me, whichever you want more."

Sora was still laughing when we turned away. Yuuto unnecessarily led me to our lightcycs, his now parked next to mine. Now we had to wait.

It felt empty and quiet (just like my chest) with none of the other Cruor around us. Yuuto knelt next to his cyc and checked it over. I was still furious at him, yet I found myself leaning over his cyc to watch him.

"Why are you the only one here tonight?"

"Because I told the others not to come."

"And they just listened to you? Just like that?"

Yuuto gawked at me, "Some people respect and listen to me." I waited, knowing there was more, and he would spill it if I didn't break away. "I had to make some threats and lock a certain someone in their room, but I got them to listen."

"Nori is going to be pissed."

"Yeah, well . . . she's not as scary as a certain *Hellcat*

I know." He rose from his spot and gripped the edge of my helmet again. "Why didn't you listen to me when I said not to be so reckless?!"

"If you are talking about protecting Reglin, then I have no regrets."

"Everyone is trying to protect *you,* and you just walk right into the lion's den regardless." Yuuto pulled on me, bringing my visor less than an inch from his face. "I'm sorry. In my hubris, I thought I could protect you and Reglin. I should have just made you both leave. And now it's too late."

"Why are you talking like this is our last time?" He smiled but remained silent, causing fear to creep up my spine. "Yuuto . . . what are you planning?"

"I'm getting you out of this mess."

Chapter Twenty–Seven

"Heroes are like angels, they're all around us... we just don't always stop to notice ..."
— ***Nanette L. Avery***

As expected, Sora had a few of his 'best men' taking part in the race. Sitting a few lightcycs away, Yuuto watched them as they started their engines, their helmets as dark as Moto's. I busied myself, trying to settle my nerves, threading my fingers through one another to tighten the hold my gloves had on them.

Since Yuuto had shown up, there was a slight tremble inside my chest. Now, with the declaration of his help and protection, it was quaking. I never needed much. An apology was more than enough, and Yuuto had done that and more. Had he always planned on taking Glin's place? I would never know, and I didn't care. Because Yuuto was here now, and I felt so much safer with his presence. Just having him near was enough to soothe my nerves, but I was still shaking. Fear and worry over his safety instead of my own now bloomed in my spine.

I dropped my hands back to my handles, hoping to hide their small shake, and leaned over to look up at him. I couldn't help but smile at him, warmth flooding my skin as he smiled back, the big one that reached his eyes—the one I loved.

Sora stepped in between us, throwing an arm around my waist. "I'll be waiting to see how you do the most, Moto."

I had to swallow my disgust, or the combination of it with my nerves would have me vomiting. Sora's overpowering musk didn't help. "Don't touch me, please."

I used my big, angry girl voice. It was how I felt, and it kept my stomach from lurching. Sora removed his touch, hands in the air as he backed away, chuckling. It was all a sick game to the prick, but I still didn't know just what he hoped to gain from it all. Either Sora didn't care about the trouble he would get in for touching a Gilded like me, or he didn't know I was one. I hoped to hide it from the beginning, but I didn't seriously think I did an excellent job of it.

Yuuto had a staring match with the other racers waiting with us. "What is it?"

He turned to me, smirking broadly. "*Please*?"

I adjusted myself, trying to dispel the discomfort of the memory. It was too late to hide my slip. My Gilded schooling showed. "Just because Sora lacks any manners doesn't mean I have to be the same!"

Yuuto chuckled at me, and it made my heart skip. It was ultimately out of hiding now. Whether I truly wanted to or not, I had forgiven Yuuto. I don't know if I should tell him that. My pride was still offended- Moto's and Josaline's- because he ignored both of them for weeks for different and the same reasons. I had twisted all that time, so I had no problem letting him do the same for a while.

Jimmy counted us down, causing Yuuto to slap his helmet over his head and grab his handlebars. The race was about to begin–time to focus.

I revived my com-motor, and he returned it, not looking over at me when I turned his way. Jimmy dropped his hands, and we took off together. The track was dark, with barely any light at all, and only the GPS kept me from flying into one of the large, rusted steel boxes that littered this section of the dock.

Pulling ahead, I dipped into the tricky turn, my knee hovering over the ground. Yuuto remained behind me, which was a shame cause I wanted to watch him. I settled for my rear mirror, seeing him as he dipped just as low. We moved effortlessly as a team. It was just like the night we raced together, with an ease to it that made it too easy to forget what we were supposed to be doing, like racing.

Sora's men showing up behind and at our sides was a reminder, waking me up to reality almost painfully. Now, it reminded me of the night Buri raced with me, Yuuto only racing to protect me and nothing more. But they went for Yuuto just behind me, surrounding him.

On both sides, they swayed back and forth, trying to make him lose his balance. So, I braked hard and hoped the creep was paying attention. If not, this would be a short race for both of us. The Kurio-chi hit his brakes in return, allowing me to be next to Yuuto in his place. Yuuto kicked the other racer, pushing the black-clad guy away to wobble.

My focus was on Yuuto, who quickly waved me on. But I hesitated even as Yuuto glared at me, flicking his head for me to go.

I retook the lead with Yuuto insisting. That's how I knew; the com-motor humming dangerously close behind me wasn't Yuuto. Both of them hit their *Lighter*, going around me to take the lead. These guys were good, but I knew better than to expect less from Sora. It was a good thing Glin wasn't here. He would never have won this race anyway.

Another hard turn. I took the inside, and Yuuto was right beside me. The two Kurio-chi weren't that far ahead, the turn slowing them down. The GPS took us safely around the huge roadblocks, but suddenly, Yuuto went off course. I followed behind closely as he zig-zagged around. We lost the Kurio-chi moments ago, everyone else sticking to the track.

It was tough, dipping back and forth for each turn. But it was fun, flying blind with Yuuto as my guide. Taking the hard route was more of a challenge. Only the two of us were willing to take it.

We pulled a U-turn at full speed, and neither of us hit the brakes. Our back wheels squealed loudly in tandem.

Flying out, the Kurio-chi fumbled at the sight of us and hit their *Lighter*. But it was too late.

Yuuto let go of the accelerator, letting me slip ahead of him as we passed over the finish line. The crowd was roaring, and both of us came to a stop. The Kurio-chi crossed the line a few seconds later.

Yuuto pulled his helmet off and looked at me as if I would do the same. Guilt twinged in my belly, but I couldn't take it off–not here, not now.

And my main reason for keeping it on was prancing over to us. "Congratulations you…"

Sora was cut short by my fist as I jumped off my cyc and took my punch as promised. I didn't want to give Sora the chance to back out. I had never hit someone before, and my hand *hurt,* but even as my wrist sang with the pain, I was satisfied by the monster's face slung to the side from my force. It was nothing compared to what he had done to Glin and Yuuto.

But it was a start.

Sora held tight to his jaw, his chuckle slowly turning into a laugh. Yuuto kept me, and I let him, not fighting to get free as I had before. I had already gotten my prize: a free shot. Still holding his chin, Sora smirked up at us, "And here I thought you'd kiss me."

"That's because you're *insane*." I spat, hoping my disgust made it through my helmet.

"Moto and Reglin are off your hook."

I stilled even more at Yuuto's words. They didn't sit right at all. "Yep. They are free to go."

Yuuto let me go, but I turned, looking up at him with tears threatening and burning my throat to ash. "Okay, Yuuto. Let's go." I softly croaked.

"He can't." I jerked back to Sora. "You won, but he didn't."

My anger was back, mixing with my tears to worsen my pain because I felt tricked and not by Sora. "You . . . you knew this would happen. Why?"

Sora chuckled, "It was inevitable."

"I wasn't asking you, asshole!" I screamed, my anger and guilt turning to rage quickly.

When I tried to go for Sora again, Yuuto grabbed me, pulling me in close. "Go home, Moto."

"No!"

"Yes, why don't you stay for a while, Moto? Get comfortable?"

Holding my arm, Yuuto pulled me away, taking me back towards the Cruor's spot. "Go now, Moto. It's over."

"Is this why the Cruor didn't come? You made them stay behind so that they couldn't stop you?!" I screeched, listening to myself as my shouts bounced back to me in the helmet.

"They would only end up getting hurt. If the Cruor attacked first, then Sora has every right to destroy them all." Yuuto whispered harshly.

"Why? Why are you letting him control you?!"

"It's one job, Moto."

Did Yuuto think he was fooling me? "For now! Until he wants you again! Then what?"

"Hopefully, you aren't around for that. Go. The Cruor are waiting for you. They will take care of you."

"Who's taking care of you?"

"Myself. I'll be fine."

I didn't believe him. There was no way it would be

About the Author

A. A. Achibane is a Muslim writer. She fell in love with a Moroccan and is now influenced with her daily life and writing by its culture. She tries to pull from what she knows and loves so you will see influences from Moroccan, Berber, Arab, Irish, Celtic, and American cultures within her works. She also loves love so romance is her genre jam.

A. A. Achibane writes contemporary, romantasy, and fantasy romance. She enjoys reading and writing horror with romance themes within.

She lives with her husband and two children as a SAM. Her writing is when she has a spare moment (usually at night after bedtime). Please stalk A. A. Achibane for more of her works and to support her growing readership. Join her newsletter for free novellas.

Be sure to check out Achibane's
website and Ream page for more
updates, stories, free novellas, concept
art, behind the scenes, and early access to
up and coming novels!

Preview

Glin watched me from his propped up position as I paced the small square that was his room. He was well-medicated for his pain, which is why (I assume) he suddenly said, "I'm sorry," I frozen and looked at him perplexed but he slowly shook his head, "I never should have let you get involved."

"You never had a say…"

"If I had walked away…" he said sadly.

I dropped to my knees before him, looking Glin in his watery eyes, "Then we would be living a lie, wondering what happened to Rene and cursing ourselves for doing nothing."

Glin's eyes hardened, "At least you would be far away from Yuuto."

I giggled back at him, "Hate to break it to you but I met Yuuto before I followed you to that race. And as many times as I've run into him since, I'm pretty sure you had nothing to do with our friendship."

"Friendship, huh?" Glin grumbled. "Is that what Yuuto is calling it? You need to be very careful, Jo."

"Yeah, I know…"

"No, you don't. I'm not talking about the Kurio-chi, you need to worry about Regulations."

My head cocked to the side, trying to look closer at his face, "What are you talking about?"

His mouth opened but my holo cut him off. Cami was calling and I had a feeling it was going to be a long conversation. "Take it," Glin replied, "I need to sleep."

I slowly retreated to the hall, going backward and

watching Glin get deeper into his bed. I shut the door tight before I answered, moving quickly towards my room for privacy. Especially when Kaito's face appeared and not Cami's.

"Kaito? What are you?.."

"Listen, Josaline, I need you to come to my location."

I didn't understand, "your location? Where are you?"

"I'm not there yet."

"Then… where are you going?"

He shook his head and I could see the background just enough to see that he was moving quickly. "I don't know. I'll send you my GPS. Hurry and start moving!"

He was on edge like I had never seen him before. "But…I don't have my cyc…"

"Get a rental! Just get here now!"

Motor Girl and the Smoking Gun

Coming Soon

Milton Keynes UK
Ingram Content Group UK Ltd.
UKHW020705290424
441924UK00017B/1021